COLD FEAR

A COLD HARBOR NOVEL - BOOK FIVE

SUSAN SLEEMAN

EDGE OF YOUR SEAT BOOKS, INC.

Published by Edge of Your Seat Books, Inc.

Contact the publisher at contact@edgeofyourseatbooks.com

Copyright © 2018 by Susan Sleeman

Cover design by Kelly A. Martin of KAM Design

1

Her life was in danger. That's what Leah said in her cryptic phone call. And now Riley was here to keep her alive.

After nearly five years apart, she needed him. Wanted to hire his team to protect her. And he'd come running. Just like that. One phone call, and he was backstage at the open-air amphitheater at Rugged Point Beach. No questions asked.

He rested his hand on his sidearm and searched the concert crowd for any hint of a threat. Tried to concentrate. Failed. How could he focus with Leah singing on stage, captivating the audience—and him?

He didn't think he would ever see her again after their big breakup. Well, not other than the superstar Leah Kent in music and celebrity news, but here he was. Someone was stalking her. Or so she thought. A man seemed to be following her, concert to concert. Hiding in the dark, then vanishing before anyone could find him. Riley wouldn't let a man, any man, come after her. Not while he was still breathing.

He moved forward to get a better view of the stage. Okay, fine, a better view of Leah. She was tall and blond, the two things he'd noticed about her the first time he'd laid eyes on her across the college quad.

Then he'd approached her, slowly, enjoying the way she met his gaze and watched him cross over to her. Eyes the color of a million sapphires compressed into a single stone had captivated him, and he'd fallen hard for her right then. She'd seemed to fall hard, too. At first, he was shocked to discover she wasn't a student and worked in the cafeteria, but that didn't matter. They started dating and were inseparable for the next two years.

Until they weren't.

Memories. No place for them tonight, but her haunting voice held him in the past. A combination of folk and country. Soft and melodic, but with a bite to it. She was singing a ballad—one they'd written together. Her first big hit. "Never Let You Go."

Did she choose to perform this song tonight to punish him? No, she wasn't vindictive. Unless she'd changed. Fame and fortune could do that to a person, and she surely had both, her songs often lingering at the top of the music charts.

She broke into the chorus, her voice and the band's rhythm swelling.

Loving you. Holding you.
Never let it end.
Never let you go.
You and me, it will always be.

The music reached a crescendo as a soft ocean breeze played over the open stage, the salty smell of waves rushing in adding to the mood. He remembered when they'd co-written it...young, deliriously happy, and in love. The song was coming to a close, and they would be face-to-face for the first time in years. But he had to force down his personal feelings.

He had a job to do—protect her.

He stepped back into the covered area of the small amphitheater to do some deep breathing and clear his head. The song ended. Applause broke out. He waited for her to join him, but she didn't. He peered out. She'd exited on the other side of the stage.

Wait, what? Was he on the wrong side? Could the stalker be over there?

He was about to dash around when she came back on stage for an encore. She sang an upbeat tune, and he scanned the crowd and the surroundings. Nothing threatening. His eyes snagged on her dancing to the beat in a silvery top and jeans, her shoulder-length blond hair and gorgeous smile captivating him. And everyone else. The crowd cheered and sang along, fans reaching up eager arms to her.

Focus, man.

She finished her song. The applause was deafening now. She bowed and glanced at him.

Good. She would step his way this time for sure.

She rose up, blew kisses to the audience then turned and walked off the other side of the stage again while the band continued to play.

Why did she keep going that way? People were swarming the stage—he had to get through them to protect her.

A loud scream sounded from the enclosed backstage area.

Leah?

His heart stuttered, and he sprinted into action, shoving past the backstage lurkers.

"Secure the area," he called to Sal Arnett, her security guard, who'd let Riley in tonight and then bolted past her manager, Kraig Moon.

Riley charged around the corner and down the hall to the wide storage and staging area. His feet came to a halt.

A woman lay on the wooden floor. Blood oozed from two bullet wounds in her back. Leah was leaning over her. The woman was blond and slender, unmoving.

Leah looked up and met his gaze. Terror filled her eyes. Her pain tore him apart, but he drew his sidearm and scoured the shadowed corners of the room. No one was there, but the shooter could be nearby. He needed to get Leah away and secure the scene.

Leah held up blood-covered hands and scrubbed them down her pants, her panicked gaze searching now.

"Someone shot...she's...she's dead." The words came out on a strangled breath. Sobs followed. Big chest-heaving sobs.

Riley rushed to her, gently took her arm, and lifted her to her feet. "C'mon. We need to move you someplace safe."

He backed them away from the area, blocking any potential gunshot to her body with his own, alert to any danger.

In the hallway, Kraig stood looking at the victim while wringing his hands. Riley moved past him and pushed open the door marked Dressing Room 1. He quickly scanned the small space. Makeup table. A love seat. Coffee table with bottled drinks and snacks. A hanging rack with clothes on it. Small refrigerator. But otherwise empty. He glanced at the door. Perfect. It had a deadbolt.

He turned back to Kraig. "Take Leah in here and stay with her until I tell you it's safe to come out."

"But..."

"No buts. A woman's been murdered. Leah could be next."

"Next?" Kraig's eyes were wide and unfocused, matching Leah's shocked stare.

4

"We'll figure that out later. The shooter could still be here."

Kraig ran a hand over his dull brown hair pulled back in a man bun.

"Move. Now!" Riley gave the shorter guy a shove.

Kraig took hesitant steps but escorted Leah in the room. Riley shut the door and waited for the snick of the lock, turning as footsteps approached him.

Sal raced into the hallway. His gaze was sharp, his muscular body poised for attack. Perfect. He would act and not falter like Kraig.

"I got the area sealed off. Heard a woman was…" Sal's words trailed off as he caught sight of the body, his wide jaw clenching.

"It's not Leah," Riley said as the woman resembled Leah —long blond hair, about five seven, and her clothing was similar. "Kraig took her into Dressing Room 1 for safety. I need you to call 911 and block access to the staging area while I clear it."

His eyes widened. "You think the shooter's still here?"

"I don't know, but I aim to find out." Gun raised, Riley cautiously approached the crime scene. Kept his gaze off the victim. Forced himself not to think about the loss of life.

He'd been a patrol officer for three years, a sniper for another three for the Portland Police Bureau, and another two years as a member of Blackwell Tactical—a protection and investigations team made up of former military and law enforcement officers. Riley knew how to tune out the horrific sight of death. How to focus and make sure no one else came to any harm.

As Blackwell's sniper, he was usually behind the scope of his rifle, but this was no different.

Assess. Evaluate. Act.

It was instinct now.

He passed the body and approached the hallway leading away from the stage. A jarring red neon exit sign at the end announced the door out of the building. Riley hoped the killer hadn't left and Riley could apprehend him. Or her? He wanted to hurry down the hall and check outside for the fleeing suspect, but he'd have to pass uncleared dressing rooms which would put him in danger. He had to take his time. Protect his own life first.

He pushed open the Dressing Room 2 door and slipped back to wait for any sound inside. Hearing nothing, he took a quick look. A small space. Empty. He moved on to the next room. And the next.

At the last door, splintered wood abutted the lock. A break-in. He steeled himself for an intruder, shoved open the door, and took a quick look. It was a much larger room with a tall dressing screen in the corner. Women's clothes were strewn across a chair, and makeup and hair products covered the table by a large lighted mirror. It was probably Leah's dressing room—unless she got ready in her big fancy tour bus outside—and the shooter could be behind the screen.

"I'm armed and prepared to shoot," Riley announced from the hallway. "Show yourself."

He waited, counting. *One. Two. Three. Four. Five.*

He swung around the corner and charged the screen, sending it crashing into the cinderblock wall. He jerked it out of the way, firearm ready. Found no one.

He blew out a breath. A long one. Drew in another and looked around. Behind him, a window was open, gauzy curtains swaying in the breeze. The shooter had likely entered through the window. Maybe exited the same way or even through the door.

Riley holstered his weapon, hurried down the hall, and bumped open the exit door to scope out the area. People were flowing around the building, but no one was running or looked threatening. Time to get official law enforcement on the scene.

Riley closed the door and dialed the county sheriff.

"Sheriff Jenkins." Blake's voice was sure and strong, just like the man.

Riley could always count on Blake. If a murder had to occur, Riley was glad it happened in their county. "Riley Glen. I'm at Rugged Point Amphitheater. A woman's been murdered."

Riley brought Blake up to speed on the situation. "We've called 911. I've cleared the area, and the crime scene is secure and protected. I don't know if the shooter exited and mingled with the people, though."

"A murder. Man, oh, man." Blake was clearly upset that a citizen had been killed under his watch—and the killer was still on the loose. "Keep the scene secure for me. I'm on my way with reinforcements."

Riley disconnected and called Gage Blackwell, owner of Blackwell Tactical. When his boss answered, Riley told him about the murder. "Area's secured, 911's been called, and I also called Blake."

"Good. Anything I can do?"

"We should get Sam out here." Samantha Willis was the newest member of their team. Before her injury, she had served as a criminalist with the Portland Police Bureau and was fully versed in the latest CSI techniques.

"You think Blake will let her touch anything?" Gage asked.

"Nah, but I want her here so the second he releases the scene, she can process the space before it's contaminated."

There was a long pause. "Sounds like you don't trust the county forensics staff."

"I do to a point, but Sam's skills are superior. If she works the scene, nothing will be missed."

"Roger that. I'll send her over."

Riley shoved his phone into his pocket and started toward the dressing room to talk to Leah. He was glad that official law enforcement officers were on the way to search the surrounding area, but he didn't need them inside. He could keep people from contaminating the crime scene and disturbing the body.

What he couldn't handle was the raw pain on Leah's face and being back in her life again. The ache was as bad as a physical knife to the chest, but he'd deal with it later. Right now he was determined to keep her safe, find the killer, and restore her life.

Of that she could be sure. Pain or no pain from their turbulent past.

2

The door opened, but Leah couldn't find the strength to lift her head and look at the person stepping into the room. Not when Jill had been murdered. Here at her concert. She hadn't even heard the gunshots. Not surprising with the music volume. And maybe the shooter used a suppressor. She knew all about them. Riley had taught her to shoot, care for weapons, and about the basic accessories like a suppressor. To this day she still went to the practice range. It was a way of remaining connected to him.

"Leah." Riley's voice was smooth like honey, and it drew her to him as it had done since the first day they'd met.

She tried to erase the sight of Jill's lifeless body from her brain, looked up, and ran her gaze over him after all these years apart, reveling in the sight of the only man she'd ever completely loved. He wore black tactical pants, a black collared shirt, and a jacket with Blackwell Tactical embroidered on the chest.

He'd gained weight since she'd seen him, but it looked like rock-solid muscles, and his hair was a little longer than his police days. When they'd first met, it was long like a surfer, and he'd always had a bit of facial hair. Then he'd become a cop, and he'd buzzed it short and was clean-shaven, but he still gave off that laidback surfer vibe. Now it was longer, but still as blond with sun-kissed highlights.

She shifted to his face and found his soft blue eyes, dark as an angry thundercloud, locked on her. Eyes the exact color of their four-year-old son's eyes.

Their son. Owen.

Riley didn't know about Owen. Didn't even have a clue.

She had to look away before he saw the guilt on her face. She knew she would feel this terrible remorse when she saw him again because she carried it with her each and every day. And...oh, man...despite the threats Riley's father had heaped on her head when he learned she was pregnant, demanding she keep quiet, she now knew Riley had a right to know he was a father. And Owen deserved to know his dad.

Her son, *their* son, had to come first. Always first. And it was time.

Riley would be shocked. Stunned. Maybe even question his parentage, but the crazy joyful night they'd gotten engaged had given them a child. She'd do a paternity test to prove his fatherhood if he wanted.

"Leah," Riley said.

She blinked a few times to wash away the guilt. To put on her stage face, leaving the personal emotions behind, performing, and forced herself to look at him. He watched her with a curious intensity.

She tried to swallow, but her mouth felt like it was stuffed with cotton balls. She didn't know if it was due to Jill's death or the thought of telling Riley about Owen. "Thank you for coming."

He came over to squat next to her. "How are you doing?"

With him nearby, she was doing better, and that made her feel even worse. She had no right to accept his help while she held this secret. She had to tell him before the day was out, even if the timing wasn't ideal. That was a certainty.

Why couldn't she have been living her faith back then? First, she wouldn't have gotten pregnant, but having Owen was the joy of her life, so she didn't regret that. But second, she would have trusted God and never have listened to Riley's father.

Simply thinking about telling Riley heaped more guilt on her head. Her announcement would rock his world. Maybe in a good way, as she knew he would embrace being a dad, but he would also be very angry at her. And at his father, who he was basically estranged from already. But worse, he would be devastated over missing four years of his son's life. And it was all her fault. She'd bought into his father's threats and taken that precious time from Riley.

Please help him understand. Please. Give him comfort when he learns.

"I called the sheriff. Blake Jenkins is his name," Riley went on, blissfully unaware of the change coming to his life. "He's on his way."

"And then what?" she asked, her focus now back on Jill laying in the next room.

"Then he'll try to ID the woman and—"

"I know her."

"You do?" Riley and Kraig asked at the same time.

She looked at Riley. His focus was still locked on her, and she resisted squirming under his concentrated gaze. She faced Kraig, still surprised at his recent adoption of the hipster craze even though he was far too old to fit in. His brown hair laced with silver was sleeked back into a man bun, and he had a full gray beard and oversized black glasses perched on a pointy nose.

"Who is it?" he asked. "Who was murdered?"

"Jill Stevenson."

"Jill. Oh my." Kraig pushed his glasses up. "You didn't..."

"Kill her?" Leah shouted, horrified. "Of course not!"

"But you wanted to."

She shook her head vehemently. "No. We may be on the outs, but I didn't want her dead."

Riley stood, his expression questioning and suspicious. "Who's Jill and why were you on the outs?"

"She was one of my backup singers."

"Until she broke up Leah's relationship with Neil," Kraig added before Leah could speak.

She clenched her jaw and looked up at Riley. "I dated Neil Yohman for a short time and caught him with Jill in the tour bus. I ended things with him and fired her."

His expression changed but she couldn't interpret it. "When was this?"

"A little over a month or so ago." She glanced at Kraig to confirm her timeline.

"Yeah, it was at the last Portland concert in August."

"Then if you fired her, why would she be at your concert, and how did she get backstage?" Riley asked.

"I don't know."

Riley shifted his questioning gaze to Kraig. Thankfully. She was wilting under his intensity.

"Don't look at me." Kraig held up his hands overloaded with rings. "I know better than to let one of Leah's enemies backstage."

Riley shot her a look. "One of your enemies? Do you have a lot of them?"

She shook her head. "But the music business is pretty cutthroat. You can't make everyone happy."

Kraig snorted. "Not even most of them."

"Maybe Sal let her in," Leah said, bringing them back on track.

"I'll go ask him." Kraig spun and raced out of the room as if he couldn't handle Riley's intensity either.

With Kraig gone, the full weight of Riley's blistering focus was back on her, almost as if he had x-ray vision, seeing inside her brain and figuring out he was a father. How on earth was she going to tell him?

He took a step closer. "Do you think the murder is related to the reason you called me?"

"To the stalker? I don't know. Maybe, but I don't know."

Riley leaned his shoulder against the wall. "Tell me about him."

"It started a few months ago with creepy emails and Twitter posts, but I blew it off as part of the job. After all, this wasn't the first stalker I've had."

Riley drew in a sharp breath. "There were others?"

"Just harmless virtual ones. Infatuated fans who took it to the extreme in social media and using the contact form on my website to profess their love. They stopped right there and never did anything else."

"But not the guy you called me about?"

She nodded, and he took another breath. This was really bothering him. She knew he'd want to protect her because that was the kind of man he was, but she didn't think after all these years and their bitter breakup that he would take these threats personally. But she had no doubt he was doing so.

She tried to hide her surprise and went on. "I blocked his emails and blocked him on Twitter. But then I started getting letters at home. I don't know how he got that address, but it freaked me out, and Sal arranged security to remain outside my house."

"The stalker probably searched property records," Riley said. "You can find most everything online these days if

13

you're tenacious enough, but it sounds like Sal's good at his job."

"He is, and he's very loyal," she said, but the fact was, she didn't trust him completely. Since skyrocketing to fame, she'd been lied to and misled by too many people with ulterior motives. Now she couldn't trust anyone.

Well, except Riley and her mother. They knew her before she was famous, and if Blackwell Tactical agreed to take on her protection, she would be glad to have someone she could completely trust in charge of her security.

Riley shifted on his feet, looking like he wanted to say something but then reconsidered. "If Sal has your security under control, why did you call me?"

"The situation escalated and I didn't feel safe anymore. The letters weren't enough for the stalker. He started showing up at my last few concerts and tried to get backstage. When Sal didn't let him through, he waited by the stage door and tried to get to me when I left venues. But what sent me over the edge—and why I called you—was that he started showing up in my personal life. I knew you worked for Blackwell and thought you could help."

He looked at her for a long moment, and she couldn't tell what he was thinking. Once upon a time, she could predict his thoughts enough to finish his sentences, but now? Now she didn't know what was going on in his brain, and that bothered her. Bothered her more than she could have imagined.

"How did you know I worked for Blackwell?" he asked.

She'd made a point to stay informed on his activities as a precaution against him learning about Owen, but she sure couldn't admit that. "I...my mom...told me. She keeps up with all the gossip from our old friends. She said she saw information on the Blackwell group in the newspaper when a reporter did a story on you."

"An unauthorized story," Riley muttered. "They wanted to do a hometown hero kind of thing. No one on the team would ever seek out publicity for what we do. I tried to convince them not to run the story, but they wouldn't listen."

He'd always been so modest when he was a police officer, and it was nice to see that hadn't changed. "Real heroes like you don't brag about what you do, but we all like feel-good stories about a hero."

"We're not heroes. Just people doing our jobs." He waved it off. "Back to your stalker. Do you know his name?"

She shook her head. "He uses a Yahoo email account and the name is *leahfan*. He signed the letters that way, too."

"Okay, first, where are these letters?"

"In my office at home."

"The murder could be related to the stalker and Blake will want those, but I need a copy of them first."

"I'll make sure you get them," she said, but she couldn't let him or Blake go to her house before she told Riley about Owen. He'd see the pictures and toys, and that would be the worst way to find out he had a son.

"Whoever makes the copies needs to wear gloves and be careful not to smudge any potential fingerprints."

"You can get fingerprints from paper?"

"Blake's team will do that," Riley said. "We have a forensic specialist on our team—Samantha Willis—who could do it, too, but I'll have to ask her if she should process them before law enforcement has a shot at it." He paused for a moment. "We also have a cyber expert on our team. Her name's Eryn Calloway. I'll have her trace the emails, but Yahoo will only hand over the stalker's real contact information to Blake, and then only after he provides a warrant."

"So it's possible that will give us the stalker's ID and he can be arrested?"

Riley shrugged. "The contact info could be bogus."

"It's all so creepy to me." She shuddered, thinking of the man as he lurked in wait for her. "Thank you for coming."

He nodded. "Have you reported the stalker to the police?"

She bit her lip. "Yes, but not at first. Like I said, I've had stalkers before. Or more like very enthusiastic fans. But when this guy showed up in person, multiple times, I did contact the police after my concert in Minneapolis. But honestly, they couldn't do much as it was my last night there. I figured because I travel a lot and his stalking spans several states that you all would be better able to deal with this."

"You're right there." He narrowed his eyes. "Did you read these emails on a phone? Tablet? Computer?"

"All of the above. Depended where I was or what I was doing."

"Blake and Eryn will want to look at every device then."

Her heart dropped. She had pictures of Owen on her computer. Not her phone or tablet. She worried about losing those when traveling and whoever found them would be happy to broadcast her personal life on the Internet. So she transferred everything to her home computer. She'd be glad to give them access to that, too. *After* she'd told Riley about Owen.

The full magnitude of what she was going to disclose to Riley weighed heavy on her, and she closed her eyes for a moment to gain enough calm to respond to him. "I'm happy to provide my phone and tablet, but I have personal files on my computer. Being a celebrity, I can't be too careful about my private information getting out, and I'd rather keep that private for now."

Riley watched her like a vulture tracking its prey. "Blake won't give you a choice. If you refuse, and he thinks it's needed for the investigation, he'll get a warrant to seize the hard drive. He would typically have the regional computer lab process it, but they're always backlogged. Eryn has taken hard drive images for him in the past. Hopefully, I can convince him to let her do it now, too. That way she can make a copy for us, and we'll have access to all of your info."

"Who is it?" The shrill voice of Leah's assistant cut through the open door.

Leah heard Sal mumble a response.

"I don't care what Riley said," Felicity snapped. "I need to see with my own eyes that Leah's okay."

Leah appreciated Felicity's protectiveness, but her outburst wasn't necessary. "That's my assistant, Felicity. You better authorize her to come back or she's going to hurt Sal."

"I'll go get her." Riley exited the room, his steps sure and strong like the kind of man she'd always known he was. A man who was a keeper. She'd known that from day one, too, and yet, she'd chosen to pursue her dream over him.

She was suddenly back on that day. In his studio apartment with the ratty old couch and scarred tables he'd bought at a thrift shop when he was trying to prove he didn't need his father's money. He thought he was slumming, but for her, it was a palace compared to the places she'd lived in with her mother after her father abandoned them. A music recording contract for a major record label sat on the table between them. A contract for both of them. A couple. Not just her.

Riley had towered over the table, glaring at her. His arms folded over his chest. His stance wide as he declared, "No way. Absolutely no way I'm signing that contract. I'm not living like a nomad. I always wanted to be a police officer, and I love my job. I won't quit. You have to choose. A career in the music world or me."

And so, she chose—her decision fueled by years of living on welfare and despair after her father's disappearing act. Incredible amounts of despair. Not having enough food to eat. Having to wear discarded clothes given to church charities and tattered shoes from the same bags. Teasing and bullying at her school because she didn't dress right.

Her mother was always busy working and had no time for Leah. For family things. For fun. Just the darkness of poverty. So dark—bleak.

She had to make something of herself to erase those horrible memories. To reach an income level that guaranteed she wouldn't live in poverty as an adult.

All because a man walked out on her. On her mother.

And yet, she'd fallen for Riley. Trusted him. He seemed different. Caring and dependable. Rock solid. Life was easy for him. He'd come from money, a ton of money, and he didn't understand how her past influenced her. Drove her to succeed.

How could he understand? It wasn't his fault. Music was a fun hobby for him, and he was glad to get by on his cop salary because being a police officer was his dream. But she'd seen the families of his coworkers break up over the stress of the job, then struggle because they didn't have enough money to live on. The couples suffered. Their children suffered.

She couldn't risk that and implored him to reconsider and sign the recording contract. He said no again, declaring she should go it alone. She'd left then. Her throat clogged with emotion. Hurried to their manager's office and tried to have the contract altered to include only her. But the label executive wanted both of them. Not her alone.

Her world crashed, and poof, they'd broken up. No warning. Nothing to prepare her. Only the cold light of the end of their relationship.

Riley—just like her father—walking away. Like every man in her life.

She was to blame. She trusted in a man when she had firsthand knowledge from her father that it was foolhardy. She vowed to go it alone from that point on. Work hard at her career. Succeed and take care of herself. No man needed.

And then...then she found out she was pregnant.

She let out a sigh so long she felt as if she was deflating.

"I was shocked when Leah said she planned to call you," Felicity's voice came from right outside the door. "She told me about your past, and you're the last person I thought she'd want to see."

"She needs help with the stalker," Riley replied.

"Sal could've handled it. He's quite capable and would've figured out who it was."

"Obviously, Leah thought otherwise."

Felicity snorted and stepped into the room. Leah's spirits lifted knowing her staunchest supporter was nearby. Felicity started as a backup singer then moved to be Leah's assistant, and they'd become close over the years. But even *she* didn't know about Owen.

Felicity tucked bleached-blond hair behind her ear, ran across the room, and knelt beside Leah to take her hands. "Riley told me it's Jill out there. How are you holding up?"

Leah looked into her friend's deep blue eyes. At least her best friend at work. Leah didn't allow people into her private life, and that included Felicity. "I'm kind of numb."

"A shock like this will do it to you," Riley said, but kept his focus on Felicity. "Did you let Jill in the building tonight?"

"No. I didn't even know she was here. I was...well, let's just say I'm having some issues and have been in the bathroom for the last hour." She blushed bright red. "How embarrassing to have to admit that."

Leah patted Felicity's hands. "I'm sorry. I know you've

been dealing with this stomach bug for the last few days, and I appreciate you coming to work anyway. And besides, it's nothing we all haven't experienced."

"Look at you, comforting me when you're the one who needs sympathy." She squeezed Leah's hands and let go. "Now what can I do to make things better for you?"

"Do? I don't know. I mean it's not like this has ever happened before, and I don't know what would make it better." She shook her head. "I just can't believe it's Jill... and now she's dead. How awful for her family. For Neil, too. How will they cope? Us, too. How do we move forward?"

"Someone will have to manage reporters when they get wind of it," Riley said.

Leah nodded, but as long as the reporters weren't circling her because they'd learned about Owen, that was the least of her worries. "Kraig will team up with my publicist Gabby Williams, and they'll handle that."

Riley looked at her in disbelief.

"What?"

"Just wondering what it's like to have people to handle things."

She frowned. "Your parents 'had people' so I know you're familiar with it."

"Yeah, but I can't picture you in that position. I need to though, right? You've achieved your dream and are living the life." He sounded disgusted by her choice, but then, she couldn't blame him.

The life of fame wasn't all that it was cracked up to be. If she didn't need financial security for herself, Owen, and her mother, Leah would leave the business. But she had no other skills and had to keep working at being the success Riley seemed to disdain.

"Kraig will be busy talking to your concert promoters,"

too," Felicity added. "And working on the schedule if it needs to change."

Her schedule. Right. She had concerts booked for the next three months. "I haven't even thought about that yet. Seems callous to go on tomorrow as if nothing happened. We need to show Jill some respect."

"Of course...sure." Felicity patted Leah's hands. "It's just...there's so much money riding on these concerts. Your career, sweetie. You know that."

"Why's that?" Riley asked.

Another thing Leah didn't want to share with Riley, but he would find out anyway. "The sales for my last album weren't as large as we expected, and this Small-Town America Tour is a last-ditch effort to bring them back up before my label drops me."

"I'm sorry," he said sounding sincere.

"No worries. It is what it is."

He frowned. "Still saying that, I see."

She'd forgotten that he hated when she used that phrase. He was a take-charge, take-control kind of guy, and he believed she had a defeatist attitude. But her childhood of poverty often left her feeling beaten down by the world. That was the way she coped when she couldn't do a thing about her situation.

He was the opposite. He could do anything if he set his mind to it. Including turning his back on his family's money and living off a cop's salary when he could have much more.

She'd worked hard to build her career, but despite doing all the right things—everything her manager and record label asked of her—it was failing. They'd decided to add smaller venues this time around, bringing her music to people who didn't have the opportunity to attend concerts in big arenas in hopes of drawing in additional fans. So far, the tour had been well received, and the current album sales were back on track with projections, but if the tour was cancelled for any reason, her label would likely drop her, and her career would be over in a flash.

Heavy footsteps sounded outside the door and a deep male voice rumbled loudly, calling out Riley's name.

Riley spun to face the door. "That's Blake. I'll go meet him and bring him up to speed."

Good. Leah needed some time out of Riley's sight. To think. To recover from the shocking discovery of Jill's body and to plan how to tell him about Owen. She had to do it right. Take his feelings into account. Because when she finally revealed her big secret, she suspected her whole world would crumble before her eyes...and his would, too.

3

Riley stood by Blake's side as he watched the county forensic specialist snapping pictures of the victim and the scene before anyone else accessed it. Large klieg lights brightened the dark area, revealing even the minutest of details, and Riley still couldn't believe he was suddenly involved in a murder investigation.

Blake planted his hands on his waist. "Has anyone but Leah been near the body?"

Riley shook his head. "I immediately cordoned off the area. No one's been near her."

"Including you?"

"Including me. I skirted around the body, sticking near the walls when I went to clear the space. Only things I touched were doorknobs and a dressing screen in Dressing Room 4."

Blake gave a nod of approval. "Any idea how the killer got inside?"

"A window is open in that dressing room. I think it's the one Leah is using. Honestly, I'm just as interested in finding out how Jill got inside. No one is admitting to letting her in, and the back door was locked."

"Interesting." Blake turned.

An inch or so taller than Riley, Blake met Riley's gaze head on and planted his feet firmly on the floor in a confident stance Riley had come to expect from him. He was five years older than Riley's twenty-nine years and clearly worked out to maintain his tip-top condition.

If eyes could frown, his did. "So Leah and you once dated, and this is personal for you."

Riley nodded. "About five years ago."

He didn't come at Riley with a follow-up question right away but seemed to ponder it first. "Why'd you break up?"

Riley didn't really want to go there, but he knew Blake needed all the facts, so he recited the past as though it happened to someone else. "We were together for about two years. During that time, we co-wrote songs and played clubs in Portland."

"You?" Blake's eyes widened. "A singer, songwriter?"

"Was," Riley said firmly removing any question in Blake's mind. "Not anymore. Not since we split up."

"That's why no one knows about it, huh?" He was referring to the Blackwell team who Riley kept in the dark about this, too.

He really didn't want to talk about it, but Blake deserved an explanation. "Picking up a guitar brings back the way things ended between us, so I quit playing."

"Tell me about the breakup."

Riley wished Blake hadn't gone here, but he did. "Not much to tell. One night we caught the eye of a manager. I was a patrol officer with PPB back then and didn't want to pursue music as a career, but I let Leah talk me into signing with the manager."

Blake gave a slow, disbelieving shake of his head. "You don't strike me as the kind of guy who could be coerced into doing anything you didn't want to do."

"I was head over heels, and she can be really persuasive."

"What happened to change that?"

"The manager brought a record studio exec to our show one night. He liked our songs, but what he really liked was our chemistry. He arranged for us to do a demo and thought it was great. So he wanted to sign us to a recording contact, starting with a long tour with another one of his big-name artists. I didn't want to live my life on the road so I said no, figuring he would give the contract to Leah. But he said it was both of us or neither. It wasn't a life I wanted, and I turned it down. She never forgave me."

"She recovered though, didn't she? Topping the Billboard Charts for the last few years."

Riley arched an eyebrow. "You listen to her kind of music?"

Blake grimaced. "You're kidding, right? Touchy-feely music isn't my thing. I Googled her on the way over."

Riley grinned. "That makes much more sense."

"Did you keep in touch with her over the years?"

Riley shook his head. "Neither one of us wanted that."

"But neither of you got married, either."

Riley wasn't going there. "Tonight was the first time I've seen her in five years. She called yesterday telling me she had a stalker and wanted to hire Blackwell to keep her safe."

"Okay." Blake ran a hand over hair the color of coal. "Then you haven't seen her in a long time, but you must still know the kind of person she is. Any way you can see her shooting this woman and then pretending to find her?"

Riley hadn't even considered that. Because of his history with Leah, he was likely thinking like a man, not a former cop. But he gave it some thought and told Blake about Neil and Jill. "I can't see Leah as a killer, and I don't like her for this. But you should know, she can shoot. I taught her how to handle a weapon and even bought her a gun for protection."

Blake relaxed his posture, signaling the end of the formal interview. "Thanks for telling me about your past. Couldn't have been easy."

"It was a train wreck, but you should know, I still don't want anything bad to happen to her." Riley widened his stance. "If you pursue her as a suspect, I'll stand by her side and fight you with everything I've got."

"I'll have to question her about it, maybe take her gun for ballistics comparison, but I'll give her a fair shake. You know that."

"I do."

The deputy who was serving as officer of record and documenting the name of every person who arrived on scene poked his head around the corner. "The medical examiner's here. Okay to let her in?"

"Yes," Blake said.

The deputy retreated, and a thin woman dressed in a white Tyvek suit and blue booties came straight over to Blake. Riley put her in her early forties with mousy brown hair pulled back in a ponytail and numerous wrinkles on her forehead that belied her age.

"Dr. Mary Zachow," Blake said. "This is Riley Glen with Blackwell Tactical."

"Call me Mary." She offered her hand and shook, her grip firm. "I've known Gage since we were kids. He was quite a few years behind me, but our families are old friends. I really respect what he's doing with this team."

Riley nodded with enthusiasm. He was incredibly thankful to Gage for his job. A gunshot took out one of his kidneys and kept him from continuing as a police officer or even finding a similar job. Gage hired only law enforcement officers or members of the military whose on-the-job injuries forced them out of their careers. Most of them were in a state of despair or pent-up anger. Then along came Gage, giving them all a second chance at a career similar to the ones they'd lost and restoring their lives.

Mary faced the victim and shook her head. "Let's get to this, shall we?"

She strode across the room and squatted next to the body.

The officer of record looked in again. "There's a Samantha Willis requesting access to the scene."

"She's the forensic person Gage hired, right?" Blake asked.

Riley nodded.

Blake frowned. "I can't let her work this scene."

"I know, but I hoped she could observe."

Blake tilted his head, his eyes narrowing. "To what end?"

"Your staff might miss something that she could point out."

Blake crossed his arms. "I don't want her making my team feel inferior."

"I don't want that either. If she has any suggestions, she could give them to you and you can pass them along if you want."

"Fine, but you make sure she understands that she stays on the sidelines and keeps her mouth shut." Blake looked at his deputy. "Sign her in and give her some booties."

"I'll go meet her." Riley stepped away before Blake changed his mind.

In the hallway, he found Sam slipping the disposable coverings over tactical style boots. She was dressed like Riley in a team uniform of tactical pants and a black shirt with the team logo embroidered in white.

She looked up and smiled. She had the friendliest broad smile, and so far, Riley could say she was pleasant to work with—always in a good mood and cheerful. But right now, he didn't want cheer. He wanted someone to commiserate with him. Of course, that would mean telling her about his past with Leah, and Gage was the only team member he'd confided in. Even then, Riley had only mentioned that he'd dated Leah and it ended badly. Nothing else. He certainly didn't say that he might still be carrying a torch for her. Admit that, and Gage would pull Riley off her protection detail due to a conflict of interest. No way Riley would let that happen.

Sam picked up her large tote bag, and Riley followed her into the other room. She started for the body. Riley held her back and tipped his head at Blake who was talking to the ME. Sam hadn't met Blake in the past, but she would have heard the team talk about him.

"Blake agreed for you to observe, but that's all," Riley said plainly. "If you see something that seems off or needs handling, talk to Blake, not the forensic staff."

"Sure thing." Instead of being upset, she bent down to get out a sketch pad and pencil. "I'll make a rough drawing of the area before the body's removed, then when Blake releases the scene, I'll take measurements and draw it to scale."

She started sketching. With her positive attitude—even when faced with a setback—and her stellar skills, she truly was a valuable addition to their team.

Mary snapped on latex gloves and moved the victim's jaw. "No rigor yet and the blood hasn't clotted. She died less than an hour ago."

Riley assumed, which he shouldn't of course, that Jill had died moments before Leah found her, and the ME was confirming that. She couldn't give an exact time of death, but this was close enough to begin asking potential suspects for alibis. Once they identified them, of course.

Mary turned the body, likely looking to see if the bullets were through-and-throughs or still in Jill's body. Riley wasn't close enough to determine the answer, but he'd made a visual search of the space when he was talking to Blake and didn't see any slugs embedded in the walls.

Mary looked up. "You'll want to see this, Sheriff."

He squatted next to Mary. She held out Jill's arm and pointed at the inside of her wrist.

"What do you think they're looking at?" Sam murmured to Riley.

"I have no idea, but I sure want to know."

Blake took out his phone and snapped pictures of the wrist then got up and called the photographer to do the same thing. Blake stood frowning down on the body and suddenly spun to march toward Riley. His booties whispered over the wood floor, belying his intensity.

"You must be Samantha." Blake shoved out his hand. "Sheriff Blake Jenkins."

Riley was glad to see she took a firm grip and shook but didn't seem the least bit intimidated. "Glad to meet you, Sheriff. I've heard a lot of good things about you."

He waved off her compliments. "Blake. It's just Blake."

Riley had noticed that when meeting Samantha, most guys took a moment to appreciate her good looks and smile, but the fact that Blake didn't and was scowling didn't bode well for what Mary had spotted on Jill's wrist.

Time for Riley to go fishing. "Looks like you located something interesting."

Blake's expression remained somber as he tapped his phone and held it out. "What do you make of this?"

Riley looked at the picture. His jaw started to drop but he stopped himself from gaping. Leah's name was freshly tattooed on Jill's wrist. Puffy and pink inflamed skin surrounded dark blue lines indicating a very recent tattoo.

Sam glanced at the phone then met Riley's gaze. "You look like you've seen a ghost."

"Ghost?" He shook his head. "No. No ghost. But I *have* seen this tattoo. Or one like it. Leah and I both have matching tats with our names inked on them."

∽

Leah should've prepared better for meeting the sheriff by thinking of what he might ask her, but when Riley said Sheriff Jenkins was a great guy, she'd relaxed a bit. Big mistake. Riley had certainly understated the way she would feel under the sheriff's scrutiny. He had that same biting intensity she'd seen in pretty much every law enforcement officer she'd ever met.

He'd powered into the room carrying himself with confidence, his posture perfect and strong. He towered over her and hadn't said a word after Riley introduced them. It was like he didn't know what to say, and not in the starstruck way.

Maybe he thought he needed to ask exactly the right question, and he wanted to ponder that. Regardless, she didn't see the nice guy Riley had mentioned. Sheriff Blake Jenkins was, in a word, intimidating.

He scrubbed a hand over the five o'clock shadow darkening his wide jaw. "Riley tells me that you called him about a stalker."

She nodded and provided the same information she'd shared with Riley.

The sheriff didn't react at all. Simply looked at her with a blank expression like he expected her to add something else. She started to squirm under his scrutiny then stopped. She didn't want him to think she was trying to hide something.

She had to find a way to handle his intensity. Maybe it would help if she thought of him by his first name instead of Sheriff Jenkins. Blake, Riley had said. A nice name. Less daunting.

"Do you think this stalker might have killed Ms. Stevenson?" Blake asked.

She wanted to look away but kept her focus on him. "I don't honestly know. He could have I suppose, but why? What would his motive be?"

"Perhaps when you refused to talk to him, he got angry. He'd seen Ms. Stevenson on stage with you in the past. He believed you were close. That it would hurt you if you lost her."

"Sounds possible, I suppose." She just didn't know anything right now, other than she wanted the killer and stalker caught. Also that Owen's identity wouldn't be revealed to anyone but Riley. "If you think the stalker might be connected to Jill's death, I could give you access to the emails he sent to me. I do most of my emailing on my phone and iPad, and I'm glad to turn those over to you."

Blake nodded, a single jerk of his head. "Thank you for your cooperation."

"And your computer, too," Riley added.

Right, that. She should count on him to remember she'd evaded that point in their conversation.

Her stomach knotted. She needed to tell him about Owen right away. She hadn't wanted to deceive him, she really hadn't, but she was young and scared, and his father's threat had forced her hand.

After she split with Riley, he wouldn't return her calls and emails. So she tried to see him in person, but he'd moved. Her only hope in finding him was to go to his parents' house and ask them for his address. His father, Philip Glen, was the only one home that day. He took one look at her pregnant belly and said she was white trash with claws trying to climb up from the gutter into his world, and he would have nothing of it. Nor would he let his son be saddled with an illegitimate baby.

Most of her believed his assessment of her. She *was* white trash. Had been called it all her life. Why wouldn't she believe it? She was the stereotype of a poverty-stricken girl pregnant by the rich boy. A joke to the world. And the desperation to prove herself grew even greater.

When his father said if she told Riley about the baby, he would sue for custody of the child, and she would never see him again, she knew he had the power and influence to do that. She'd slunk off like a naughty child.

She couldn't lose the little boy in her womb who she now loved more than life itself and vowed to be a good mother. She planned to use those claws Riley's father accused her of having to succeed in the music world and make a good living to support Owen.

Oh, you were so young and foolish back then.

Wiser and stronger now, she hoped she and Riley could defend themselves against his dictator of a father.

"I'm sure Eryn's available to image the devices if you want to fast track this," Riley told Blake, bringing Leah back to the present.

"I'll give her a call," Blake replied.

"I also have handwritten letters from the stalker," Leah said. "And he was very active on Twitter until I blocked him from my account."

Blake took out a small notepad and pen then scribbled something down. "I'll look into that, and if it seems as if we have cause to request a warrant to get his personal information from Twitter, we'll request it."

"Thank you. He used the same Twitter name, *leahfan*, as he did with his email."

Blake added that to his notepad. "What about other social media?"

"I have a Facebook fan page and a business Instagram account, but not personal accounts. My publicist handles all my social media, and so far, the stalker only ranted about me on Twitter. After a while, I asked her to stop telling me when he posted because there was nothing I could do to stop him."

Blake rested on the edge of the makeup table. "Tell me about your—Ms. Stevenson's—boyfriend?"

"He's all hers," Leah said quickly. "As far as I know they're...they were still together."

Blake flipped through his notepad. "Neil, right? Could he have killed her?"

"I doubt it. He hates guns. He had a childhood friend who was killed in a drive-by and refuses to touch one."

That bit of information went into his notebook, too. "Can you think of anyone else who might want to kill her?"

Leah hadn't even considered it. She'd once been fairly close to Jill. Not outside of work, of course, but on the job. During rehearsals. Breaks. Meal time. Traveling on the bus. Hours and hours on the road either brought you closer to someone or made you want to run the other way. She liked Jill and had gotten close to her.

And look what happened. Jill betrayed her. And then there was Carolyn, her financial advisor. She'd embezzled millions of Leah's hard-earned dollars and spent every penny of it, pretty much draining Leah's accounts, and she was nearly broke now.

"Ms. Kent," Blake said.

Could Carolyn be involved? "You should talk to my former financial advisor, Carolyn Eubanks. I had to fire her four months ago for embezzlement. Jill was her client, too, and I think she lost money as well." Leah shook her head.

"My fault. I thought Carolyn was amazing and I referred several of my employees to her. In hindsight, I regret doing that."

"Backup singers and musicians make the kind of money that requires a financial advisor?" Blake asked.

"Not all the time, but I want people I can trust around me," she replied, catching the irony in her own words. "People who are talented and will be loyal to the team, and who won't bail on me for a better offer. Means I pay far higher than the going rate. Most of my team have been with me since the beginning."

Blake stared at her. "Except Jill and Carolyn."

"Yes, except them," Leah said sadly. "And I wish that was different. You don't know how much."

"I get that Jill might have a reason to want to kill Carolyn," Riley said. "But why would Carolyn want to kill Jill?"

Leah shrugged. "She just came to mind as someone in my world who was devious. Plus Jill will...uh, would have been testifying against Carolyn along with me."

"Ms. Eubanks could be trying to stop that, I suppose," Blake said, but he didn't sound like it was a good lead. "Give me her contact information, and I'll talk to her."

Leah scrolled through her phone contacts to Carolyn's name and shared it with him, very aware that Riley was still in the room and watching her every move. She was surprised he wasn't grilling her along with the sheriff.

Blake made a note of the details.

With all his notes, how many pads must he use in the course of his job?

He looked up. "Do you own a gun, Ms. Kent?"

What? Where'd that come from? Surely, he didn't think she — "You think *I* shot Jill?"

"Just covering all bases." He gave her a pointed look. "You didn't answer my question."

"Yes, I own a gun," she said and didn't care that she sounded belligerent.

Pen poised over his notepad, he stared at her. "What's the make and model?"

So, yeah, he honestly thought she could've shot Jill. Unbelievable. She hadn't done it, so it didn't matter if she told him about her gun. "It's a Ruger LC9S. The purple model if it matters."

That went into his notebook, too. "If we find Jill was killed with a 9mm, would you be willing to surrender your gun for ballistics testing?"

"Of course."

His eyebrow went up as if he didn't think she would really comply. "When was the last time you had contact with Jill?"

"The day I fired her."

"Tell me more about that."

"There's not much to tell. I was dating Neil, and I caught them in the bus in a compromising situation in my bed. I told her to pack her things and leave as well as ended my relationship with Neil on the spot. For what it's worth, she said he started things with her, but honestly it didn't matter to me. She had a choice. She could've told me about his advances and not gotten involved with him."

"And when was this?"

"I'd have to check our tour schedule for the exact date, but it was a little over a month ago in Portland."

Blake tucked his notebook and pen into his pocket and pushed off the makeup table.

Leah nearly sighed with relief. He was done, leaving, and this was almost over.

He met her gaze and held it, and she didn't like the fire

35

burning there. "Can you think of any reason why she would have your name freshly tattooed on her wrist?"

"What? My name?" Leah gaped at him.

Blake nodded. Riley opened his mouth to say something, but Blake silenced him with a look. "Answer my question, Ms. Kent."

But how? "I have no idea why she would do that. It's pure craziness. She hated me for firing her. Why would she want my name on her arm?"

"Do you have any tattoos?" he asked.

She glanced up at Riley. Had he told Blake about their matching set? Didn't matter. She had nothing to hide. She held out her left arm and tapped her wrist. "I have one here. It has my name and Riley's on it. But I either wear long sleeves or cover it with concealer anytime I'm in public. I don't want gossip reporters to go looking for Riley and make his life miserable."

This was true, but even more she didn't want Riley's father to find out and sue for custody of Owen.

"Seems like a lot of work," Blake said. "Why not have it removed?"

Indeed. Why not? A thought she had most every time she covered it up, but she couldn't get rid of it even if it would make her life easier. She had no idea why, but she couldn't.

She shrugged.

Blake narrowed his eyes. "Can you wash off the concealer so I can look at the tattoo?"

"Sure." She got up and went to the sink.

She pumped soap on her wrist and soon the blue-inked infinity tattoo appeared. She resisted running her finger over the figure eight shaped loop, her name on one side, Riley's on the other. He'd gotten a matching tattoo, but he was a rookie police officer, and though tattoos were allowed back then, they were frowned on, so he hid his on the underside of his arm where his shirt sleeve would cover it. Even if he was shirtless, the only way it was visible was if he lifted his arm.

She'd suggested he put it on his shoulder, as honestly it wasn't very romantic having her name near his armpit, but he said when he went to Oregon's recruit training academy, he'd change clothes in front of other recruits, and he didn't want even a chance that the tattoo could rule him out. In her mind, he'd overreacted, but becoming a cop was everything to him, so she didn't mention it again.

She dried her arm and returned to hold it out for the sheriff. He studied it, his eyes narrowing. He pulled out his phone and held it out. "This is the tattoo on Jill's wrist. It's in the same location."

Dumbstruck, she stared at the screen. This tattoo with the telltale pink skin of a recently inked image really did match Leah's. Her name was in the correct location on the figure eight, but a question mark was inked where Riley's name should be located.

How had this happened? How?

"No one even knows about my tattoo to have one made like this. Except for people closest to me like my mom, no one knows. Not even Felicity or Kraig."

"And me, but then we aren't close anymore, are we?" Riley's tone and expression were stony.

For some reason he was acting hurt. Maybe he didn't believe her story about covering the tattoo. He could think she was ashamed of having been in a relationship with him and that's why she hid it. Or she actually wanted to erase him from her life.

"Did Ms. Stevenson know?" Blake asked.

"I can't see how she would. Like I said, I covered it in public. I either wear something that covers it or blot it out. I do so before ever leaving home, and I never forget." She looked at the photo again.

Jill's other hand was in the picture, too. She wore a ring. One that Leah recognized, shock traveling through her. She held out the phone to the sheriff and tapped the delicate silver cross in a circle. "This is my ring. Jill must have stolen it before she left the tour."

He took the phone and enlarged the picture. "How can you be sure it's your ring?"

"A fan made it for me. She said it was a one-of-a-kind and no others exist."

Blake furrowed his high forehead. "Didn't you notice it was missing?"

Leah shook her head.

"Then you haven't worn it after you fired Ms. Stevenson."

Leah thought back, trying to remember her outfits and jewelry for the concerts. "I don't honestly know. I only wear it for performances, and there have been so many concerts since then. Felicity might remember, though. I can ask her."

"Go ahead, but don't tell her where we spotted the ring."

Leah got out her phone and was surprised to see her hands still trembling. Okay, maybe surprised wasn't the word. Shocked was more like it. Jill had been murdered. Leah was seeing Riley for the first time in five years, and she feared her past would be revealed like Pandora's box exploding open. Of course she was shaking.

"Everything okay?" Felicity asked.

"I'm putting you on speaker so Riley and Sheriff Jenkins can hear you." Leah tapped the speaker button. "You know that circle cross ring I got from a fan?"

"Yeah."

"Do you remember the last time I wore it?"

"Hmm, let's see." Silence filled the phone. "I'm not sure

if it was the *last* time, but you definitely wore it at the Chicago concerts. You were nervous because of the bigger crowds after playing the smaller venues, and you wanted to have a reminder that God was with you."

"Oh, right. I remember now. I wore it every night in Chicago."

"When was that?" Blake asked.

Felicity rattled off a date about six weeks ago.

Leah muted the phone. "Is it okay if I have her check for the ring in my jewelry box? Just to be sure it's gone?"

The sheriff shook his head. "If Ms. Stevenson stole it, her prints could still be on the box, and we'll want to preserve those."

Fingerprints. Stolen. Murder. Leah could hardly believe what was happening. She wanted to crawl in some hole and hide until it was all resolved. But with her tour schedule, she couldn't hide for even a day. She would face things head-on like she always did and get this resolved.

She unmuted the phone. "Thanks, Felicity. That's all the questions I have."

"Can I help in any other way?"

"I'm good for now, but thanks for asking." Leah quickly disconnected before Felicity started to ask questions Leah couldn't answer.

"I'll have my team look for the ring and fingerprint the jewelry box when they process your dressing room." Blake frowned. "Is there anything more you can tell me about the ring or the tattoo?"

Was there? Her mind was a muddled mess, and she just didn't know. "I suppose Jill might have liked my ring and had a copy made, but I doubt it. And as far as the tattoo, I honestly don't see how anyone could've even known about it."

He crossed his arms. "Well someone knew, and for some reason, Ms. Stevenson chose to have it inked on her arm."

"Or someone did it to her while she was held captive," Riley said.

Leah shot him a look. "What are you saying?"

"That whoever killed her arranged to have the tattoo done before he killed her. Likely as a message to you."

What? Even more craziness. "But what kind of message?"

Riley widened his stance, a move she knew well. He was digging in. Putting his foot down and either creating a line he wouldn't cross or committing to something. "I don't know, but I won't stop looking into it until I have the answer and I'm positive you're safe again."

Her heart beat hard but not from fear. It was hard to believe that she had a good man in her life again who genuinely cared about keeping her safe. Since she'd become famous, the men she'd encountered were shallow and wanted to use her in some way.

It was a heady feeling to have a fine man like Riley defend her, but the moment she told him about Owen, that would change, and odds were good that he would walk away from her.

Then who would defend her from the stalker who now might also be a killer?

4

Leah knew it was time. Not that a tiny dressing room—a murdered woman laying a few feet away—was the right place to tell Riley that he was a father. But then, where was the right place to tell a man he had a four-year-old child? To bring up a painful past?

Help me do it right. For Riley. For Owen. Please.

She steeled her resolve and looked up at Riley where he leaned against the wall, his attention fixed on his phone. She opened her mouth to speak. Tried to find the words. Tried to start. Failed. How did she start a conversation that would irrevocably change his life?

She desperately searched the room as if the right words hung in the air and she just had to grab hold of them. She spotted her phone laying on the table and an idea formed. She tapped in a text for her mother who cared for Owen when Leah was working.

Send me a really cute picture of Owen.

Leah sent the text and waited, her heart pounding so loudly that she was sure Riley had to hear it thump in her chest, but he didn't move. Not a bit. Not even an eyelash.

What he was doing on his phone she didn't know, but it captivated him.

Her phone dinged, and she looked at the screen. She'd received a photo taken at a recent zoo outing. Owen stared up at a tall giraffe, his eyes alight with wonder and excitement. Owen was beyond adorable in the picture. A perfect photo for a man to see his son for the first time.

"Riley," she said and held her breath.

He lowered his phone and looked at her. "Yeah?"

Here goes. "I have something to tell you, but I need you to promise not to share it with anyone else for the moment."

"Does it have to do with the investigation?"

"No."

"Okay, then. I promise."

She woke up her phone and handed it to him.

He studied the picture and looked up. "He's cute. Who is he?"

"That's Owen. O—my son." No matter how hard she tried, she couldn't say "our son." "He turned four two months ago."

"You have a child?" The gaping surprise on his face was beyond anything she could imagine. "Who's his—wait. Four years. You said he was just over four."

His gaze locked on hers, digging deep for an answer. "Is he—"

She took a long breath, gathering the strength and presence of mind to speak the words after years of keeping them silent. "Yes. He's our son."

Riley's eyes opened wide, a look of wonder in his eyes. He shook his head and turned his attention back to the phone, staring at it hard. Emotions raced across his face. He closed his eyes for a long time, and his free hand curled into a tight fist. She prepared herself for the anger she knew was coming.

He looked up, an icy coolness froze his expression. "Ours. You said ours." He took a step toward her and paused. "Unbelievable, Leah. Just unbelievable. How can you stand there calmly and say that when you didn't bother telling me about him? Not once in four years. Four years! So much time. So very much."

She'd expected his anger, but the sheer force caused her to shift back. "I wanted to tell you, but your father—"

"What in the world does my father have to do with this?" The words exploded from his mouth. He glared at her, his eyes harder than she'd ever seen, even stonier than the day they'd split up.

"Does he know about the boy? About Owen?" he demanded.

"Yes."

He sucked in a long breath. "You're kidding, right?"

She shook her head and waited for him to explode again. She felt terrible about this. Just awful, but she couldn't think of a way to convey that to him so she said nothing.

He raked his hand through his hair and started pacing. "I have a boy. A son. I'm a father."

He suddenly stopped and looked at the phone again. "I can see it now. The resemblance." He gently touched the screen, his anger fleeing for a moment, amazement settling in.

Her heart shattered, and she didn't know if it could ever be mended. This is the look he would've had when Owen was born if only she'd told him instead of believing his father. Riley would have been there. Held his son in his arms. Loved him from day one. That was the kind of man Riley was.

And maybe that played into her decision, too. Her fear that he was such a wonderful, stable, calm man that he could easily have gotten custody of Owen if he'd wanted to. With or without his father's help.

She was on the road all the time. Playing concerts. She didn't neglect Owen and leave him home. Her mother often came on tour, traveling in her own vehicle, and staying in an adjoining room with Owen, allowing Leah to spend time with her son yet keep him a secret. With her nomadic life, a judge would've sided with Riley, not her. She could never lose her son, so she had to hurt Riley in the process.

He lifted his head, the sadness apparent in the downturn of his lips. "Tell me what my father has to do with this."

She didn't want to speak. Didn't want to hurt him more, but he had to know the truth. Every bit of the ugliness.

She took a sip of water, and then pulled in a long breath. Finally, she met his gaze. "When I first learned I was pregnant, I didn't know what to do. I did nothing for the first few months, maybe hoping it would go away. But then the baby started moving, and I knew it was real. He was real. So I tried to get ahold of you. I texted. Emailed. Called."

"And I didn't answer. Or respond. I was hurt, and I didn't want to talk to you, but if I had…" Shaking his head, he dropped onto the nearest chair, set down the phone, and propped his elbows on his knees to rest his head in his hands. "Man…wow. This is my fault. All my fault. I missed so much."

"No. No. Don't blame yourself." She rested a hand on his shoulder, reveling in touching him and hoping she was transmitting her concern. "Sure, I gave up then, but the last few months of my pregnancy, I knew I had to try harder. So I came to your apartment."

He lifted his head. "But I'd moved."

She nodded. "And the manager wouldn't give me your forwarding address. I figured your parents could tell me where you lived. I knew your father might not. He didn't

44

think I was good enough for you. Your mom would've told me. At least I hoped she would. But she wasn't home."

"So you talked to my father, and let me guess, he still thought I was too good for you, and he wasn't glad to see you."

The raw pain of that visit came flooding back in living color—standing before Philip Glen, his head high and haughty as he belittled her and called her white trash.

Tears filled her eyes as she nodded.

Riley curled both hands into tight fists as anger burned in his eyes. "And he obviously knew you were pregnant."

She nodded again. "He said if I told you about the baby, he would sue for custody. He said with his connections, he could easily get custody, and he'd make sure I never saw the baby again. He sneered at me and told me if I didn't obey his demands, he would give the baby a 'proper upbringing.' I know how you hated your childhood and what a tyrant he was. I couldn't let our son live that way."

"If you would've told me, I would've stepped up. Done the right thing and my father wouldn't have had any part in things."

"How could I know that when you wouldn't even talk to me? For all I knew, you would hate our child as much as you seemed to hate me."

His hand went to his chest. "You really think I would've done that. Really? That I'm that kind of a man?"

His pain cut her to the quick as if he had stabbed her. She had just inflicted the worst pain of all on him since he prided himself in being an honest, trustworthy, genuine man. He strove to be the very opposite of his father, and she'd all but accused him of being his dad.

She grabbed his hand. He tried to pull away, but she held tight. "I'm sorry, Riley. I was young. Hurting. Alone with a baby on the way. No money. No hopes of continuing to sing to support myself and the baby. Emotional and not thinking clearly. I know in hindsight you would have been there for Owen but think about it. Even if you were, your dad could have trumped any effort you made to get custody."

He jerked his hand free. "I'm Owen's father. I would have prevailed."

"Would you have? Against your father and all his money. His connections. He would've called in every lawyer he could and fought until he won—just to spite me. You know that. I knew that back then, and I couldn't take a chance. Wouldn't you rather I raise Owen and not tell you then to have your father raise him?"

"You," he admitted, his tone and posture dejected. "So what do we do now? He can still fight us."

"I don't know. We think about it. Pray about it. Maybe seek legal advice. All I know is you deserve to know your son, and I had to tell you."

Riley dropped to his knees in front of her. He clutched her hands. "I'm sorry, honey. So sorry. If only I wasn't so pigheaded and answered your calls, this wouldn't have happened."

She never expected this response and wasn't prepared to handle it. "No. It's all my fault. I should have stood up to your father, and then gone back to get your address when your mother was home."

Riley shook his head. "I can't blame you for running. No one stands up to him."

"You did. You left home to become the person you wanted to be and cut all ties."

"But that was after years of him trying to control me, and honestly, it was done out of desperation. You didn't have the same motivation."

"Don't let me off the hook this easy. I take full responsibility for my actions, and I'm so, so sorry that you missed out on Owen's first years."

"Wait. Owen. His name is Owen." Riley's eyes widened. "You named him after my grandfather."

She nodded. "I knew how much he meant to you, and I wanted you to be a part of your son's life even if I couldn't tell you about him."

He squeezed her hands, and then got up to grab her phone. "Wake this up and let me see him again."

She pressed her thumb on the reader and gave the phone back to Riley. He stared at the screen, a smile sliding across his face. He looked at her, and a blistering, painful moment passed between them. "When can I meet him?"

Right, meet Owen. Become part of his life. Maybe try to take custody.

Fear grabbed her by the throat. That kind of fear that left you paralyzed—not physical, not like a stalker in the shadows—but the kind that told you no matter what you did, your life was about to fall apart, and you were helpless to do anything about it. That kind of fear left her unable to speak.

Leah had paled and looked like she might be physically sick. Riley stood unmoving. Thinking. He had a role in this mess. He should have talked to her back then, but he was young, too. Hurt. In anguish and licking his wounds. He just couldn't face her. And the result was that he missed four years of his son's life. He should forgive Leah. Now. Here. It was probably terrifying for her to tell him about Owen...and his father. But now that he thought—really thought—about what happened, he was angry. Good and angry. And honestly, he couldn't get beyond it. He didn't know who deserved his anger, but it was there. Simmering in his gut.

He hadn't felt this deep raging disappointment and resentment since the day he left home. But now it came alive in his every pore, and he couldn't get past his emotions. He had to think about everything she'd said. Process the news.

But first...first, he had to see his son.

"When, Leah?" he demanded, his tone sharp.

She lurched back, her eyes flashing in surprise.

"Now that I've had a moment to process, I'm angry," he said. "Not sure if it's at you. My father. Me. Maybe all of us. Or even at God. But I won't apologize for how I feel."

"You deserve to be angry," she said, sounding contrite. "And if I could leave so you never had to look at me again, I would, but selfishly I need you and your team. I know that makes me a terrible person, but there it is. I wouldn't blame you if you walked away and didn't look back. Just know that whatever you decide about my protection, I want you to get to know Owen."

He tightened his fists, letting the nails bite into his flesh. "You really know how to drive that knife into my gut and twist it, don't you? No matter how angry I was at you, I would never walk away and leave you in danger. I thought you would know that, too. And now you can't blame your comment on being young and naive."

She cringed. "I'm sorry. I...I don't know what else to say."

"It's simple. Tell me when and where I can see Owen, and we'll move on. Once I have time to process this we can talk again."

"Mom and Owen are back at the hotel," Leah said. "You can meet him in the morning when he wakes up."

Riley imagined stepping into the room. His child, the precious blond boy in the picture, would be playing, look up, recognize him as his father, and smile. That same eager, enthralled smile in the picture. Riley's anger evaporated, and his heart lifted like a feather floating in an ocean breeze.

He was a dad. A *dad*, for crying out loud. Him. Riley Glen, a dad. And he'd meet his son in the morning.

His anger completely vanished. He couldn't explain his roller coaster of emotions. Mad one moment. Glad the next. But he did get one thing.

He was a dad. A for-real, honest-to-goodness dad.

He'd been dreading the all-nighter waiting for Blake's team to finish processing the scene, but now he was grateful for it. He wouldn't sleep a wink anyway, and the investigation would help pass the time. That was when he could quit staring at Owen's face.

Riley got out his phone and held it up. "Text me Owen's picture."

He gave Leah the phone but didn't bother giving her his number as she'd called him before. He was eager to look at his son again. *His* son. An adorable blond-headed boy with a big smile and bright eyes. Kind of a Mini-Me.

Riley couldn't even grasp the thought, it was so foreign to him. A parent. He was a *parent*. And he wouldn't be an absent one. Not like his father. He would be there for Owen. Each and every day. For the big things. For the small things. He'd already missed so much. He wouldn't miss more.

Then it hit him. Hard. Like a punch to the chest, and he couldn't breathe.

How could he be there every day for Owen with Leah traveling all the time? He couldn't. Not unless he gave up his life and traveled with her. Or sought custody of Owen. Neither option a good one. The first would destroy him. The second would destroy her. And would it completely destroy Owen?

His phone dinged, and he glanced to be sure the picture

had arrived, but then he shifted his gaze to Leah. "What are we going to do about this?"

"Do?" she asked, but she had to know what he meant. She was likely stalling.

It made him mad all over again. He took a firm stance and didn't look away. "I want to be part of Owen's day-to-day life, but how can I be when you're always on the road?"

She raised her chin. "I'm not *always* on the road."

"A lot of the time, though, right? Especially with this make-it-or-break-it tour you're on. How long is that?"

"Three months, but I don't perform every day. I have time off. I'll be home."

"So I can what?" He stared and didn't bother to hide his anger. "See my son for five or six days of the month? After you kept him from me for four years? *Four years*."

"It's my job, and I have to provide for Owen."

Riley shook his head and looked up at the ceiling for a moment to gain a smidgen of calm before he acted like his rigid father. He sucked in a breath and let it out, then locked gazes with her. "And here we are again. Right back there. Our last day together. You touring the country. Me staying at home. But this time?"

He paused and locked in on her eyes. "This time there's a little four-year-old boy caught in the middle. How will you make that right, Leah? How?"

5

Riley was sure the sun was high in the sky by now even if the windowless backstage area gave no hint of it. But he felt the time changing in his bones because the morning brought the biggest day of his life.

He would meet his son for the first time.

Riley wanted to race out of the amphitheater and rush to the hotel, but the crime scene was still being processed. He touched the picture of his son's face one more time and stowed his phone in his pocket to pay attention to the activity around him. County's forensic crew was finishing and loading up their equipment. Time for Riley to get his team members started on this case and move forward in finding the stalker, then get to the hotel.

He dialed their cyber expert, Eryn Calloway, quickly brought her up to speed on the situation, and gave her a brief explanation of his past with Leah. "I'm sending you a picture of Leah's tattoo, and I need you to search the Internet for any photos where her tattoo is shown. As soon as possible would be great," he added as Eryn had a young daughter and they tried to be cognizant of that and help her work around parenting.

"I can start right away. Bekah's still sleeping," Eryn said. "Sounds like you're thinking someone close to Leah leaked the tattoo to the media."

"It's either that, or Leah's responsible for Jill getting inked, which would make her a suspect."

Eryn didn't respond, but silence left an uneasy tension.

"And how likely do you think that is?" she finally asked.

After Leah had dropped a bomb on him, he had to think about that for a moment. She could be keeping other secrets, too, but she wasn't a killer. Or at least he didn't think the mother of his child could do that. He gave Eryn the same answer as he gave Blake. That he didn't know.

"I'm glad to see you're at least allowing for the possibility," she said. "Something that can't be easy to do when you were once so close."

Riley had to agree. Not easy at all. But he wouldn't linger on that. "Also, Blake is going to call you about imaging Leah's electronic devices for email information on the stalker. You'll make a copy for us to review, too, right?"

"Only with Leah's permission."

Say what? "We need that information if we hope to catch her stalker."

"Then I'm sure she'll be glad to give it to us."

Would she? "Actually, she seemed a bit hesitant about her computer. Said as a celebrity she had to protect her private life."

"Well, she does, and I can understand her being cautious."

Not the response Riley expected.

"I'll talk to her," Eryn continued. "And ease her mind about that, but ultimately it's up to her."

Riley paced to diffuse his mounting frustration. How could he be expected to find a stalker—who could also be a killer—if Leah tied their hands? He would have a talk with her, too, and if she still refused, he wouldn't let up until she gave in.

She was still sitting in the dressing room, and he could do that now, but Blake would be turning over the scene in moments and that took precedence. Riley had wanted Alex to take her to her hotel and stand guard outside her room to keep her safe as well as to stop her from running with Owen. He didn't really think she might do that, but after the bombshell she dropped, he felt like anything was possible. But when he suggested she leave, she asked to stay in case she was needed. If they located any other evidence as to who killed Jill, Leah thought she might be able to help interpret it.

"Is there something else you need from me or are we done?" Eryn asked.

He focused his thoughts. "The guy also stalked her on Twitter. Name is *leahfan*."

"Okay, I'll look into that, but you know Blake is the only one who can get actual identification from social media and this guy's email account."

"I know. Just do what you can, okay?"

"Of course, and Riley...try to relax. You sound like you're wound up tight, and that won't do anyone any good."

"I'll do my best," he said and meant it, but how could he relax when a woman had been murdered and Leah had a stalker?

He had so much on his plate right now. He needed to work each and every moment to find the killer, and yet, make time to meet and get to know his boy. He needed help. Thankfully he could call on his top-notch team to support him.

"Before I go, can you get the team together for a meeting?" he asked. "Sometime in the next few hours."

"Most of the guys are holding trainings."

"We could meet on their lunch break," he said, not willing to give up that easily. "I'll have food delivered."

"Then they'll be there because you know they never pass up free food." She chuckled and ended the call.

Riley wished he could laugh with her, but he was still stinging from the way he and Leah had left things, and he had to figure out their future before his mood could improve. He'd never take Owen from her. Never. She was his mother. The only parent he'd known for four years. That would devastate him, but Riley would find a way to be part of his son's life, and if that meant joint custody then he wouldn't settle for less.

Blake turned from his conversation with a forensic tech and started across the room. If Blake had finished, then Sam could begin working, so Riley motioned for her to join them.

"We're done here, and I'm releasing the scene." Blake ran a hand over his face, his five o'clock shadow dark and out of character. He'd always been clean-shaven and well groomed, but then, Riley had never spent all night at a murder scene with Blake.

Blake let his hand fall, and it landed on his service weapon where it remained. "I suppose you're planning to do your own forensic evaluation."

"I am," Sam said.

"I hope you plan to share anything you find that we overlooked."

Sam didn't answer right away, and Riley could tell she wanted to say no. After all, Blake wouldn't share anything he'd located unless he had questions about it. But that wasn't because Blake didn't want to share. Department regulations prohibited him from doing so.

"I will," Sam finally said.

Blake responded with a clipped nod and looked at Riley. "I'll keep you updated."

"Appreciate it."

"And I assume you'll be seeing to Leah's safety until we apprehend the suspect," he added.

"I've got her back," Riley said and tried his best to look in control.

Blake cocked his head and watched Riley. So fine. Riley didn't exactly hide his emotions. One of his weak spots. Except when he was on duty as a police officer. There he'd managed to hide everything he was feeling, and he needed to take the same attitude now.

"Okay," Blake said not changing his focus, which told Riley he knew something was up. "I'm out of here."

He strode across the room, keeping to the walls. He was doing his best not to disturb forensics before Sam had a chance to do her thing. Something most law enforcement officers wouldn't have considered, but Blake was a cut above, and Riley often wished Blake was part of the Blackwell team. But then if Blake joined them, they wouldn't have a strong law enforcement contact. Also, to work on the team, Blake would need to suffer a serious injury that took him out of his current job, and Riley didn't wish that on anyone.

Sam turned to Riley. "I didn't see a ring on Blake's finger. Is he single?"

Riley shot her a surprised look.

"Not for me." Sam shook her head as if her being interested in Blake was out of the question. "I would never date anyone in law enforcement. It's for my friend. I think she'd be into Blake."

"He's married."

"Then why no ring?"

"Cause he's married to his job, not a woman."

"So he doesn't date, then?"

"Never heard of him doing so. Feel free to try to set him up, though." Riley smiled, trying to let his sour mood go. "But promise me one thing."

"What?"

"That I can be there when you tell him. It's bound to be good for a laugh."

Sam playfully punched Riley in the shoulder. "Just for that, you'll be the last person I tell."

Riley chuckled but then remembered the reason for being there and quickly sobered. "If you've got this, I'd like to escort Leah back to her hotel."

And meet my son.

"Actually, I could use help with measuring the scene before you go. Will only take a minute or two."

Not what he hoped to hear, but first and foremost, he had a job to do. A woman had been murdered. That trumped his personal turmoil, even if it was life-altering. "I'm all yours."

He followed Sam to the far side of the room where she set down her bag to withdraw her tape measure and the drawing she'd made earlier. Together they took the measurements, and she jotted them down.

She stowed the notepad and got out a camera. "You can take off now. I'll take pics of the scene then process any forensics I find. FYI, I took a few shots of the body with my cell when no one was looking if you need them for any reason."

Riley opened his mouth to weigh in on her actions, but she held up a hand. "I know Blake said not to do anything but observe, but come on, you would've done the same thing." She grinned. "I was *observing* through my camera."

"It's just a good thing Blake didn't catch you, or he would've asked you to leave."

"I know how to be discreet." An impish smile brightened her face.

As he grabbed his jacket from a chair in the corner, she quickly moved around the room to snap photos and then squatted near the area where Jill had fallen. "The blood spatter is consistent with a close-range shot. Means she was murdered right here, and the body wasn't moved."

He shrugged into his coat. "Good to know that for a fact, though I never really thought otherwise. I've been going on the theory that the shooter was on the premises. If he didn't wear gloves, you might be able to find his prints."

"I'll start with the doorknobs." Sam stood. "But you should know, knobs aren't always the easiest to print because of their shape. That will be especially true after the forensic team has already dusted them."

"I know you'll do your best."

"I might even have to remove a knob to bring it back to the compound to fume it for prints."

"We're talking murder here, so do whatever you need to do. Gage will smooth things out with the amphitheater owner."

"Gage is great to work for, isn't he?"

Riley nodded. "And I'm thankful for him every day."

A faraway look claimed Sam's eyes, and she seemed to forget all about him. He had to believe she was thinking about her life in limbo. That time between being told she could never again do the job she loved and finding hope and a promising future with Blackwell Tactical.

She tapped her notepad. "I'll have to call in a few favors to get the prints analyzed, but I've still got contacts at PPB who'll run them for me."

Riley nodded. "Then I guess I'll owe you."

"Oh yeah, you will!" She smiled and any remnants of her distress vanished.

Riley honestly didn't know anyone who smiled as often as Sam did. Not only was she a great team member, but he suspected she would be an amazing girlfriend or wife. But though Riley was already fond of her in only a few weeks, his feelings were all sisterly. Nothing romantic at all.

Why couldn't he fall for someone like her instead of Leah? And why couldn't people choose who they were attracted to?

Why, God?

Riley didn't want to feel anything for Leah, but it was painfully obvious that his strong feelings remained. Hearing her scream earlier had taken years off his life. Then learning about Owen? His feelings for her were suddenly all mixed up with having a child together.

His emotions were so raw, he feared he'd turn into a blathering idiot in front of Sam. He quickly said, "If Blake didn't take the jewelry box into evidence, you'll want to print it and the windowsill in Leah's dressing room."

"Will do. And what about the murder weapon? I should do a thorough search. Any theories on that? I mean, obviously, Blake's team tore the place apart and did a grid search around the building's exterior but found nothing. It's looking to me like the killer took it with him."

"Unless he ditched it outside the radius of their search."

"When I finish inside, I'll expand that area and do my own search."

"Sounds like a good idea." He zipped his jacket up." Okay, I'm out of here."

"I'll let you know if I recover anything that I think Blake's team missed."

"Thanks, Sam. I'm glad to have you on the team."

"Glad to be on it. I'm not glad for the injury. Not because it took me out of the job, because this one is even better. But

I could do without the pain and stiffness." She rolled her shoulder. "Anterior shoulder subluxation. Affects my shooting accuracy, and since criminalists are sworn officers and work patrol at times, I had to choose between a desk job and unemployment. What about you?"

"Lost a kidney after taking a bullet outside. I was just coming off duty. Outside the precinct with other guys coming off, too. Didn't have a vest on and this guy decides to open fire. Thankfully, no one died, but we all had our share of injuries. Some life-altering like mine."

"Wow, that's rough."

"Maybe, but it's easier to live with one kidney than a painful shoulder."

"Yeah, but another injury and you could lose that one. Seems like you might want to be a little more cautious."

"You lost a kidney?" Leah's shocked voice came from behind.

He turned to find her standing there openmouthed. She'd changed into different jeans and a pink T-shirt since the forensic team had taken her clothing. Because she'd found the body, she was a suspect until proven otherwise—standard procedure in a homicide investigation. They'd also swabbed her hands for gunshot residue, but they came up clean. A good thing, but honestly, not all shots left residue, or she could have worn gloves. They couldn't rule her out as a suspect yet. He hated thinking about her that way, but as Eryn said, he had to keep an open mind.

"It's why I left PPB," he replied to her question. "They wouldn't let me work with the risk of another injury."

"I should say not." She crossed her arms and her nostrils flared.

Look at her—acting all protective. Was she considering him as the man she used to date or as the father of her son?

Neither were familiar to him, and he didn't know what to say.

"I need to finish those prints." Sam started to leave, then turned back to Leah. "I'll need your prints for elimination purposes. Can I take them before you go?"

"Sure," Leah said, keeping her focus on Riley.

He still had no clue what she was thinking and why she seemed unwilling to look away, but he didn't like the feeling at all.

"Okay, then," Sam said, her tone declaring she'd picked up on the vibe between them, making her uncomfortable. "I'll grab the supplies."

Since Leah was still watching him, he would use her undivided attention to float his upcoming plan past her. "After Sam takes your prints, I'll drive you back to the hotel, but then I'd like for you to stay at our compound."

She tilted her head. "Compound?"

"Gage owns fifty acres near the beach in Cold Harbor. He and his family have a house there. The rest of the team members live in cabins on the property. The entire area is fenced in with state-of-the-art security which would be perfect to keep you safe."

She narrowed her eyes. "Why such tight security?"

"We have a large weapons cache for our law enforcement classes. We also have a ton of expensive equipment. So it only makes sense to protect it."

"The security sounds intimidating."

"It is. Or at least we hope it is. And it's the safest place for you right now."

She tapped her chin with a finger, looking lost in thought, then shook her head. "I'd rather not. I haven't seen the stalker in Rugged Point. It should be safe for me to go back to the hotel."

He stepped closer to her to keep Sam from overhearing him. "It's not optional, Leah, now that I now know about Owen. I won't risk a stalker harming him."

"No one but you and my mother know about him or that he's here. He's staying in a different room with my mom. He'll be fine."

Riley crossed his arms. "As I said. It's not optional."

"Please, Riley. If we stay there it will only take one look from your teammates to figure out Owen is yours. Then the word will get out about him. I can't have that happen. Not now. Not while I'm on this important tour. The gossip could take over. Ruin things. My career will all but be over."

"My teammates can be trusted not to tell anyone."

"I don't know them. I can't trust them."

He planted his feet firmly on the floor and wasn't going to budge. "I can, and I do. End of story. After I meet Owen, we'll pack your things and head out to the compound right away."

She took a sharp breath and blew it out. "I insist on my mother coming along, too."

"Sure, that's fine." Riley almost sighed in relief that she'd agreed.

"Be sure to add the costs for our boarding to my bill."

"Bill?" He stared at her. "Do you honestly think I would charge you for this?"

"Your whole team is working on finding the stalker. I have to pay you."

"You may think that paying me erases what we had together, and this is just a business relationship now, but it's more than that, and you know it. Particularly after your bombshell. So no." He planted his hands on his waist and held her gaze. "You aren't paying for my—our—services and that's final."

She watched him for a long moment, emotions racing so quickly across her face he couldn't pin them down, but not one of them looked positive. "I don't want anything more than business between us. We'll see each other for Owen's sake, but that's all. Nothing romantic for sure."

"We finally agree on something," he said, sounding sure of himself, when he was anything but sure.

"I..." Leah started to say, but Sam joined them, and Leah closed her mouth.

"This should only take a minute." Sam carried a hand-held fingerprint reader, and she quickly recorded Leah's prints.

The moment Sam packed up the device and moved away, Riley took Leah's arm. "C'mon, let's get going."

"Wait." She shrugged free. "My wrist. The tattoo. I still need to cover it up. We certainly don't want reporters contacting your father right now."

He had a son to meet and waiting for her to hide any evidence that she'd once cared for him was the last thing he wanted to waste time on. Especially since he believed it was more. He suspected she was embarrassed to have a public display of their failure on her wrist.

He eyed her. "Why didn't you get rid of it? It's easy to do."

"Do you still have yours?"

"Yes, but I don't spend time every day covering it up."

"I considered having it removed, even made an appointment with a doctor, but for some reason I couldn't go through with it. I don't know why. Maybe I couldn't erase you from my life that completely."

He didn't know what she meant exactly, but fool that he was, her behavior gave him hope that she still cared about him. Why that made him happy, he didn't know, but he needed to get control of his volatile emotions soon or he was in for a world of hurt again.

~

Leah stepped out with Riley into unusual sunshine on a cold September morning. Normal weather for this time of year was misty rain with occasional downpours. Leah wished she could take a moment to lift her face and absorb the warmth to soothe away the terrible events, but Riley clutched her arm and urged her forward. He was likely in a big hurry to meet Owen.

She didn't know how she was going to tell her precious son that Riley was his dad, and she dreaded the moment. She'd expected the tough part was telling Riley, but telling Owen trumped that in spades. How could she possibly do that? Did she say right off the bat that Riley was his dad or let them get to know each other first? Owen was an easy-going child, taking after Riley in that regard, but what if Owen didn't like Riley?

She'd dreamed about this very situation many times, and it always ended badly. She had no idea how to proceed. She'd simply have to play it by ear, and that scared her to death.

A biting wind whipped across the lot, and she snuggled into Riley's jacket. He'd allowed her wear his coat to cover her tattoo, and the warm fleece lining kept the cold at bay. She appreciated his typical kindness, but with the scent of his soap lingering on the fabric, memories assaulted her, and she didn't want to go down memory lane. Didn't want to remember the good times and the love they'd shared or how much he meant to her. She'd loved him so intensely it was a wonder she was ever able to walk away from him to pursue her dream.

Riley unlocked the passenger door of his black SUV, and she shook her head as if she could knock the thoughts from her mind, but they stuck like Velcro to a fuzzy sweater. Since Carolyn had stolen Leah's nest egg and her latest album didn't generate the sales she needed, she'd been thinking a lot about her life, her career. She may have succeeded in becoming a professional musician with chart-topping hits, but with the theft, it didn't bring the financial stability she desperately needed.

She'd once believed her future was all set. She'd lived modestly and saved, saved, saved, but then Carolyn embezzled. Leah could never go back to the poverty of her childhood. Never.

Angry at Carolyn all over again, Leah climbed into the vehicle and yanked hard on the seat belt.

"You trying to kill that thing?" Riley asked, grinning at her. One of his charming features that she'd loved. Her anger dissipated, and she smiled.

"Sorry," she said. "I was thinking about something, and it made me mad."

"Like?"

"Just stuff."

He eyed her for a moment, like he was dying to ask for additional details, but then closed the door and ran around the front of the SUV and climbed behind the wheel.

The hotel was only a few miles away, but the tension in the confined space felt like a heavy blanket of fog, suffocating her as they drove. She didn't want to bring up anything personal. She was still too raw from their discussion about Owen—though she had to admit Riley had taken the news better than she'd expected—and talking about Jill's murder wasn't something Leah wanted to do either.

Riley didn't seem to notice her turmoil but kept checking his rearview mirror as if he believed someone was following them. Maybe her stalker, but there was no indication that he'd come to Rugged Point.

Riley suddenly glanced at her and caught her watching him. His eyebrow went up in a perfect arch, but then it fell as fast as it raised. "I scheduled an update with the team. I assume you'd like to freshen up at the hotel before that."

"Thank you." She smiled at his consideration. "Also you should know that I need to make time this afternoon to meet with Kraig and my publicist. We decided to go ahead with the concert tonight. I'd rather we didn't, but I won't go into all of the logistics of cancelling a concert, which Kraig impressed on me before he left. We're in danger of losing our promoter, and if that happens, it's the end of my tour and the end..." She shrugged, as she couldn't say the end of her career. It was bad enough to think about failing, much less speak it out loud.

"I kind of figured with the way Kraig was acting that the concert would go on."

"We'll dedicate it to Jill." She folded her hands together and stared at them. "I feel like a hypocrite since we were on the outs, but I realize in hindsight that she did me a favor with Neil as it showed his true colors."

"About the concert." He met her gaze and held it for a split second before facing the road again. "I'd be remiss if I didn't mention that it's virtually impossible to protect you on stage. Not with the size of the crowd. The team will be there and your security will be the best anyone can provide, but your safety isn't a given."

She could almost see her stalker in the audience, the same gun that killed Jill in his hand. Was she being foolish to do this concert? Maybe if it was just her she had to think about, but she had to think about Owen and her mom, too. And also all the people she employed. She couldn't suddenly put them out of a job.

"I have to keep going with the tour," she said, then took a deep breath. "You know about my sales slipping and about Carolyn. I can't believe I'm telling you this, but I'm...I'm nearly broke. I thought I had a nice nest egg for Owen, me, and Mom to fall back on if anything happened."

He sat, not responding, his gaze on the road. He tightened his fingers on the wheel then relaxed them. "I'm sorry things aren't going as well as you hoped. Our team will do our very best for you so you can keep up with your tour and make some of that money back."

He'd sounded genuinely sorry, and she appreciated his compassion after she'd badly hurt him. She faced him again. "I know you will, and I appreciate that more than I can say."

He pulled under the hotel's portico and glanced at her again, his expression unreadable. "Do you want to freshen up before or after you introduce me to Owen?"

"Before," she said and waited for him to complain at the delay in meeting Owen, but he simply nodded.

He killed the engine and quickly jumped out to open her door. Ever the gentleman. Leah slid out and hurried inside the lobby. She took a good look around before proceeding to the front desk. Though she hadn't seen her stalker in Rugged Point, it wasn't hard to imagine him hiding behind the large potted plants. Or behind the coffee cart. Waiting for her to pass so he could pounce. If he was the killer, did he plan to shoot her, too?

Did Jill know the shooter was behind her and had a gun and planned to use it? Was she running away or simply walking to the stage entrance?

After years spent with Jill, Leah could vividly imagine her in the moment. Could put herself in Jill's shoes.

Wait. Jill wore similar clothing as Leah. Their hair, height, and build were very close. She wore Leah's special ring. Could the killer have thought Leah had already left the stage and mistakenly killed Jill instead?

Leah's knees went weak, and she clutched the counter.

Riley faced her. "Are you all right?"

She nodded, but she was far from all right. If not for Jill coming into the theater, would Leah now be laying in the morgue?

6

Riley searched Leah's hotel room and bathroom and pronounced it safe for her to enter. She'd lost her color in the lobby and still hadn't regained it. He'd asked about her quick mood swing, but she'd said she wanted to get to the room safely and then she'd tell him her concern.

He closed the door, and she handed his jacket back to him. "What if the bullet was meant for me?"

"What?" Riley tried not to stare at her, but he couldn't help it with her outrageous statement.

"Jill and I were similarly dressed. She wore my ring. Her hair, height, and build are near enough to mine that from the back the shooter could have believed it was me."

She could be right, and Riley didn't much like it. So why didn't he see that? Or Blake or Sam? The resemblance was close enough, that was for sure. But what about the tattoo?

"You could be right."

"Really, you think so?"

"Yeah, but only if Jill's recent tattoo was unrelated to the murder. If the killer did the tattoo or had it done, he would know it wasn't you."

Looking confused, she dropped onto the corner of the

bed. "Do you really think the killer had something to do with the tattoo? Maybe, like you said before, that it's some sort of message to me?"

He nodded. "Either way, I'll mention this theory to the team to get their opinion."

"Good," she said, but didn't look happy with the fact that he agreed with her.

And why would she? He'd admitted that someone might have killed her if Jill hadn't been there.

If Leah was right, he could have lost her. Permanently. Right there, not far from him before he had a chance to talk to her again. He would've never seen her again. He couldn't imagine that. Even when they'd been apart he always wondered if he would run into her again someday. But death was so final. So very final.

His stomach knotted. He didn't want her to see how much this affected him. He breathed in, held the breath, and released it slowly.

"Why don't you go ahead and freshen up," he suggested, hoping he came off as lighthearted. "And I'll be in the hallway making calls."

She nodded and got up. When she reached him, she grabbed his arm. "Do you think it's a good possibility or far-fetched?"

He considered not answering, but her wounded gaze was locked on him, and he couldn't refuse. "Good possibility."

She gasped for air and dropped her hand to wrap her arms around herself while looking down at her feet.

"Hey, hey." He rested his hand on her shoulder. "I won't let anyone harm you. You know that, right? I'd give my life before letting that happen."

"I know, it's just..." She shrugged.

"Just what?"

She looked up, her eyes murky pools of anguish. "After a few betrayals, it's hard for me to trust people right now."

He jerked his hand away, feeling burned like touching a hot stove. "You don't trust me. That's rich after the secret you kept for years."

She took a step back as if he'd physically struck her. He hadn't, but he did hit her where it would hurt, and that wasn't the kind of guy he wanted to be. Why did he always let her get to him like this? React—then think?

"Sorry," he said and meant it. "That was a low blow, but hearing you don't trust me after everything? It was too much."

"I trust you. Totally. But..." She sighed. "After the recent betrayals in my life, my initial reaction is to be suspicious. I hate that, but when you're a celebrity, people want to ride on your coattails. It's hard to know people's true motives. Yours are right, though. Just bear with me if I have knee-jerk reactions, okay? I trust you. Totally. Completely."

He believed her, but he probably shouldn't. "I don't know how you live like that. It must really hurt. Especially losing your money. I know how important that is to you."

"Don't," she snapped, and her eyes flashed wide open. "Don't say it like that. Like money is a dirty word. I have to support myself and Owen. My mother, too. It's not a crime to work. To take care of the people you love."

"I wasn't aware I put any emphasis on the word."

She sighed. "Nothing has changed, has it? We're older. Maybe wiser and experienced at life, but you still detest money, and I still need financial security."

"That about sums it up." He'd hoped that she'd changed her opinion on money, but why should she? He didn't. And honestly, he knew his feelings on the matter were skewed. But he'd seen how having a nearly unlimited supply corrupted. How it gave people ultimate power that should be reserved for God. How people made gods of themselves. He supposed there were exceptions, but he'd never met one.

"And there's no point in talking about it," she added.

He tipped his head at the door. "I'll be in the hall."

He exited the room and tugged the door closed. He took a look down the hallway, both directions, and was pleased to see it empty. He couldn't deal with trying to protect Leah from an immediate foe right now. Not with raw emotions.

Why did it still hurt so much to see that she chose her career over him? She didn't have the same money-grubbing personality as the people he'd grown up around, willing to do anything to get more and build their influence. Or did she? Had he been so blinded by love that he didn't see it back then? Was his father right that he needed to be cautious around her?

If so, he would find out. They would be spending a lot of time together until the stalker and killer were apprehended, and Riley knew she couldn't keep up an act for that long, and he would see the real Leah.

Because there was one thing he was an expert at—spotting a phony who cared only about growing their wealth. His family had taught him that skill.

Riley stood at the door to Owen's room and almost didn't want Leah to open it. His future lay behind a closed door, and he was so concerned Owen wouldn't like him that his palms were sweating.

She swiped the key and pushed open the door. The joyful laughter of his son spilled into the hallway. Riley's heart lurched with joy. Owen was here. Not just a picture. Riley really and truly had a son.

Riley stepped into the room that matched Leah's. Two

beds with floral bedspreads, a long credenza, and a small round table with chairs. But in this room, one of the beds was covered with colorful Duplo building blocks, and a woman he had to assume was Leah's mother, sat on the edge of the bed, the giggling child hidden behind her. She was thin with shoulder-length blond hair, and when she turned to look at them, Riley caught his first view of his son.

He clutched red blocks in his chubby hands and pushed them together then added them to a tall tower.

"Oh," Leah's mother said. "You brought...is this..."

"Yes. Mom, meet Riley."

He heard Leah speaking, but his brain couldn't process her words because at that very moment, his son turned to look at them. His eyes, the same soft blue as Riley's, locked on him. Riley didn't know what he expected, but the overwhelming, mind-crushing wave of pure love caught him off guard, and he had to sit down on a nearby chair.

Owen quickly shifted his focus to Leah. His eyes lit with joy. "Mommy."

He scrambled off the bed and ran past Riley as fast as his short legs carried him to leap into Leah's arms. She swung him around, and Riley memorized every inch of his son's face and body.

He wore a black-and-white striped shirt with blue jeans, and had a smudge on his cheek, dirt or crayon. His hair was blond and tousled with an adorable cowlick in the back. It was in the exact same place as the cowlick Riley worked to tame after every shower.

Leah set him down and sat on the bed. "I brought someone special to meet you."

Owen spun to look at him, curiosity burning in his eyes. "Who is he, Mommy?"

Riley dragged his focus from Owen to Leah. She chewed

on her lip for a moment. "Remember when I told you your daddy had to go away?"

Owen nodded, his expression now serious.

"Well, he's back now. This is your daddy."

Owen's cute mouth formed an O of surprise.

Riley hoped he would come over to talk to him, but he scooted behind Leah.

"You don't have to be afraid of him," Leah said. "He's a wonderful man and a lot of fun. He wants to get to know you. Do you think you'd like that?"

Owen gave a shy nod but grabbed Leah's hand and held onto it.

"Don't worry. Grandma or I will be with you, too." She turned and stroked her hand over his hair.

Riley longed to be there next to them running his hand over his son's head, too. Holding him. This little person who resembled Riley in so many ways his heart almost burst from the pure joy of it.

He now understood why Leah didn't tell him about Owen. She loved Owen with the same intensity, and she was being a fierce mother bear protecting him from Riley's controlling, manipulative father. Riley still didn't like what she did, but he could forgive her now. Totally and completely. How could he do anything else after experiencing this unexplainable love?

But then fear filtered in. Fear that the boy wouldn't like him. He had to find a way to get through to him and eliminate any concerns he might have. At six feet and around two hundred pounds, to a four-year-old used to mostly women in his life, Riley must seem like a monster.

He knelt on the floor to make himself smaller. "Can I see what you're building?"

Owen nodded and scooted back on the bed, tugging Leah along with him. Riley got up and suddenly noticed

Leah's mother watching them. "Sorry I blew you off before, Mrs. Kent. This is all just so surreal." He extended his hand.

"It's Vivian." She shook his hand with a firm grip. "I'm very glad to meet you, and Owen will be, too, once he adjusts to the idea."

"I hope so." Riley went to the far side of the bed. He gently sat to keep from jostling Owen.

Owen looked up, his eyes narrowed. "I'm building a castle. This is the tower."

Riley nodded, keeping his expression serious to match Owen's. "It's a fine tower."

A half smile quirked his mouth, revealing a dimple in the exact spot as Leah's. He'd always found hers adorable, but a dimple on his son's innocent face? Beyond adorable— whatever that word might be. Something totally not in Riley's vocabulary.

"Want to help?" Owen asked.

Riley nodded.

"You can make another tower with the green blocks. Make sure it's as good as mine."

Riley loved his son's spirit, even though it bordered on bossy. He collected green Duplos and started stacking them. He felt Leah watching him but wasn't about to look up to see what she was thinking. He simply wanted to enjoy his son. He took his time connecting blocks and waiting for Owen's approval, which was generously given.

"I have something special to share," Leah announced.

Owen and Riley both looked up.

She smiled at Owen. "Your father invited all of us to stay at his cabin. You know, a place like the cabins you build with your Lincoln Logs. Would you like to do that?"

Owen's eyes got wide. "Can we?"

"It's a great place to visit, and you would have friends to play with," Riley jumped in, hoping to up the enticement.

"They have a fort, a swing set, and a puppy. His name is Barkley, though he's more of a young dog now, I suppose. And it's located on a big wooded property where we have campfires when the weather is nice, but it's still close to the beach."

Owen got to his feet and jumped up and down. "Can we go now, Mommy? Can we?"

She smiled at Owen, the happiness in her gaze one Riley remembered from the past, and he nearly gasped at the way it sliced into him. How he would like to have that look cast in his direction again.

"As soon as you clean up," she said. "And we get everything packed."

"Yay." Owen clapped his hands then launched himself at Riley.

He caught his son in his arms and had no time to think about how it felt to hold him before Owen backed away and rested his hand on Riley's shoulder for balance. His eyes narrowed. "Are you going to go away again?"

Riley wasn't prepared for the heart-rending question, so he opted for the truth. "Sometimes. Just for a few days at a time. I have to do that for my work, but otherwise? No. I'm never going away from you again, Son. That's a promise."

7

The compound's big metal gate clanked closed behind them on a fenced property deep in the woods near Lost Creek. Leah had never been much of an outdoorsy person, but Riley was, and she'd gone camping with him in the past. She didn't hate it, but she would much rather be in a house with a bed and bathroom close by. Still, back then she'd do almost anything to make Riley happy.

When had that changed? Was it the day they'd broken up, or had it been building up to her leaving? She never really considered that, but maybe it would be worth giving it some thought.

Not now, though. Not when she was entering Riley's world.

He glanced in the rearview mirror, a hint of a smile on his face. Her mother and Owen sat quietly watching out the windows for the entire drive which was so unlike Owen. Riley had been checking the mirror for the entire trip—first for a stalker as they left the hotel, and he might be doing so now, too, but his gaze kept lingering on Owen.

It was clear that he was truly enamored with his son, and it made her happy to see his love. But it worried her, too, as she didn't know what he planned to do about wanting to see Owen on a regular basis.

The tires crunched over gravel, drawing her attention. They wound down a hill, and the wooded lot opened to a large clearing with a ranch-style house and large yard. Two bikes lay next to the door, one purple, one black.

"This is Gage's house." Riley glanced at Leah. "I mentioned him, right? He owns Blackwell Tactical and is an all-around amazing guy. He's married to Hannah, and they have two children. Mia and David."

Riley clearly respected Gage, so Leah instantly did, too. Riley was a great judge of character, and he always seemed able to identify a phony. She sure could use him in her world. Maybe then she wouldn't have had the recent betrayals.

Riley looked up in the mirror. "They're the ones with the puppy, and you'll like playing with them."

"Puppy!" Owen clapped.

Riley grinned as he turned down a narrower road and soon they came upon cabins on both sides of the road, each of them unique in their design. Five in all, and at the far end, a sixth one was framed and under construction.

"This is where we all live," he said. "We each built our own places with help from the team. Sam's is the one that's not finished. She just joined the team, and we're helping her finish it."

"Which one is yours? No wait." She held up a hand. "Stop to let me take a good look and guess."

He braked, and she studied the buildings. She knew it wasn't the one with a small porch holding two rockers and children's toys laying out front. He wasn't a sit-in-a-rocker kind of a guy. He was a doer. And he didn't have children— at least none that she knew about. Except Owen, that was.

Nor did the very contemporary structure fit him. The big

77

picture window in the front was too exposed, and he liked his privacy. Plus that cabin and the one with the porch were made of logs, and he was a more linear thinker and liked straight, clean lines. Another one was so plain and simple, she didn't see that as being his, either. He'd developed good taste and design sense in his upbringing.

His had to be the A-frame, with a metal roof that continued down the sides. Sleek white wood lined the peak in front and slatted boards with a natural finish were mounted vertically across the front. Natural-finish French doors served as the entrance, and steps ran the width of the building, adding to the stylishness.

Private. Clean lines. Simple, yet architecturally interesting. Yeah, this place screamed *Riley*, and she could hardly wait to see the interior.

"Well?" he asked. "Not as easy as you thought, huh?"

"No, it's very obvious," she replied. "It can only be the A-frame on the left."

He cocked an eyebrow, and she chuckled. She loved feeling happy for a moment. Knowing her stalker couldn't get to her here, she could relax for the first time in weeks.

"How did you know?" he asked.

"It's you. Not fussy or intricate. Interesting without trying. And very few windows on the front keeps it private."

"Wow, that's amazing. You're right, but I would never have seen it. I just built what I liked."

"Go, Daddy," Owen said. "Want to meet Barkley."

Riley whipped his head around, a shocked expression on his face. Owen calling Riley *Daddy* had shocked her, too, but what else would he call him? She'd told her son that Riley was his daddy.

Riley reached back and patted Owen's knee then turned around and pulled into the parking space near his cabin. He was out of the vehicle like a flash and opening Owen's door.

Leah leaned over the seat. "I need you to be on your best behavior, Son. Put your listening ears on and don't wander off. Okay?"

"K."

Leah's mother undid his straps, and he bolted from his seat. "Want to see inside."

Riley held out his hand, and Owen took it, his earlier reticence long gone. She sighed.

"That a good sigh or bad?" her mother asked.

"I honestly don't know," Leah said as she gathered her things together.

"They do look adorable together."

Leah watched them walking hand in hand to the door, their blond hair standing out in the shady woods. "They both toe in on the right foot. I never noticed that on Riley before."

"You'll be noticing a lot of similarities, I think." Her mother picked up Owen's toys and books and put them in his backpack. "You did a good thing, Leah. Telling him, I mean. I know you're scared, and you don't want to share Owen, but it's the best thing for Owen."

She glanced at her mother. "I hope you're right, because right now, it feels like my world is collapsing around me."

"We'll just have to trust God, won't we?" She got out of the vehicle.

Leah climbed out, too. "Always your answer for everything. Even in the worst of times."

"You have to live beyond your circumstances. Trust God beyond them."

"Even when your child is hungry and you have no food?"

Her mother frowned. "I tried my best, sweetie. I really did. And took every bit of help that was offered so you didn't go hungry for long."

"I know you did, Mom, and I am forever grateful that

you did and kept trying to make things better. But I hope Owen never has to experience the humiliation of getting free breakfasts at school when all the other kids know they're just for the low-income families and make fun of you. Or standing in a soup kitchen line." The memories were too painful to think about, so she willed them away.

"There's no shame in needing help like that. Only shame is in how you've always seen it." Her mother sighed. "Look at you now. You have abundance. Way more than is required for everyday life, and you still have needs. Deep unquenched needs."

Leah hadn't told her mother about the embezzlement yet as she didn't want her to worry. "Not physical ones. Owen has never known, nor will he know what it's like to wonder where his next meal will come from."

Her mother looked hurt, and Leah gave her a hug. "I'm not dissing you, Mom, or the way you raised me. You did everything in your power to take care of me. I know that and I appreciate it. I'm doing the same thing for Owen. I hope you can understand that."

Riley's gut churned with acid as he looked at the interior of his home. He'd never shown his cabin to anyone who meant as much as his son did. He wasn't close to his parents. Didn't have siblings. Hadn't dated anyone seriously in years. That meant he never brought anyone home with him except his teammates, and they'd been to his cabin more times than he could count—no big deal.

So touring Leah, Vivian, and Owen through the space seemed as personal as laying his heart on the table for close examination.

"Is this my room?" Owen asked as they stepped into the guest bedroom.

"I thought your grandma could sleep in this room, and you and your mom can stay in my room."

Owen looked up at him, a quizzical look on his face. "I mean my *always* room."

Riley didn't know how to answer that. "I...ah...I'm..."

Leah knelt by Owen. "Why do you think you would have an always room here?"

"Because Daddy lives here and mommies and daddies live in the same house. Now that Daddy's back, we will all live here, right?"

"Um, well." Leah flashed a glance at Riley. "That's something we're still talking about."

Owen scrunched up his face, and Riley held his breath in wait for the next question he probably had no answer for. He wanted to be a good dad, but how? He'd never done it before and had no idea what to do.

Owen looked around the room. "Where are the toys?"

Riley whooshed out a breath of relief. "I didn't know you were coming here until today, but if you tell me your favorite things to play with, I can make sure I get them."

"Really? Do you mean it?" Owen's face lit up as he beamed a smile up at Riley.

How would he ever be able to discipline or say no to a boy with such a precious face? He knew dads had to do that, but how? Just how?

"Really," Riley answered and set aside his worry about parenting to deal with on another day. Leah could take care of the hard things while they were together, and he would watch and learn.

"I want to go play with the puppy," Owen said.

"That might not be possible right now." Leah stood. "I have to go to a meeting with Ri—your...your dad. We can get your toys and books from the car. Grandma can read to you, and you can play here."

Owen's lower lip poked out, and if Riley thought he would have a hard time saying no before, he was now certain it wouldn't be possible. Riley half enjoyed seeing how adorable Owen looked and half hated that his son was disappointed when he could likely fix it. "I can call Hannah to see if it would be okay for Riley to play over there during our meeting."

Leah frowned.

Riley met her gaze. "If it's okay with you, of course."

"Please, Mommy." Owen's pout grew larger.

"I wouldn't mind the time to rest," Vivian said.

Riley flashed her a smile of thanks.

"Then, yes, you can go if Hannah says it's okay."

"Yippee!" Owen jumped up and down and bounced out of the room.

"I'll grab a snack for him from his backpack before he goes so he doesn't crash." Vivian followed Owen out the door.

"Help yourself to anything you can find in the kitchen, too," Riley called after her. He got out his phone to call Hannah but felt Leah's gaze on him. He turned. "I'm sorry. I don't want to go against your wishes and won't suggest something again before asking you."

"It's okay," she said.

"We need to talk tonight about the future. It's not fair to Owen not to know what to expect."

"I agree we need to talk, but not tonight. Not after my concert. I'll be wiped out." She shook her head. "I don't know what I'm doing here or what we should do next, and I want to be fresh for that discussion. We have to make sure we put Owen first."

"Absolutely," he replied, longing to spend every second with his son.

He loved Owen. A love he never knew was possible. How could he take one look at a child and have his life changed forever? This had to be the same kind of love God had for His people. Riley truly got that now, and he would always put Owen first. From today until the day he took his last breath. But from what Riley could tell in the little bit of time he'd spent with Owen, the boy wanted his mother and father together, living in the same place, and there was no way that could happen without a huge change in the way he and Leah lived.

God could do amazing things, and now Riley fully understood that God's love went beyond words, and He would do the very best for the three of them. Problem was, Riley had learned in life that the very best came with great pain designed to help him grow. Mature in his faith. Into the man he was meant to be.

He'd experienced so much pain and abandonment in the past, could he survive even more? Something he also had no answer for, and with Leah watching him, it wasn't the time to figure it out.

He held up his phone. "We need to get going. Let me arrange things with Hannah."

She answered right away, and he made his first ever playdate for his son. How weird was that? He didn't mention to Hannah that Owen was his son, only said he was a friend's boy. She'd know the minute he arrived at her house, but he didn't want to spring it on her over the phone. It would be crazy enough to tell her in person.

When Owen finished his snack, they said goodbye to Vivian and headed out.

Leah started to lift Owen into his car seat, and he shook

his head, a stubborn expression on his face. "I want Daddy to put me in my seat."

A flash of hurt registered on Leah's face, and Riley's heart broke for her. "I don't know how to do the buckles, but your mom does."

Owen crossed his arms.

"How about if Dad puts you in the seat, and I teach him how to do the buckles?" Leah suggested.

Placated, Owen nodded. Riley was fast learning what an amazing mother Leah was.

He picked Owen up, and he circled his arms around Riley's neck and hugged hard. "I'm glad you came back."

"Me, too, buddy." A lump formed in Riley's throat, and he had to swallow hard as he settled Owen in his seat and stepped back to allow Leah access.

She scooted in front of him, and he caught a whiff of her scent. She used to smell like apple pie, but now she had a flowery scent he couldn't place. He liked both. Too much for his own good.

He forced his attention to the straps. She fastened them easily from years of practice, but Riley wasn't sure he'd caught it. At Hannah's house, he would try to remove the harness and learn it for sure. He'd likely get a car seat if he planned to have Owen on his own. Or maybe Leah would bring the seat. That might be easier.

He shook his head and got in the car. He could jump out of helos, fire and maintain the most complicated of sniper rifles and other firearms, but he was totally helpless in figuring out a simple car seat. Seriously, his life was never going to be the same again and he thought that was a very good thing.

Owen hummed "Itsy-Bitsy Spider" all the way to the Blackwell residence, and the song stuck in Riley's head even after Owen stopped.

"Carry me?" Owen asked.

Riley was happy to oblige and scooped him up in his arms. He received another hug and smile that Riley tucked away to remember when things got tough in their meeting.

"I want to push the button," Owen said at the door.

Riley bent forward, giving Owen access to the doorbell.

"He can walk, you know," Leah said, but instead of sounding put out, her voice held humor.

Riley smiled and enjoyed the moment. Just the three of them. On their first family outing of sorts.

The door opened and Hannah stood there, a wide smile on her freckled face. She wore her typical jeans and knit shirt, and her vivid red hair was pulled back in a ponytail. She ran her gaze over Owen, and her smile suddenly faltered and disappeared.

"Oh, he's...not a friend...he's..." She let her words fall off and moved her focus between them.

Riley understood her feelings. He'd experienced them not too long ago when Leah told him about Owen. Hannah frowned. Right. She was mad because she thought he'd kept this from her. She saw herself as the team mother and wanted all of her children to be happy. That often meant prying and long talks, but he couldn't have possibly shared about his son.

Barkley came bounding out the door, David running after him, stealing everyone's attention.

"Puppy!" Owen squirmed to get down, and Riley set him on the ground. He charged after David.

"Stay close, Owen," Riley called after him and refused to take his eyes off his son. He wasn't about to let him wander off into the woods on the first day he was in his life.

"I'm Hannah Blackwell," he heard Hannah say, but he didn't turn to look at the women as they got acquainted. "And that's my son, David."

"Leah Kent. Owen's mother."

"As in *the* Leah Kent?" Hannah's voice shot up. "Oh my goodness, yes. I was too shocked at...well, you know...to even look at you. But it's really you, isn't it? Here. And you're Owen's mother."

David and Owen came back toward the house, Owen carrying Barkley who was almost the same size as he was and didn't look comfortable as he dangled from Owen's arms. But Barkley didn't complain. He was used to being handled. Not only did Mia and David play with him every day, but Eryn's daughter, Bekah, was often over here, too.

Owen stopped and looked up at Riley. "This is Barkley and David. He has a sister, Mia. We're going to play with her. Bye, Dad."

Hannah took a quick intake of air, and Riley faced her.

"Bye, Owen," Leah said.

"Oh, bye, Mom," he called over his shoulder as an afterthought.

When the boys were inside and out of earshot, Hannah grabbed Riley's ear and pulled him close, treating him like a wayward child. "You kept this from me? All of us?"

He freed his ear. "I only found out last night. So yeah, kept it from you for a whole eight hours or so."

Her gaze went to Leah. "You didn't tell him."

Leah blushed and shook her head.

Riley felt an irrational need to stand up for Leah. "It's complicated, and I'll tell you all about it when I come back, but for now, thank you for letting Owen play with David and Mia."

She planted her hands on her hips. "You also didn't mention Leah. Not once in the year I've known you, and you've had plenty of time to bring her up."

He looked at Leah. "Hannah thinks she's the team mom and sometimes gets a little bossy."

She cuffed him gently on his arm, but grinned. "I prefer to call it overprotective and nosy."

Riley laughed, but Leah simply smiled.

"I look forward to getting to know you, Leah," Hannah said.

"Translated, grill you for every detail of our past." Riley snagged Leah's hand and backed away. "Let's get out of here before it's too late."

He laughed and ran for the vehicle, towing Leah along. He heard her giggle, and for a moment he was back five years ago, and he wanted to spin. Lift her into his arms and swing her around. Because despite the stalker, despite the murder, and not knowing about his son for years, delirious happiness curled through Riley like the best surfing waves.

He had a son. A healthy, bright, adorable son. Riley had been called *Dad* or *Daddy*. Not once. Not twice. But so many times he finally quit counting.

"You will pay for this, Riley Glen." Hannah laughed and went inside.

Riley opened his SUV door for Leah and stood back.

She was still grinning as she climbed inside. "Hannah seems really nice."

"She is. We all love her and give her a hard time." He closed the door and jogged to the other side thinking what a wonderful family he had in his teammates. And his family! He had a family of his own now. Sure, Owen was sprung on him in a way he wouldn't wish for any man, but Riley wanted to look on the bright side. Embrace his fatherhood.

Thank you for my son. For his health. For everything to do with him. He's amazing, God. Amazing!

Blessings wrapping around him, he got behind the wheel and took them down the drive past the team cabins and past another grouping of log cabins all the same, all utilitarian. "For our class participants."

She looked at him. "Do you teach?"

"I do. Several classes actually. One on concealed carry and one on long guns. But my favorite is one for urban snipers." He pointed ahead at a large building about the size of a gym and pulled into the parking area. "This is where we'll be meeting. Down the road a bit, we have a town with storefronts, and in my urban sniper class, I get to teach new snipers how to hit their marks no matter the situation. We even take them up in the helo, though they'll never likely shoot from one. It adds a thrill to their day and makes them want to come back for other classes."

"You really like your job, don't you?"

"Like? Nah. *Love* it." He flashed her another smile and got one in return that stole his breath.

It was one of those smiles she had on stage that every man wished was for him alone, and wow! Just wow! It was something else having it directed his way after only seeing her lately in concert a few times on YouTube. His hand started to lift of its own accord to sink into her thick hair, but he forced it down before he did something he'd regret. "I'll get your door."

By the time he got to her side of the vehicle, she'd already opened the door, and he remembered why they were there. His joyful mood vanished, and he sobered. They were there to figure out who killed an innocent woman and who was stalking Leah. Both things needed his undivided attention, and she needed to know what to expect inside.

"Okay. Just a warning," he said. "We have five guys and two women on the team. You've met Sam, and you'll really like Eryn as she's pretty easygoing and friendly. She's a working mom like you, though Bekah is a bit older than Owen. She just turned five. The guys are great, but they can be a bit intense at times. They mean well even if they aren't always the most diplomatic."

"Like the sheriff who you said was a great guy?"

"He *is* a great guy, but yeah, he can be over-the-top, too." Riley smiled to try to make up for his warning as she was starting to look uneasy. "I just wanted to give you a heads-up as they can be a bit intimidating at first."

"Thank you. I'm pretty sure I can handle them. I've dealt with a lot of crazy fans, the rabid media, and cutthroat music biz people. And—" She smirked, "I handled them all just fine. Let's see these big, bad guys of yours."

Riley laughed, loving her strength and ability to roll with the punches. He wanted to sweep her in his arms and swing her around again. Instead, he took a deep breath and pushed open the door.

8

After Riley's warning, Leah prepared herself for the worst. She knew how to act confidently and had learned how to disarm the most intimidating people, but meeting Riley's team had a personal element to it, leaving her uneasy. She stepped inside the big building and stopped in the entryway. Ahead of her was an open area set up with tables and chairs in a classroom style. The space as large as a gym with a high ceiling, giving the place a cavernous feeling.

Riley pointed at a smaller room off to the side where voices drifted out of the open doorway and echoed through the big space. "Straight ahead is the conference room."

She stepped forward and searched for her usual confidence. At least she'd had a chance to take a quick shower, cover her tattoo, and put on some makeup at the hotel. She often felt less than others from her upbringing, but she could always hide behind her makeup and her celebrity status. Though she doubted these guys would care about any of that.

She paused at the door so Riley could go first. He entered the room, she followed, and all conversation stopped.

A woman about Leah's height with jet black hair pulled back into a ponytail hopped to her feet and vigorously shook Leah's hand. "Okay, you'll have to forgive me, but I'm having a little bit of a fangirl moment here. I love your albums. Play them all the time. My daughter and I dance to the upbeat songs."

"She really does. I've seen it with my own two eyes." A man with fiery red hair sitting next to her stood up and extended his hand as he towered over her in his six foot plus height. "Trey Sawyer, and the woman gawking at you in shock is my soon-to-be wife, Eryn Calloway."

"Sorry." Eryn clutched Leah's arm. "I should have introduced myself."

Leah chuckled and then gave Riley a smile. He was right about Eryn, but totally wrong about Trey. He wasn't intimidating at all, even though he was a big muscular guy.

"If Eryn can let go of your arm." Riley laughed. "I'll introduce you to the others."

"Oh, sorry." Eryn released Leah's arm and brushed the sleeve off as if she needed to remove her touch.

Leah experienced this kind of behavior all the time, but she never got used to it. She didn't deserve it. She simply sang songs, so why did that make her special? It didn't. It was these men and women sitting at this table who were special. They deserved the applause and the crazy salary.

"This is Cooper, Coop Ashcroft." Riley rested his hands on the next man's shoulders. He was a burly guy, and she noticed he wore a wedding ring. She took a quick look around at the others and found a ring only on the next man. Interesting. The team was mostly single. Not surprising, she supposed, with the dangerous work they did. Having dated Riley when he was a police officer, she knew how it was excruciating to wonder if the man you loved would come home every day or if someone would gun him down.

"Coop's a former Army Ranger and teaches our air assault classes—among others," Riley added.

"Nice to meet you," he said, his expression serious and intimidating. He must be an okay guy, though, because obviously a woman fell in love with him and married him.

Next came a man with dark black hair and a genuine smile.

"Gage Blackwell." He stood and offered his hand.

"Thank you for allowing your team to take this assignment," she said. "I'd like to talk about paying you."

He released her hand. "Riley's already got that covered."

Riley looked upset that she brought it up, but he didn't say anything and moved to the next man. He also had dark hair, but a close-cut beard where Gage was clean-shaven.

"Our team joker, Alex Hamilton," Riley said.

Alex didn't stand but looked up at her, a dazzling smile crossing his face. "I'll skip shaking hands because I'm having a fangirl moment, too, and don't want to embarrass myself."

"Right." She chuckled. "The joker."

"No, I'm serious. Well, not about the girl thing, but I do like your music."

"Thank you." Again, not too intimidating. So far Coop was the only one giving off-putting vibes.

"Alex was once a recon Marine," Riley said and stepped to the other side of the table.

The guy on the end looked at her like a bug he wanted to swat.

"Jackson Lockhart, former Army Green Beret," Riley said. "And I should have mentioned Gage was once a SEAL."

Jackson's mouth curved into a half smile, and he shook her hand. "Welcome."

"Thank you," she said and released his hand.

"And you already met Sam."

Sam nodded, a broad smile on her face. "I echo Jackson's comment but with a bit more enthusiasm."

Riley pulled out a chair between Sam and Eryn. "Go ahead and have a seat."

She slipped into the chair and scooted her chair in and took a quick look at the women beside her. Their focus was on Riley standing at the far end of the table. Had he placed her between the women on the team hoping she'd feel more at ease? It was just the kind of considerate thing he would do.

"Eryn said you promised lunch," Coop said.

Riley glanced at his watch. "It'll be here in thirty minutes at most."

"Better be." Coop grumbled. "I gotta get back to class and I don't want to teach on an empty stomach."

"No one wants that," Alex laughed.

Riley rolled his eyes and launched into describing the murder. She was impressed with his command of the room as the others listened quietly. She glanced around the faces and could see the respect his team held for him. She honestly didn't like that he'd lost a kidney and could be hurt, possibly losing the other one while working, but it was clear he loved his job and the others loved him.

He grabbed a marker and turned to the whiteboard. He jotted down *Stalker* and *Murder* before facing the group again. "We really have two investigations going on here, but there's a chance that they're one and the same. Here's what we know about the stalker."

Facing the board again, he wrote down *emails*, *letters*, and *personal appearances*. "I've asked Eryn to review the emails Leah received from the stalker. The letters are still at Leah's house in Portland and someone will have to retrieve those."

The blood drained from Leah's head. She had pictures of

Owen there. His toys...they'd find out. *Wait. No.* They could go to her house now. She no longer needed to hide Owen from everyone. Not this team. How long would it take until she stopped reacting in fear when anything regarding Owen came up? But she couldn't fully relax as she was still trying to keep reporters and Riley's father from finding out about him.

"Gage, with your permission I'll take the helo to Portland and pick them up," Riley said. "We might be able to pull prints from them and that could be our biggest lead."

"Of course," Gage said. "Just keep me updated on your schedule."

She didn't like the thought of him in her house without her. "I'd like to go along."

"Um, yeah." A sheepish expression crossed Riley's face. "I assumed you would since it's your house and all."

Riley jotted his name next to *letters* and Eryn's by *emails* before looking at the group again. "Leah, can you give us a list of the concerts where you saw the stalker, along with the times and dates?"

"Felicity and I can come up with everything you need."

He shifted his focus to Eryn. "Once we have that list, can you pull CCTV for the area to see if we can get this guy on video?"

"Absolutely."

Leah swiveled to look at Eryn. "You should know when I filed the complaint with the police in Minneapolis, they said there were cameras, but the video was too dark to make anything out."

"I'll still look at them as I have tools and resources to improve video that local police don't have."

Gage, his expression skeptical, locked his focus on Leah. "I take it you got a good look at this guy."

94

"Yes. He didn't try to hide his face. Felicity and I both saw him."

Gage gave a clipped nod, and she was beginning to think he was a man of few words. "Then we should get a sketch made. My wife, Hannah, is a sketch artist. You can meet with her ASAP and get that done so we know who we're looking for."

Leah nodded. "I just met her. She seems really nice, and I'd be glad to work with her. I have another concert tonight, but I'm free all afternoon."

Gage fired a questioning look at Riley, probably wondering why they'd talked with Hannah, but Riley either didn't notice or was ignoring it. Leah figured it was the latter.

"As Leah said, the concert is a go. Means I need everyone on protection detail tonight," Riley said. "And the sketch will tell you who to be on the lookout for."

Gage stood. "Let me call Hannah to see if she can do it after our meeting." He stepped from the room.

Riley looked at Leah. "Can you get Felicity here ASAP to work with Hannah?"

"I can call her." Leah dug out her phone.

"There's a buzzer at the gate. Tell her to ring that and one of us will let her in."

Leah nodded and stepped out to the area where Gage was talking to Hannah whose excited "yes" came over the phone. Was Hannah excited about the getting to work in her area of expertise or was she planning to question Leah about her past with Riley? Leah would need to prepare herself for that and be ready and on guard, not revealing anything more than necessary. There was too much up in the air to say more. Especially not before she met with Riley tomorrow and they worked some things out.

Tomorrow. Less than twenty-four hours. A face-to-face

meeting. That was going to be some meeting, and she was honestly afraid of what he might say—ask for. For a man who just found out he was a father, he was taking to fatherhood just fine, and he seemed eager to make up for the lost years. Which meant Leah would have to allow Owen to spend time with him when she wasn't around. Her stomach knotted, but there was no point in thinking about it now. Not when she couldn't do anything about it.

She stepped out of Gage's earshot and dialed Felicity. When she answered, Leah told her about the sketch. "Could you drive out here?"

"Sure." Felicity's usual zest for life lifted Leah's spirits. "Glad to help. Tell me how to get there."

Leah gave her directions and considered Felicity's reaction when she drove up to the imposing gate. Just like Riley warned Leah about meeting the team, Felicity deserved a heads up, too. "It's like this massive secured compound. With a crazy fence and gate. You have to ring a buzzer, and then someone will meet you."

"Sounds like something you'd see on TV or in the movies."

"It really is kind of surreal." Leah said, thinking about everything she'd learned from Riley. "I can't tell you how thankful I am for the team's help. And how completely defenseless I feel around them."

She didn't say anything for a long moment. "Them or Riley?"

"Both," Leah said quickly as she didn't want to lie, but she didn't want to draw attention to her interest in Riley. "The team members are very intimidating. Riley is, too. But in other regards, he's the same easygoing guy I once knew." *And loved.*

Silence filled the phone again. "You need to watch yourself with Riley, sweetie. Unless he's changed and is ready to travel with you."

She was so right. "No. He hasn't changed in that regard."

"But in other ways?"

"Yeah, he's still laid-back, but there's a quiet strength about him that he didn't have before. Probably from his years as a cop and sniper and now on this team." He'd really matured into quite a man, and she was very happy for him and the success he'd found in the job he wanted to do. But what if he lost his other kidney? Or worse—his life?

"Okay fine," Felicity said. "Your silence says it all. There's something going on. I won't stop until you tell me all about him and this team—and you know it."

Leah laughed with her friend, and she loved the light feeling. It also felt good to know that she was safe at the compound and didn't have to hide Owen. *Wait*, she did have to hide him from Felicity. She'd have to get to Hannah's house before Felicity arrived, bring Owen back to Riley's cabin, then swear Hannah to secrecy and hope her kids didn't say anything.

"You know you're still in love with him, don't you?" Felicity asked.

"What?" Leah had been too focused on Owen to catch Felicity's comment. Or at least she didn't think she'd caught the right thing.

"You. You're in love with Riley."

"Hah. You're crazy."

"Nah, just observant. I watched you last night. Every time he came in the room your eyes lit up for a moment before you hid it. And when he wasn't looking at you, girl, you were so checking him out."

She didn't doubt that she'd been doing just that. "Don't you dare mention this to anyone. Especially not Riley."

"Mention, what?" Riley's voice came from behind, and she jumped as her heart plummeted toward her stomach.

She took a second to gather her thoughts and calm down. "I gotta go, Felicity. Buzz when you get here."

"It's him, isn't it? The person who just said something. See? I can even tell on the phone because your voice is all breathy."

"Goodbye, Felicity," Leah said pointedly and put on a fake smile before turning to Riley. "Felicity's on her way."

"Great," he said and watched her expectantly.

She started back toward the room.

He clutched her arm to turn her to face him. "You're not going to answer my question, are you?"

No way. She shook her head.

Intensity darkened his eyes a few shades from soft blue to storm-cloud gray. "What are you hiding from me?"

"It's nothing really. Just Felicity being crazy."

"You're sure that's all it is?"

She nodded, but Felicity was very intuitive, there was likely some truth to her observations, and Leah needed to think about it before she did something she regretted.

She rushed back to the room, putting everyone around her so Riley wouldn't continue to badger her. He went back to the whiteboard, and she took her seat but couldn't concentrate. She knew Riley was jotting something down, but it was like her mind had a will of its own and wanted to think about the mess her life had become instead.

"Leah, did you hear me?" Riley's insistent voice broke through her fog.

"Sorry, no. What did you say?"

"Eryn found a picture online of your tattoo."

Leah turned to Eryn who held out her phone. "This photo was posted on a gossip blog a few weeks ago. Do you recognize where it was taken?"

Leah stared at the picture of her running down a street lined with large, well-maintained houses, Neil by her side. Her hand was lifted as if she was waving at someone or hailing a cab and her tattoo was clearly visible.

She was stunned. "That's impossible. I didn't want the press to hound Riley and his family, and I never left home with my tattoo exposed."

"Never?" Coop asked, clearly doubting her.

"Never, but let's say that I somehow forgot. If I was meeting with Neil, I definitely would've covered it. I was always very careful around him." She stared at the photo. "I don't even know where this is. It doesn't look familiar at all. It's definitely not my neighborhood."

"If it was taken the day it was posted, you could look at your calendar and see where you were," Alex suggested.

"Good idea." She found the date in the corner of the screen. "I broke up with Neil long before the day the photo was posted. Whoever put this up has been holding on to it for a while."

She looked at her arm and shook her head. "Which is weird. Usually when a fan catches me doing something in my everyday life, the pictures show up right away."

"Could this be near your house?" Riley asked. "Have you lived in the same place since you started touring?"

She nodded. "Well, nearly anyway. I lived in an apartment until I could afford to buy my house. That was two years ago. But I don't recognize the area."

"Eryn can you put this up on the screen so we can see the details better?" Riley asked.

Eryn nodded and went to a small projector in the back of the room. Her back was to the group, blocking what she was doing, but within a few moments the image appeared on the large screen on the front wall.

Leah studied the picture carefully. She had her hair

99

pulled into a ponytail as she always did for a run and was wearing clothes she only wore for exercise. Clearly she was out for a jog. "I try to run most every day, even when on tour. There are tons of neighborhoods that I have jogged in and wouldn't recognize again. But I only ran with Neil a few times. Problem is, I don't remember all of the places we went. I know we ran in a few different parks, but a neighborhood doesn't seem right. And exposing my tattoo is not something I would have done. Ever."

"You must have this one time," Riley said, sounding suspicious. "Since you seem so adamant about not showing it, I would think you could remember the one time that you did."

She didn't like how he was looking at her. He clearly didn't trust her anymore, but she understood that after she hid Owen from him and refused to answer his earlier question. "The other question is, am I waving at someone? Hailing a cab? What? Maybe waving hello at a fan? But the tattoo. That's the oddity here."

"All of that's possible," Eryn said.

"And who took this picture?" Leah squinted at the screen. "Maybe it was after Jill started seeing Neil, and she followed us. Then she posted it online. Maybe to reveal the tattoo to create a publicity nightmare and get back at me. But then she would've sold this photo to media outlets, not hide it in a blog comment."

"It would explain how she knew about the tattoo," Gage said. "But not why she recently had it inked on her own wrist."

Leah didn't get it. Any of it. "A better explanation is that my stalker took the picture and posted it, but again, why put it in a comment? And how did my tattoo end up exposed?"

"What about the clothes you're wearing?" Coop asked. "Might that narrow it down?"

"I still have them and wear them when I run, so not really. I just can't explain any of it." She squinted at the screen. "Could this have been Photoshopped? Maybe I was running another time, and I was put in the picture with Neil? Or what if the tattoo was added as well? Whoever took the picture could've talked to people in my past and found out about it, then added it."

"I can't tell you if the photo was altered," Eryn said. "But I can do some measurements of the tattoo placement and compare it to your actual arm. The process is called photogrammetry, a science of making determinations about objects in an environment based on visual evidence. That way we'll know if it was added."

"Don't you think that's pretty far-fetched?" Riley's skepticism was growing.

"That's the only explanation, though it does sound like a crazy one." Leah wrung her hands together. "I just don't remember this. I'm sorry. I really am. I wish I could."

"It's okay." Eryn patted Leah's hand. "If you run every day, there's no way you can remember every location."

"Maybe this was when I was on tour. Neil visited me several times then. I run with a few of my staff, too, and there could've been other people with us that day who aren't in the picture. Can you remove the tattoo from my arm so no one learns about it, and then show my staff the picture to see if anyone remembers the area?"

Eryn nodded enthusiastically. "We could ask them tonight at the concert if they'll be there."

"Yes, they're all still on my team. Just three people." She smiled at Eryn. "Maybe you could ride with me when I head to the amphitheater and come backstage to talk to them."

"Are you kidding?" A wide smile spread across Eryn's face, and she grabbed Leah's hand. "I'd be all over that."

"Good."

Eryn suddenly jerked her hand back. "Sorry. Fangirling again. But, yeah. I'll get this tattoo removed and bring the picture on my phone."

"Thank you, Eryn," Riley said moving Leah's focus back to him. "Any chance you can enhance it, and we might catch an address on one of the houses or something else that might identify it?"

"I'll try, but the quality isn't good to begin with. I'll also try to track down the person who posted the photo. The section where it was posted was about celebrities in their everyday lives. The comment was pretty generic and basically said Leah Kent was out for a run."

"You know, it's odd that my publicist didn't get an alert on that. I know she set up Google alerts so that every time my name is mentioned online, she's notified."

"Their algorithms aren't infallible, and they don't capture everything on the Internet," Eryn said. "Or maybe she thought it was no big deal and not worth telling you about."

"But it would mean she knows about my tattoo."

"We'll need to show her the picture, too."

Leah looked at her watch. "I was supposed to meet with her this afternoon, but with doing the sketch I'm running behind. I can ask her to come to the concert tonight instead. Let me text her to see if that works for her." Leah grabbed her phone from the table and tapped in a text.

"And her name is what again?" Riley asked.

"Gabby Williams." Leah's phone dinged, and she checked the message. "She said yes."

Riley wrote Gabby's name on the board then added Eryn's name next to it. He turned and focused on Eryn. "You sure you're good with doing this? I mean the whole 'fangirl thing' might have you distracted. I'm sure Leah would let you come hang backstage, and I can do the interviews."

"Sure, that's fine with me." Leah smiled at Eryn. "I'm glad to give you a full access pass."

"Okay," Eryn said a ready smile on her face. "I'm glad to just hang."

Trey groaned. "You should not feed her addiction."

Eryn looked at Trey, and her smile turned mischievous at the same time as a loving expression crossed her face. Trey's gaze heated up, and an intimate smile spread across his mouth.

The temperature in the room seemed to rise fifty degrees, and Leah had to admit she was jealous of the pair. They were crazy in love. In love like Leah had once been with Riley. She glanced at him from under her lashes only to find him watching her, his expression unreadable.

Did he wish for the same thing?

She doubted it, but if she was being totally honest with herself, she wanted to have a man in her life. One to come home to and share everything with, because even with her mom and Owen by her side, plus a career she loved with wonderful fans, life could get lonely. Very lonely indeed.

9

Riley didn't know what Leah was hiding, but he didn't like it. He wanted to take her out of the room, sit her down in a chair, and interrogate her with a hot light over her head. Okay, fine. He didn't actually want to do that, but he did want her to trust him enough to confide whatever it is that she shared with Felicity but couldn't tell him.

Once upon a time they kept no secrets from each other and were each other's best friends. Eventually, they'd let their other friendships suffer as a result. They were that into each other. A love you read about in books or see in movies, but never expected to encounter in life. And a love Riley knew he'd never find again.

"I've also done some searching on Twitter." Eryn looked at Leah. "Your *leahfan* stalker has been silent lately. He's had a flurry of posts, talking about how you and he were meant for each other, and he just needed to find a way to let you know. He kept polling his followers, asking for ideas on how to approach you. But then, nothing for the last three weeks."

"Can you get his name from his Twitter account like the sheriff said he could do?" Leah asked.

Eryn shook her head. "Twitter won't release a speck of

information without a warrant, but that won't stop me. Guys like this are often active in forums or like to leave comments on blog posts. So I've written an algorithm to search for *leahfan*. It's running now. I can often piece together enough information to figure out an ID by comments that are left. Also I set up an alert to be notified if he posts anywhere. Oh, and I'm running one for the tattoo as well to see what I can find."

"You go." Leah clapped her hands. "You're really great at what you do."

Eryn beamed at Leah. Riley got that Leah was Eryn's favorite singer and she was enthralled by being with her, but he wished the regular Eryn was present so she wouldn't miss anything. Fangirl Eryn might. Riley would need to make sure he kept an eye on that.

"Eryn, I assume your algorithm will also look for other social media and pictures," Jackson said.

Eryn looked at him, but it was with reluctance. "Yeah, it'll scrape the databases for every bit of info."

Riley noted the social media information and then tapped the word *emails* that he'd written on the board earlier. "To do this, you'll need Leah's devices."

"Right. Blake has already asked me to take an image of them. I need to preserve and record the system state before doing that. Means I have to physically access them. I can tag along with you and Riley on the helo to do the computer."

"Perfect. Thank you." Riley smiled at Eryn. He didn't know what they would do if she quit her job to have the house full of kids that Trey wanted to have, but it was seeming like she was leaning that way.

Eryn faced Leah. "I suppose you've ridden in a helicopter like a zillion times."

"Actually, I've never been in one."

"Then you're in for a treat." Eryn grinned. "If you give

me your phone and iPad, I can image them while you meet with Hannah."

Leah nodded. "With everything so unsettled with the concerts, promise me if I get any 911 texts from my manager while you have my phone that you'll make sure I get word."

"I can text Riley."

"Perfect."

Riley added the device information on the board that was fast filling up. A good thing as that meant they had leads to follow and maybe they'd find Leah's stalker. "Next up is the tattoo recently inked on Jill's wrist. I need someone to visit local tattoo shops to show them the picture and ask if any of the artists did the tat."

"I finished my classes for the week, so I can do it," Alex offered. "Who knows? Maybe I'll come back all tatted up." He wiggled his eyebrows in a playful way.

Riley knew there was no danger of that. Alex cared too much about his appearance to permanently change it with tattoos. At least he wouldn't get inked without giving it a solid evaluation first.

"C'mon, pretty boy, do you really expect us to believe that?" Coop said, a tight smile on his lips.

"Pretty boy?" Alex mocked being upset, but this wasn't the first time Coop had teased Alex about his precise grooming standards.

Gage rolled his eyes. "Focus people. I'd like to get home before it's time for dinner."

"Me, too," Jackson said. "Maggie has a rare day off, and I want to spend as much time with her as possible."

Alex rolled his eyes. "You're getting married in a few months, and you have a lifetime of days together."

"Doesn't mean I don't want this one, too." A slow smile crossed Jackson's face.

Riley was glad so many of his teammates were in solid relationships, but right now he needed them to focus.

Talk about the pot calling the kettle black. Tell yourself the same thing.

"I should also tell you about Carolyn Eubanks," he said.

Riley heard Leah gasp, but even if she was upset that he brought Carolyn up, he explained about the embezzlement.

"Man, that's rough," Coop said, surprising Riley.

Coop wasn't the most sensitive of guys, but he'd gotten married. Maybe spending more time with Kiera was softening him up. "You did file a complaint, right?"

Leah nodded. "She's awaiting trial."

"No one deserves to be treated this way." Thunder consumed Gage's expression. Not a surprise. He always, *always*, stood up for the underdog. "Let us know if there's anything we can do to help with her prosecution."

"Agreed," Riley said. "We're here to help."

"Thank you," Leah said and looked down.

Yeah, she was hiding something all right. Did she not want them to get involved in Carolyn's prosecution? Is that why she looked away? When they were alone, he would do his best to get to the bottom of it.

"Blake will interview her," Riley said, fixing his gaze on Leah to assess her response. "But he'll likely be tied up with more promising leads. So I'd like to talk to Carolyn right away. Since we're already headed for Portland, I can interview her then. I'd like to leave first thing in the morning. To get everything done in one trip, we'll have to get going early."

Leah groaned. "Maybe not first thing. Late concert and all. It's the last one in Rugged Point and final concerts in a location usually stretch out extra long, which is more draining. No one wants to say goodbye."

Riley rubbed his chin. "I suppose we can push it back an

hour, but not too much longer." He turned to Sam. "I'll scan the letters and you can process them for fingerprints. Or... would that be wrong to do before we turn them over to Blake?"

Sam frowned, an unusual look for her. "I could lift prints, and would love to do it, but it would really call into question the validity of anything his forensic staff recovers. Could be problematic when this stalker is caught and goes to court."

"What about DNA?" Riley asked.

"Same thing. Even photocopying the letters could be problematic as you could transfer touch DNA from the machine. You're better off taking pictures or trying to get pictures from Blake's team."

When Riley was a police officer, he had access to information like this if he needed it. He loved his current job, and he wouldn't give it up for anything, but he sure didn't like being on this side of the law at the moment.

Gage leaned forward. "Blake won't share. He's too much of a stickler for protocol. The best thing for us to do is have Sam take pictures since she's familiar with evidence procedures."

Sam nodded. "I'd be glad to handle that."

"Then I'll use gloves and bag the letters to bring them back to you before turning them over to Blake." Riley added it to the board, and then took a look at everything he'd written down. "Okay, that's all I have."

"FYI," Sam said. "I'm not sure of the value yet, but I lifted quite a few prints from the area. It's a public place and that's not surprising. After my friend at PPB runs them, we'll see if they return anything of value."

"What about the jewelry box?" Riley asked.

"It held only one set of prints, Leah's, so that's a dead end. I need to get elimination prints for Felicity, Kraig, and

Sal. I can do that tonight at the concert. Also, my expanded search for the gun was a bust. It's looking like the killer took it with him."

"Good work on the prints, Sam," Riley said but he was distracted by her last comment on the gun.

The killer either wanted to dispose of the weapon somewhere far from the amphitheater, or—a thought Riley really didn't want to have—the shooter was holding onto the gun because he was going to kill again.

Leah was instantly drawn to Hannah's gentle nature and kind spirit. Felicity, who sat next to Leah on a barstool in Hannah's kitchen, seemed to like Hannah, too, but then Felicity was an extrovert, and she could mix and mingle with anyone, anywhere.

Hannah took the sketch from her portable easel and passed it to Leah for what seemed like the tenth or eleventh time in the last two hours. During that time the sun had disappeared behind clouds and Hannah had turned on bright overhead lights in her kitchen that gave off warm and welcoming vibes.

"Well?" Hannah asked, lifting a cup of tea to her mouth.

Leah forced herself to look at the drawing. Hannah's artistic talent was obvious, but the picture wasn't right. Leah couldn't put her finger on it. She wished she could. All she knew was the guy didn't look like the man she'd seen. She sighed.

"Okay," Hannah said. "It's not right yet."

"But I don't know why." Leah handed the sketch to Felicity. "What do you think?"

She took a long look at it then shook her head. "I agree with you. Something's off."

Hannah stood, took the sketch, and set it aside. "It's time for a break. We'll have some tea and chocolate chip cookies I baked yesterday. We can eat our fill of the gooey yumminess and forget all about this man for a while to clear our heads."

"Thank you," Leah said, knowing it would take a whole lot more than cookies to help her clear her mind. "I'm sorry I'm not able to pinpoint his features better. You must have other things you'd rather be doing."

"Are you kidding?" Hannah grabbed plates from the cupboard and turned. "I love being a stay-at-home mom. Our kids are amazing and I adore them. But I need grown-up time and things that challenge me, too. Plus, this is what I love to do. The more complicated the better."

She set the plates on the counter and grabbed a cookie jar shaped like a cute clown. She'd no more than set it in front of Felicity and Leah when the sound of little feet came running their way.

When Leah had first arrived, she'd taken Hannah aside and told her not to mention Owen was her son, but Leah didn't know what Owen or the other children might say. Thankfully, Riley agreed to keep Owen outside while Felicity was here, and if he tired of playing out there, he would take Owen back to the cabin. She wished she could join Riley to watch Owen playing with the other children. He didn't have much socialization outside of his preschool, and she could easily imagine living here and him making fast friends with Mia and David.

David raced around the corner, and though Leah had met the children earlier, she was still struck by the intensity of his red hair, his million tiny freckles, and how much he resembled Hannah. He was dressed in worn blue jeans and an Oregon State University sweatshirt, and he slid onto a barstool. "I'm hungry, Mom."

"Me too," Mia said as she rushed in. She had wispy blond hair held back by a lime green headband that matched a polka-dotted shirt. She took one look at Leah and Felicity, and she darted behind Hannah to peek out.

"They have cookie radar." Hannah laughed, reached behind her back, and gently brought Mia forward to introduce Felicity. "This is David and Mia."

David ignored Felicity and solidly met Leah's gaze. "Don't I like know you already?"

"It's Leah Kent, silly," Mia loud-whispered to David. "You know. The famous singer. We see her on TV all the time."

David frowned. "Yeah, don't know her."

Leah leaned forward and smiled at the children. "Well, you do now."

"Okay, kiddos," Hannah said. "Go wash your hands and then take a seat at the patio table. I'll bring out cookies and milk."

"Owen wants some, too. And so does Riley."

Hannah laughed. "Riley really is a big kid at heart."

"Who's Owen?" Felicity asked.

Leah was dumbstruck and couldn't respond.

"A friend of David's," Hannah said before the kids could speak.

Felicity nodded. "I would think Riley would have something better to do in finding out who shot Jill instead of playing with kids."

Leah didn't like Felicity mentioning the murder in front of the kids, and Leah also had to stick up for Riley. Why, she didn't know. "He's doing all he can, and if he needs a few minutes to play, then I think we need to cut him some slack."

Felicity gave Leah a questioning look but didn't say anything else.

"Scoot." Hannah pointed to the door. "Outside both of you."

David ran off, but Mia seemed a bit off balance for some reason, and she bumped into the wall.

"Slow down, sweetie," Hannah said, gently righting her, then plated the cookies.

As a parent, Leah didn't understand why Hannah wasn't more concerned with Mia's loss of balance, but Hannah went to the refrigerator to grab milk. She glanced over her shoulder in the direction where the kids had gone. "I didn't want to say anything while Mia was in here, but she suffered a brain injury in a car accident a few years ago and has some residual issues."

"I didn't even notice it," Felicity said.

"Ah, that explains it," Leah's statement came out at the same time, gaining Hannah's focus.

"You have a mother's eye," Hannah said.

"Can I help you carry their food?" Leah smiled and got up to draw attention away from the comment.

Hannah nodded, and Leah grabbed the plates before Felicity asked any questions. Leah rushed to the back patio where she set the plates in front of the children and Riley who were all seated at a large patio table.

Riley had Owen on his lap and had taken wipes out of Owen's backpack and was cleaning his hands. Seeing them together in such a casual setting, seeming totally at home with each other, hit her with such intensity that it brought tears to her eyes. If she hadn't hidden Owen and chosen financial security, she'd still be with Riley. Owen could be here all the time. Playing with these children. Coming home to Riley's cabin—their cabin—at the end of the day. Together. A family.

Sorrow flooded her body, and she clutched the back of the chair as a sob escaped. She heard Hannah's footsteps behind her, and she took a long breath to pull herself together and will her tears away. She wiped her eyes and put on a big smile before heading back into the house. She stood in the living room, her heart ripped open. Unending questions raced through her mind, mingling with regret.

Leah heard the door, and she turned to see Hannah enter. Leah wished it was Riley. Wished he'd come to comfort her, but he hadn't. Of course not. It was just business between them. She'd even asked him to keep things that way.

Hannah didn't say a word but took one look at Leah and swept her into a hug. "Everything will be okay. I know it will."

Hannah's caring snapped Leah's tight control, and she couldn't hold her tears back now. She heard the door open again, and fearing it was one of the children, she came to her senses enough to push back and look up. Riley stood watching her, concern evident in his gaze.

"Is everything okay?" he asked.

No, it's not. Not at all. I need you.

"I'll let the two of you talk." Hannah gave him a pointed look that Leah didn't understand, but Riley seemed to catch on.

Hannah left the room, and Leah didn't know what to say to Riley. She certainly couldn't share her thoughts on what might've been, but right now she wanted to discuss their past more than she ever had.

Is that you, God? Working on my heart. Trying to change it?

Riley took a step closer but stopped to watch her carefully. "What's going on?"

She pointed at the children through the door. She couldn't put her feelings into words or she'd really fall apart. She shook her head and started for the powder room on the other side of the foyer.

He came up next to her and slid his hand in hers to stop her.

"Tell me." His tone was gentle and inviting.

How could he be so kind to her after she walked out on him? He simply was a wonderful man, and he was here, ready to help. Her tears intensified, rolling down her cheeks.

"I'm just overwhelmed," she managed to get out.

"Aw, honey, don't cry."

Honey. She hadn't heard that endearment in such a long time. Not since they went their separate ways.

He peered into her eyes, his filled with the honest caring she'd always received from him.

Oh, Riley, how could I have let you go?

Her crying ramped up, and she was beyond holding anything back.

"C'mere," he said and drew her into his arms. He wrapped them securely around her but held her gently like precious china. She felt like she'd come home after a long absence, and this was where she belonged. She'd missed a man's touch. No—*correction*. She'd missed Riley's touch.

Neil was the only man she'd dated since Riley. She hadn't been able to date and keep Owen a secret, but Neil came into her life at a particularly vulnerable time, so she'd given in. Gone out with him for a few weeks. If he hadn't taken up with Jill, Leah would've ended their relationship soon because it could go nowhere with her secret. Her life had been on hold from the moment Riley's father issued his ultimatum. She didn't realize how completely and totally the secret affected every bit of her life until now.

Help me. Please help me.

Riley drew back and looked her in the eye. "I know we're not close anymore, but there's something you're not telling me and it's bothering you. I want to help with that. What can I do?"

There. That was the Riley she loved. An amazing man with a heart of gold all wrapped up in a handsome package that sparked her senses and made her heart swoon.

She tentatively touched his cheek. "Thank you for asking. It means a lot to me, but I have to work through this on my own."

Just like that, his face closed down tight. Like a metal door slammed shut and tightened every muscle into a rock-hard slab.

She'd done it again. Not physically leaving but emotionally withdrawing, and she was on her own again.

The way she wanted it, right?

Usually, she'd think about the stability and security her nest egg had brought. Her reason for leaving him in the first place.

But thanks to Carolyn, Leah had nothing now. Totally and completely nothing.

10

————

Riley was a fool. Holding Leah like that. The warmth of her body next to his, a closeness he'd had only with her and missed. Her vulnerability and his inability to help her only made him want more. So much more.

And then what? She turned around and closed him off like slamming a book. Done. Finished. She still didn't need him. Didn't want him. Other than to keep her safe. Talk about a gut-ripping pain. One he would have to get over. Just like when she'd walked out.

But he hadn't gotten over that, had he? His reaction to having her in his arms again was proof positive. He wanted more of it. A whole lot more.

Well you can't have it. Have her. So let it go. Get over it. Do what you always do. Swallow it down and move on.

He changed the subject. "Did you finish the sketch?"

She flashed him a surprised look.

What? Did she think he'd be licking his wounds because she refused to share? Well, she was right. But he was older now. More mature and able to handle her rejection better.

"No," she said.

He tipped his head at the mantle clock. "You wanted to leave for the amphitheater in a half hour."

"Then we better finish up." She stepped around him, giving him a wide berth as she headed to the kitchen.

He instantly felt the emptiness of the room. What did he do now? Go watch them work on the sketch? Stand here like an idiot and ruminate over what could never be?

Neither. He would spend more time with Owen until the sketch was finished. He'd fill his heart with joy and build memories to make up for the years he'd missed.

He found his son on the top of the huge wooden play structure that Riley had helped build. At the time, he'd thought nothing of the size or the height from the ground, but now, seeing his son, his adorable son, a huge drop below him, panic set in, and he charged across the yard.

"Daddy, look!" Owen plopped onto the slide and whooshed down, bounding to his feet on the ground. His face was alive with joy, and Riley hated to be the bad guy here, but he'd already learned that being a dad meant you had to be the bad guy sometimes.

"Did you see me?" Owen asked.

Riley knelt beside him, his heart still thundering in his chest. *Craziness.* He'd faced down criminals with guns, and yet, he'd never experienced such terror. He brushed Owen's hair back and took a moment to calm himself so he didn't come across as demanding and rigid as his father.

"I saw it was a lot of fun for you, but I need to ask you something."

"What, Daddy?"

Riley had to smile at Owen's constant use of *Daddy*. "The play structure is really high. Too high for you, at your age. If you want to go to the top, you need to have a grownup with you. Can you do that for me?"

He frowned. "David and Mia don't need anyone."

"They're older than you. Bekah is another friend you'll meet soon. She's closer to your age, and I know her mom won't let her climb up alone. Maybe you could play with her when Mia and David are on the top. Or even play with Barkley." He pointed at the puppy who was sleeping in the shade.

"Barkley!" Owen's eyes lit up, and he started to run off.

Riley caught hold of him. "You promise not to go up high without a grownup?"

"Promise."

Riley kissed his forehead.

"I love you, Daddy."

Riley's heart burst with happiness.

"I love you too, Son." Riley released him. Owen bolted across the yard and scooped up a bewildered Barkley who recovered quickly and licked Owen's face. Owen giggled and dropped to the grass to wrestle with the puppy.

Satisfied that he'd handled that well, Riley got up. His phone rang, and he spotted Eryn's name on the screen. He answered and headed for the house to keep the kids from overhearing his conversation.

"I've got an update for you on *leahfan*," Eryn said.

Riley closed the door behind him but kept an eye on Owen. "What do you have?"

"My algorithm found comments he made in several places on the Internet. From them, I can tell you he's thirty-six. Lives alone in an apartment. Is very opinionated about current politics and leans toward the conservative right. And he claims to be a Christian, but he's interpreting the Bible to fit his views. He's not a vegetarian, and he despises people who are. He's single but is desperately seeking a mate. He likes blondes. In fact, it looks like's he obsessed with them. He mentions Leah often, only by her first name, which is interesting, but he most always talks about her hair."

Riley stood in awe of Eryn's work. "It's amazing the profile you can create from people on the Internet. Freaky actually."

"It's why most law enforcement officers refuse to use social media."

And Riley was one of them. "Jill was a blonde. Coincidence?"

"Maybe, or maybe the stalker saw Jill performing with Leah and because he couldn't get to Leah, Jill's a substitute. And adding the tattoo satisfies something in him. Or maybe because he can't get to Leah, the tattoo is his way of saying he loves her."

"Sounds possible, but first he would have to know where Jill was, and she hasn't performed with Leah in a while. But say he tracked her somehow, he would've had to get backstage to kill her. That would be a challenge. Couldn't he just have waited for her to exit and try to abduct her, or kill her, or whatever he wants to do with her?"

"Stalkers or murderers don't always think logically."

"Say we're right and Leah's stalker is the killer," Riley said, though he wasn't fully convinced. "What's our next step in finding him?"

"I reviewed his Twitter account, and he's obviously obsessed with her. At first the tweets are gushing and quite beautiful, but then as time passes and Leah doesn't return his love, they get uglier and uglier until he threatens her. In case Blake hasn't had anyone review it, I compiled a report so he can get a warrant for the account holder."

"I'm sure he appreciates that, as do I."

Leah stepped into the room and handed a sketch to Riley.

"Hold on a sec," he said to Eryn and looked at the guy's bald head, wide nose, and a thick goatee. His eyes were narrowed in a glare. That tough exterior fit with a man who would be willing to stalk a woman. And just looking at him made Riley's blood boil. He had to find this creep and do it now.

He turned his attention back to Eryn's call. "What're the odds that the account holder's information will be legitimate?"

"Not high, but there's often something to be learned even when false details are given to open an account. Problem is, I don't think Blake will share that information with us, so it's a dead end for me."

Riley resisted going off on an anger-filled tangent. "I hope he realizes with Leah's life on the line that sharing with you could be the very thing that stops this stalker before he kills again."

From the moment Riley stepped into the amphitheater, he had his hands full. He'd started by meeting with Sal and Alex to get security set. Then while Sal moved his men into place, and Alex determined the best location for the Black-well team to take a stand during the concert, Riley interviewed Leah's staff.

What a bust. They didn't know anything about the photo. Not a single thing. They could be lying, Riley supposed, but he was a good judge of character, and he believed them.

Now he stood on stage, his focus on the empty amphitheater watching for threats while Leah did sound-checks with her band. Eryn sat on a stool in the middle of the action, her usual intense focus absent as she listened to the music.

Riley had to admit he was surprised by her behavior. It was so out of character for the strong, independent woman he'd known for years. But then everyone had a side to them that they didn't show on a regular basis. Case in point, his issues with his father. No one but Leah knew about that and how deeply it affected Riley. But now that he had a son, Riley would work hard to let that go so he could be a great father.

Leah's song ended, and Eryn clapped liked the rabid fan she was.

Leah smiled at Eryn. "It's so sweet of you to encourage us."

"Just wait until the concert. I'll show you what encouragement looks like." Eryn wrinkled her nose.

Leah chuckled and turned to the band. "Okay, everyone, let's run though the closing number. We botched it a bit last night."

Riley hadn't noticed, but then he'd been too busy staring at Leah and watching for the stalker. And he wouldn't be listening much tonight either. He had to focus better. Not on Leah. He'd been doing plenty of that. No, he had to keep his eyes on the crowd. On the building. On the shadows and stay one step ahead of any danger.

Sudden movement across the stage caught his attention, and he reached for his sidearm. Sal strode out of the shadows and crossed behind the musicians heading Riley's direction. Riley blew out a breath and let go of the butt of his gun. But he didn't relax. Sal had purpose to his steps. Hopefully that didn't mean bad news.

"We're as ready as we can be," Sal announced the moment he stopped in front of Riley, his tone raised above the music. "Metal detectors are in place and the additional staff I've contracted will search all bags. Fans are going to grumble, but no one will get a gun inside the amphitheater."

Riley nodded his thanks. "Leah's going to hate inconveniencing her fans, but I just saw that the murder has spread on social media, so they're going to know the reason soon."

"And that will make our job harder as curiosity seekers are going to come out in droves and clog the area around the building."

"Sheriff Jenkins is setting up a perimeter, and his deputies will keep them off the property."

Sal didn't look convinced.

"Hey, I get that you're concerned. You think we're just small-town hicks. But I've served on a city police force, and I put Sheriff Jenkins and his men on the same professional level."

"I'll have to trust you on that." Sal narrowed his eyes against the sun beating down on the stage. "And your team. When are they arriving?"

Riley glanced at his watch. "Thirty minutes or so. Which is in plenty of time to clear and lock down the entire facility before the concert starts."

"Perfect. I've got a few more details to take care of, and then I'll join you all in the final sweep." Sal strode away as fast as he'd arrived.

The music ended, and Riley shifted his focus to Leah.

She faced her band. "Okay, just a reminder. We'll open tonight with a brief announcement about Jill and then run the slideshow Gabby put together to honor her. I'll step to the side and you'll accompany it with the medley of her favorite songs. Then I'll say something else, we'll dim the lights for a moment of silence, and slowly move into the concert. Any questions?"

"Yeah," the drummer called out. "Don't you think this is going to be a real downer for the fans?"

Leah didn't respond for a moment. "I'm usually all about the fans, but Jill deserves our respect, and I'm going to give it to her. Hopefully I can do it in a way that the audience can understand."

A woman in the back scoffed.

Leah eyed her. "You have something to say, Jaz?"

The woman with long hair dyed the color of black ink stepped forward. "Just that you and Jill didn't exactly part as friends. So why do this? Seems hypocritical."

Leah lifted her shoulders into a hard line. "I'm not disputing that Jill and I had our differences. She made a mistake. We all do, but it doesn't mean she doesn't deserve our respect." Leah's chin went up as if daring Jaz to argue, but the woman gave a clipped nod and stepped back.

Leah clapped her hands. "Okay, then. Let's get dressed and despite the somber opening, give these fans what they came for. Are you with me?"

The group grumbled a yes.

"No. That won't do. Are you with me?" Her voice went up and she kept at it until the group was pumped and eager.

Riley was impressed with her ability to fire up her band much like she brought a crowd to their feet. She'd always been an amazing entertainer where he was merely adequate. She'd told him she'd learned how to perform on cold, dreary, hungry nights in her room when she needed to take her mind off her world. She would become someone else, and for those moments, live a happy life. And she'd also said she performed most every day of her school life, pretending that barbs and insults about their poverty didn't sting.

He'd wanted to make up for that somehow. She always felt less than others, and he'd tried to make sure she knew that no one person was better than another. All people sinned. All people had moments when they were ugly to others. All people hurt the ones they loved at times. But that was the beauty of God's grace. He showered His love on everyone, even when they didn't measure up or messed up badly. He cared about each person's heart, not outward circumstances. They didn't define a person in God's eyes, and Leah shouldn't define herself by them, either.

And now, she'd risen above this difficult situation and was still determined to do her job to the best of her abilities. And he was determined to make sure she was free to do so without coming to harm.

She turned and started his way, locking gazes with him. Her feelings for Jill's loss burned intently in her eyes. He knew her genuine emotions would shine through when she spoke to the fans tonight as she acknowledged Jill's loss, and they would be with Leah.

"Ready?" she asked, her voice breathy and tears glistening in her eyes.

He wanted to say something to encourage her and remove her unease. Maybe take her into his arms, but he knew she wouldn't want that in front of her band so he nodded and led the way to the side entrance where her bus was parked. He'd prefer she would get dressed in the building, but she couldn't even stomach the thought of stepping backstage where Jill had died, and he didn't blame her. So he'd had the bus moved close to the building and a canvas walkway erected, allowing her to access her vehicle unseen.

He nodded at Sal's guard who pushed open the door for them. Another guard, mirrored sunglasses hiding his eyes, stood at the bus door. Riley took comfort in their professional appearance and focused attention.

Leah paused and glanced into a narrow opening between the walkway and the building.

Riley followed her gaze and spotted several reporters with microphones and TV cameras lingering by the front of the bus, but he urged Leah ahead. "Keep moving."

"They must have found out about Jill."

"They did. Saw it on social media."

She glanced back at him, worry now added to her expression. "I hope they don't cause problems."

Riley hoped so, too, but if they came between him and his job of protecting Leah, he would move them out of the way, because he wasn't going to let anything stop him from his protection job tonight. Even if it meant he stopped the concert. Whisked her off stage. Or if he had to, give his life for hers. Nothing was out of the question to keep her safe. Nothing.

Leah breathed deep and bowed to the deafening applause. She'd successfully honored Jill and they'd moved through two thirds of the concert lineup. The fans jumped, screamed, reached up, obviously enjoying themselves.

Leah dipped in another bow as Jaz's earlier word came back. *Hypocritical.* Jaz thought Leah was being hypocritical. She didn't disagree. She felt bad about Jill's murder and about holding a grudge against Jill then standing before the fans and not telling them how she ended things between them. But then, show business was often filled with hypocrisy. Fake. Unreal. You name it, she'd seen it. But that didn't mean that was who she wanted to be.

Forgive me for not painting the full picture for the fans.

Emotionally drained, she wanted to slink off stage to her bus and sleep for days, but her drummer started the next song. Even if Leah wanted to sleep, maybe linger in her guilt, she had an amphitheater filled with people waiting for her to embrace the music and give them a show.

She plastered a smile on her face and started clapping as she charged around the stage to pump them up even more. A commotion in the back of the structure caught her attention, and she came to a stop. She lifted her hand over her eyes to block the blinding spotlights and get a clear picture of what was happening. Sal and one of his men were taking down a man. Wrestling him to the floor, the guy fighting for all he was worth.

Images flashed through her mind of this man getting free. Lifting a gun. Firing at her. Everything around her seemed to slow. Freeze in time.

She shot a look at Riley standing in the wings. His finger was pressed against his earpiece, concern on his face as he gazed over the crowd.

Why wasn't he reacting? Warning her? Coming to get her?

She started clapping again. She kept it up and made her way to his side of the stage.

He met her gaze and gave her a thumbs up.

A false alarm.

She whooshed out a breath, trying to focus on the performance. She moved in a trance back to the middle of the stage. Vaguely heard the guitars playing and missed the intro. The fans were belting out the words. She held out the mic, smiling and pretending she'd planned for them to start without her. They loved it, so she continued until she could gain her breath and composure.

Somehow, she muddled through the rest of the concert, handled two encores, then ended the performance even when they clamored for more. She just didn't have it in her to go back on stage for another song or forced smile. Nor walk to her bus to change.

She sank to the floor just offstage and rested her head on her knees.

She heard Eryn, who'd been seated on a stool for the entire concert, drop down next to her and take her hand. "It's over and no attacks. You can relax now. You're safe."

"Thank God for that," she managed to get out.

Eryn nodded.

Out of the corner of Leah's eye, she caught a glimpse of Riley heading their way, his sure, strong strides bringing him closer. She'd already gotten used to having him in her life again and had to admit she enjoyed it. He would likely help her up, escort her to get changed, and then drive her home. All the while coddling her and making sure she came to no harm.

She could easily get used to his attention on a regular basis.

"I'm so impressed," Eryn went on obvious to Leah's musings. "I know you're suffering, but you kept it hidden, and no one could tell you're going through so much."

"Thanks," Leah said, but it wasn't an accomplishment.

She was good at hiding things. Failing to let them out was what had ruined—and continued to ruin—her life, and with Riley bearing down on her, she knew tonight would be no exception and a rift would remain between them.

11

The next morning, the helicopter's rotors thumped a steady rhythm as Riley helped Leah climb in through the side door. She noticed he hadn't helped Eryn get in. He was such a gentleman with his private school manners that he likely wanted to offer Eryn his assistance, but Leah got why he didn't. She already knew Eryn was such an independent woman that she'd likely deck him if he tried.

Imagining that very thing brought a smile to her face.

"What's so funny?" he asked.

"I was imagining you helping Eryn into the helicopter."

Eryn frowned. "I'd sock him if he tried."

"Exactly." Leah smiled again.

Riley rolled his eyes and shook his head. "There's a headset for you hanging by the seat allowing us to communicate during the flight. If you need anything, let me know, okay?"

She nodded and noticed Eryn settle her headset over her ears.

Riley started to close the door then paused, his forehead knotting.

"What is it?" she asked, fearing there was some kind of mechanical failure.

"Owen." Riley scrubbed his free hand over his face. "I don't want to leave him behind."

She got that. Totally. Owen had begged to come with them, so Riley promised he'd take Owen up in the helicopter another time. That was good because it at least kept Owen's tears at bay, but it didn't take away his pouting lip that even she had a hard time refusing.

She was sad to see Riley suffering, but she was thrilled he was embracing fatherhood. Not that she should ever have doubted he would.

He took a long breath and exhaled loudly. "Is it always like this? The leaving."

"You never get used to it, but it does get easier and you can look forward to coming back. The joy and happiness they feel when you return. That's always a special moment."

Riley nodded, apparently satisfied, and yanked the door closed. He slid into the cockpit, and she had to admit it was totally cool that he'd branched out to become a helicopter pilot, or like the team members like to say, a helo pilot.

She settled the headset over her ears and adjusted the small mic. She'd chosen to sit in the back with Eryn instead of up front with Riley because she could look out both sides of the helicopter. And maybe because when she'd come out of his room this morning and discovered he'd made breakfast for all of them, her heart had melted even more, and she needed to put some space between them before she did something stupid like kiss him. Something she desperately wanted to do when she'd seen him barefoot, wearing a white T-shirt and worn-in jeans, looking altogether too appealing.

"Here we go," he said and the aircraft lifted off smoothly into the sky, whirring up higher and higher, leaving her stomach behind. She reveled in the feeling and loved being able to look out the windows. He piloted them out over the ocean then banked back inland over soaring pines and lush greenery.

Wow! Just wow! What a view. God's creation was like no other. Only He could craft such beauty. And only He could help her with her struggles.

Wait, what? Where did that thought come from?

If it could help her, did it matter? She closed her eyes and prayed, lifting her cares and needs to God. For some reason, winging over the treetops she felt closer to Him. Like He might have an answer for her if she just listened hard enough.

Her mother was a strong believer, and Leah had believed in God since she was young, but when she was with Riley she forgot all about the garbage from her childhood for a time, and she learned what it meant to live her faith. But after getting pregnant when she should never have been so weak as to be in that situation, her faith suffered. She'd regained her relationship with God over the years, but she'd never committed herself this fully before. Maybe that was what it took to find peace in her life. To set her priorities. If it was, she would try starting now.

I will listen, Lord. I will. I'm committed now. Show me the way. Please show me the way.

She opened her eyes and looked at Eryn, face buried in her laptop. She'd probably taken this flight so many times, it was second nature to her, but oh, how could anyone take God's amazing creation for granted? The greens, browns, whites, blues were vivid shades only God could create.

It hit her then how minuscule she was in comparison to the vast landscape below and the endless skies above, yet God cared about each little bird and flower. That meant He cared about every detail of her life, too. She'd only been praying for God to make things work out the way *she* wanted, but what if God had something else in mind for her? Could she trust Him—completely—even if He didn't want her to continue her career?

Her attention was drawn to the blond-headed man in the pilot seat. What would it be like if they reconciled and raised Owen together?

That would never happen, would it? Or was God urging her to consider it? Maybe she was wishing for it because it would make life easier, and she wouldn't have to share custody of Owen. Thinking about spending extended periods of time away from him left her breath catching in her throat, and a panic attack like she hadn't had since she was younger threatened to take her down.

She closed her eyes and concentrated on breathing to ward it off. The solid thump of the rotors settled her mind as time ticked past, but she kept her eyes shut tightly until she was in control again. When she opened them, she found Eryn looking at her.

"Everything okay?" Eryn asked.

Riley glanced over his shoulders. "Leah?"

"I'm fine." She forced out a smile to ease his concern. "Go back to flying this thing."

He took a final lingering look and turned his attention back to the front. Leah released a silent sigh drawing Eryn's attention again. Leah smiled but Eryn didn't respond with one, which was unusual for her and that worried Leah. Had she somehow heard about Owen and was wondering about him?

Hannah and Gage promised not to tell anyone until Riley could meet with the entire team and let them all know at the same time. The soonest they could do that was breakfast the next morning. And though they agreed to keep things quiet, that didn't mean David and Mia wouldn't say something to Bekah. But since Eryn would see pictures at Leah's house, Riley would tell her before they got there. Leah just didn't know when he planned to do that.

Man, it was going to be hard to see Eryn's response when she found out. Leah had already come to care for Eryn. Would she think badly of Leah for a decision she made years ago?

A sigh formed deep in Leah's body, but Eryn was still watching her, concerned, so Leah held it in.

"What are you working on?" Leah asked to break the awkward silence.

"I'm reviewing the CCTV files from the different venues where your stalker showed up. I was hoping to get a look at him, but the only video that he appears in is the Minneapolis one."

"And it's too dark to make him out."

Eryn nodded.

"Is there any way you can enhance it?"

"I can lighten it a bit, but I don't have the skills to improve it enough. It will take an expert."

So much for their most promising lead. Leah hoped it would pan out, but with her recent prayer she wouldn't let the setback get her down. "Do you know anyone like that?"

"I don't, but my friend, Piper might. She's an FBI agent. Right now she's on vacation and is staying with me. I'll ask her when we land and I can get a cell signal."

"Approaching our landing pad," Riley said over the headset. "If you want to call it that. Basically, it's a dirt field surrounded by trees. A tricky landing, but we use Lee's place all the time when we come to Portland, so I've got this. Just didn't want you to worry when you saw the clearing that looks the size of a postage stamp."

Leah turned her attention to the area below, and she couldn't even see the clearing, only a forest of trees. He kept lowering the helicopter and finally she could see the small spot. He wasn't kidding that it was postage-stamp sized. She grabbed her seat and held on.

"Don't worry." Eryn closed her laptop and relaxed back. "Riley might be a relatively new pilot, but he was trained by Coop, who's the best of the best. And this helo is his baby. No way he would let Riley get near it if he wasn't capable of landing in all situations."

Leah was glad to have another opinion on Riley's abilities and tried to relax. He proved Eryn right by safely touching down with a soft landing.

"Lee will have his old truck waiting for us," Riley said. "You two go on and get settled while I shut this down and do the post flight inspection."

Leah released her seatbelt and hung up her headset. Eryn led the way out of the helicopter into the crisp air.

Leah locked eyes on the tiny clearance surrounding the helicopter. "The helicopter is dangerously close to the trees. Why doesn't this Lee guy clear more land?"

"He doesn't want the liability of inexperienced pilots landing on his property. This pad keeps them away."

Leah could certainly see why. "But doesn't it make it a greater risk for all the pilots who land even if they're experienced?"

Eryn grinned. "He says life's an adventure, and that's the fun in landing here."

Leah shook her head. "I never did understand that mentality. I'm not much of a risk taker."

"Really?" Eryn tilted her head. "I'd think it was a risk every time you stepped on stage. Not physical but emotional. You have thousands of people counting on you not to let them down and you pour your heart out in song. That's riskier than anything we do."

"I've never even thought of that. I just go out and do what I love and have fun with it."

"Which is why you're so great. It's authentic. Especially when you sing 'Never Let You Go.' That's still my favorite of all your songs. It just touches me for some reason."

Leah wished Eryn hadn't brought that one up, but it wasn't unusual. She was told often enough that people loved that song. And they asked for it at every concert whether she'd put it in her lineup or not.

"Riley and I wrote that song together," Leah said, wondering why in the world she was mentioning something she didn't want to talk about.

Eryn stopped walking and stared at Leah. "That's why it's so special, isn't it? Because you wrote it for each other, and when you sing it, you still think of him and that time in your life."

Leah shrugged.

"What happened? Why'd you break up?"

Leah didn't want to answer, so she started walking again.

"Wait, I'm sorry, Leah." Eryn caught up to her. "It's none of my business. I shouldn't have asked."

"It's okay. I'd explain it, but you're Riley's teammate, and if he wants you to know, he'll tell you." Leah expected Eryn to get mad.

But she simply nodded. "You're a good person. Putting Riley first like that."

Leah smiled her acknowledgment, but she really hadn't done anything special. Her response was simply motivated by caring about Riley.

She continued on until she reached a pickup truck with rust spots over faded blue paint and enough dents that it looked like it had barely survived a demolition derby. She guessed it was from the fifties and had lived a hard life.

Eryn located the key in a metal container under the

front wheel well and opened the door. She motioned for Leah to slide in and she did.

Eryn got in, too. "Mind unlocking the door for Riley?"

Leah leaned over to pull up the lock. In moments Riley would be right here, snugged up close to her. She moved a little closer to Eryn who gave Leah a knowing look. Leah didn't care. She was better off getting a look from Eryn then riding for the next forty minutes touching Riley.

He soon slid in and got the truck going, the rumble of the old engine oddly comforting as they started down the road.

"As you can tell, there's no GPS in this truck." He glanced at her and smiled. "You'll have to give me directions."

Just like she'd often done in the past. She smiled back at him. "Remember your old station wagon? We'd take your surfboard and escape to the beach."

His grin widened. "I'll never forget those beach days."

"It would be nice to do it again," Leah said. "To get away from the fast-paced world and all the technology competing for our attention."

Eryn looked up from her phone and gaped for a minute. "Speak for yourself."

They all laughed, lightening the tension and making the rest of the drive more comfortable. Leah spent the time thinking about Riley entering her house. Her home. The most personal place of her life. And oddly, after years of letting only service people through the door, she was okay with giving him access.

Had she come to accept him in her life again so quickly, or was this more of God's prompting?

"Mind telling me where I have to turn?" he asked.

She gave him directions, and he soon pulled into the drive of her simple home. She took a moment to enjoy looking at the single-story contemporary house she'd bought the moment she'd saved enough to pay cash for it. It was the ugly duckling on the block, but she'd painted it a nice cool gray color and added minimal landscaping that a professional maintained for her, leaving it always well-manicured. Over the years, she'd remodeled all the rooms, one at a time, and now it fit her family perfectly.

Her family. Her mother, Owen, and her. And now Riley was part of their family. They'd all stayed at his place. Surprisingly, she felt equally comfortable in his little cabin. It had everything a person needed.

It had Riley. Not something she should be thinking.

She opened her bright blue front door and Eryn and Riley followed her into the vaulted foyer.

Riley drew his weapon. "Wait here while I clear the place."

Leah shot him a look. "You think my stalker could be waiting here?"

"Anything's possible." He turned to Eryn, his look professional and intense. "Stay alert."

She nodded, her hand drifting to her shirt and lifting the hem to reveal a holstered gun. Riley stepped off, heading into Leah's home.

Leah hadn't expected this. Not at all. She'd expected to walk him in. Follow her lead and gather only what they needed. She was okay with that, but not this. She always prepped carefully before anyone entered the house. Before a repair person arrived, she scrutinized the place, removing all traces of Owen. The work orders were in her mother's name. And most importantly, she never stayed around for the workers to see her. She didn't want to take any chances.

And now Riley was just waltzing through her house, looking at every nook and cranny. She waited, holding her breath until he returned. It whooshed out. Maybe her anxiety was more about his safety than anything.

Maybe, or maybe she had much more work to do on her personal insecurities.

Riley holstered his weapon. "We're clear."

"Great." Eryn let her hand fall away from her gun. "Then let's get after it."

Riley held up a hand. "There's something you should know first."

"Okay."

"And I need you to promise to keep anything you see to yourself," Leah added.

Eryn cocked her head. "You're scaring me with your serious tone."

"Sorry," Leah replied, trying to lighten her tone. "It's not bad, honest, it's just that I'm in the public eye, and I have to be careful about what gets out. I haven't let a stranger in my house in years, and I'm a little rusty at trusting people. I want to trust you, as I think you're worthy of it, but..."

"You can't." Eryn waved a hand. "No worries. I get it. And even if I didn't, you're our client and I won't tell anyone. Not even Trey, if you don't want me to."

"You can tell him as the rest of the team will hear about it at breakfast tomorrow."

"Okay, c'mon." She wrinkled her nose. "Spill. I'm dying of curiosity."

Riley bent to the lower shelf of Leah's small entryway table to grab a frame with Owen's picture. He handed it to Eryn. "This is my son."

She took a quick look then her head popped up. "You're a dad?"

He nodded and smiled at Leah—love, pride, and joy all comingled in the smile. "Owen is our son. I didn't know about him until yesterday. And before you get upset with

Leah, she had a good reason for not telling me. I won't go into details, but it involves my father who I'm estranged from."

Eryn looked at the picture again. "He's your spitting image. I mean like a mini you."

"I know. Isn't it great?" Riley beamed with happiness.

Leah's heart warmed clean through. Man, oh, man. She knew right then—right there standing in the home that had been her only sanctuary for years—that she was a goner, and her life would never be the same again.

Good or bad, she didn't know, but she'd let Riley Glen get under her skin and into her heart once again.

Riley could see Leah was upset as they got out of Lee's beat-up truck in front of Carolyn Eubanks' house, and she had every right to be. The woman had done her wrong. Seriously wrong.

He wished he'd thought to bring Eryn along instead of leaving her at Leah's house to prepare the computer for transport. Eryn and Leah had gotten past the fangirl moments and seemed to enjoy each other's company. And Eryn was such a compassionate person, she would be better able to comfort Leah right now. Still, he would do his best to support her.

She paused on the curb, staring at the lavish house, anger radiating from every pore. "Take a good look at this place because I paid for it. Hopefully it'll be sold after Carolyn's found guilty, and I'll get a bit of my money back."

The home was a sprawling two story painted crisp white with black shutters and roof. Gray stones wrapped columns and the garage corners while wrought iron railings ran the length of a long walkway leading up to the front door.

Extravagant landscaping covered the front yard, including an elaborate bubbling fountain with huge dolphins and mermaids leaping in the spray.

"Okay, let's do this," she said her voice hard, her shoulders raised.

He walked next to her up the stone paver walkway and knocked on the door with wrought iron trim. It swung in, and Riley noticed the lock had been pried open.

"What in the world?" Leah asked.

"Someone broke in. We need to get you back to the car and call 911."

Leah didn't budge. "What if Carolyn's hurt? We need to check, don't we?"

How did she have the heart to check on someone who'd wounded/betrayed her so badly? But she was right. If Carolyn was injured, immediate assistance could mean the difference between life or death.

He drew his weapon. His patrol days came back to him, and he went on autopilot.

"You carrying?" he asked her.

She jiggled her purse. "Yes."

"Get out your gun and stay in the foyer while I check on Carolyn. Yell if you see anyone or anything odd happens. Meanwhile, call 911. Got that?"

"Yes. I won't move." She dug out her gun and phone, and he had to admit there was something exciting about a woman with a gun.

He didn't like leaving her behind, but he had to. He stepped around the corner into a large living room, decorated to perfection like it came straight from a designer magazine. More of Leah's money went into that, he supposed.

Anger mixed with his unease, and he started for the back of the house. He rounded another corner. A familiar smell hit him in the face, thick and putrid. It felt like he slammed into a thick wall of odor.

He flinched and covered his mouth and nose with his hand as he backed out. He couldn't see Carolyn, but he didn't need to. He couldn't help her.

She was dead—and had been for some time.

The smell of decomposition was unique, and he knew without looking that somewhere in the back of the house, Carolyn had died, and with the broken door, he also knew it wasn't an accident.

Leah had called 911 and now she waited. Hand clasped around her gun, her hands shaking and her palms moist. Fat lot of good the shooting range did her. She'd always been so proud of her prowess there, but her hands weren't shaking, and she wasn't afraid like she was now. If someone came at her, she had no idea if she could even fire, much less hit them.

Footsteps sounded on the wood floor from the direction Riley had gone, and they were moving fast. Had he found something? Was someone chasing him?

She lifted her gun. Planted her feet. Focused. Prepared.

He charged around the corner. Alone.

"You scared me," she said as she lowered her weapon.

"C'mon." He took her arm and propelled her out the front door. "Let's go to the truck."

"Did you find Carolyn?"

"Sort of."

"What do you mean *sort of*?"

"As I got closer to the back of the house, I noticed a unique smell, so I didn't go any further and risk contaminating a crime scene."

"Smell. What smell?"

He looked at her then, long and hard. "A body decomposing."

"Oh my word, are you kidding? Carolyn's dead?"

"No doubt in my mind, but I didn't go in far enough to confirm." He opened the truck door, and she was glad to sit, as her legs were wobbly, and she feared she would drop to the ground.

Carolyn was dead.

Another person Leah had quarreled with was dead. Her house lock broken. She was likely murdered, too.

Murdered. Another person. Unbelievable. Totally unbelievable.

Leah's pulse raced.

Who would've killed Carolyn? Maybe someone else whose money she'd stolen. Leah had once been mad enough to murder her over that very thing. She'd never do such a thing, but would the police think it was her? She had no idea when bodies started to smell, but it had to be a day or two. Leah had been in Rugged Point for the last two days, but if Carolyn had died three days ago, Leah may or may not have an alibi for time of death.

Craziness. She was thinking about finding an alibi. For murder no less. She didn't even know what city she was in three days ago. Tours were so hectic that days ran together and mixed and mingled in her head. She could figure it out but would wait until they had an official time of death and the police insisted on knowing.

Listen to her. Thinking *official time of death* like it was an everyday thought. Seriously, what had her life become?

Riley got behind the wheel and dialed his phone.

Leah faced him and heard his cell ringing. "Do you think Carolyn was murdered?"

He looked at her. "Did she have any serious health issues?"

She shook her head.

"Then it's likely she was murdered." He paused for a long moment. "Or because of the upcoming trial she took her own life."

"Suicide? Really? But it seems like you think murder is more likely."

He nodded. "I have nothing to base it on except the jimmied door, but I do. I'm calling Blake."

"The sheriff? But why?"

"My gut says this is connected to Jill's murder."

She could hardly wrap her mind around that and didn't know what to say.

"You need to prepare yourself for the PPB detective to interview you. And when we head home, Blake will want to interview you, as well."

What? "But why? I didn't even go into the house."

"If we assume this is related to Jill, who was killed at your concert, then it has a connection to you. And you have motive to want to kill Carolyn. So like it or not, your status as a potential suspect has just gone up."

12

_____

Dinnertime was fast approaching, and Riley stood baffled in his kitchen. Leah was still in shock from Carolyn's death and the ensuing trauma brought on by the PPB detective's pointed questions. Riley hated seeing her like that and had encouraged her to rest while he took care of Owen. Where that offer came from, he didn't know. Her mother had given him a knowing smile and retreated to her room, too. He knew she was giving him time alone with Owen, but Riley didn't know what to do with a four-year-old boy. Didn't know what to do with a child at all. So many things were a mystery to him.

Did kids this age eat regular food? Were they potty-trained? He thought so, but he had like zero experience with kids and didn't know for sure. Did they brush their own teeth? Dress themselves? Riley's list of questions went on and on, but food was the priority.

He settled Owen on a barstool, hoping he could provide answers. "What do you want to eat for dinner?"

He shrugged.

Right. Big help. Riley thought back to his childhood. He'd have eaten a burger every day if his mother had let him, but she'd insisted on developing his dining palette. What did a preschooler know about palettes?

Riley always kept patties in the freezer. "How about a burger?"

"Yes, please. Can I play now?"

Riley nodded and helped Owen down. He ran to the coffee table where he'd stacked his Duplos and started building. Riley would quickly get dinner going and then go play with his son. *His son.* He would never tire of those words.

Riley found the burger and buns and put the meat in the microwave to thaw.

"I have to go outside to light the grill to warm it up," he called across the room.

Owen looked up with an eager expression on his face. "Can I help?"

Riley could let him push the ignitor button, but the grill wasn't a toy, so he shook his head. "When it's ready you can help me carry the burgers, okay?"

"K." Owen went back to building.

Riley was so proud of himself. He averted the first major hurdle that could've caused tears. Mentally patting himself on the back, he fired up the gas grill and returned to stare into the refrigerator.

Thanks to Hannah insisting he go grocery shopping with her instead of living off frozen meals, he had fresh fruits and veggies. He selected a head of lettuce and other salad fixings along with apples that he would slice. Feeling totally domestic, he prepared the items then put them in the refrigerator to stay fresh. Finally, he plopped down on the floor by Owen. Riley picked up a few blocks and connected them.

"No." Shaking his head, a stubborn look on his face,

Owen took the blocks from Riley's hands. "I don't want those like that."

He continued to stare at Riley, his expression exasperated. The boy might resemble Riley, but his look, especially this one, was all Leah. He was a combination of both of them. A good reminder that Owen needed them both in his life. Of that, Riley was sure. He just didn't know how to practically implement it.

The timer rang, and he got up. "Time to put the burgers on the grill. Do you still want to carry them for me?"

Owen nodded. Riley headed for the kitchen, and his Mini-Me stepped alongside him, his expression so serious Riley had to smile. He handed the plate to Owen who held it tightly and took careful steps toward the patio door.

Riley loved every step. He could easily imagine teaching Owen tons of things that Leah could never do, and he was thrilled with the chance to try.

On the patio, Riley stepped in front of Owen before he reached the grill. "The grill is very hot. If you touch it, it will burn you, so I need you to stay back. Understand?"

"It's like the oven. Mommy and Grandma won't let me touch that."

"Exactly." Impressed with his son's reasoning skills, Riley took the burgers and put them on the grill, the sizzle and instant aroma making his mouth water.

They went back inside and Riley was stunned that Owen offered to help set the table, and he knew exactly how to do it. Leah and her mother were doing a fine job raising him, and Riley was thankful for that.

The entire family settled down to dinner, and despite Leah's worry and unease over the recent murder, she was upbeat and cheerful through the meal. Riley assumed she was putting aside her emotions for Owen.

After the meal ended, she looked at Riley. "Do you want to give Owen his bath?"

Bath? Another new challenge. "I have no idea how to do it, but sure."

"I'll show you, Daddy." Owen jumped down and ran for the bathroom.

Leah smiled at Riley. "I'll grab his bath toys and meet you in there."

Riley soon learned bathing a kid was pretty easy, but staying dry in the process wasn't easy at all. Nor was helping a tired boy put on his pajamas. But they eventually accomplished the task. It likely took far longer than if Leah had dressed Owen, but Riley was proud of finally having all arms and legs in the places they should go.

He scooped up his freshly bathed son. He smelled like bubblegum soap, and Riley reveled in the scent and memorized it. Overtired, Owen suddenly crashed and was nearly limp in Riley's arms, his pudgy body resting solidly on Riley's chest. Owen's arms snaked up around Riley's neck, and his baby-soft skin evoked emotions in Riley that he couldn't even put words to.

"I love you, Daddy." Owen's sleepy voice melted Riley to the core.

"I love you, too, Son," Riley got out over a big lump in this throat.

He started for the bed and sat on the edge. Owen clung tight, so Riley sat there, simply enjoying the feel of his son in his arms. The scent of his sweet shampoo. The warmth of his little body. The shared love.

It suddenly hit Riley. Being a father was his new calling in life. To be a dad. To raise a child in faith. In God's Word. To bring him up with the love Riley didn't always feel growing up. To help Owen become a godly man and father himself one day.

To be there for his son each and every day.

"Need to pray now." Owen squirmed free and knelt beside his bed.

If Riley thought he couldn't experience any more joy, the sight of his son kneeling by the bed, hands folded, eyes scrunched closed made his heart overflow.

"God bless Mommy and Daddy and Grandma," Owen said. "And me, too. Amen." He started to get up then settled back on his knees. "And God, please don't let Daddy have to go away again. I want him with me."

Riley's heart constricted, and as Owen got up to look at him, his eyes sleepy, Riley made a promise to himself. He wouldn't leave Owen more than was absolutely necessary for his work. How he would resolve that with Leah he had no idea, but his son had to come first.

Riley tucked Owen into bed and brushed the hair from his forehead to give him a kiss. "Good night, Son."

"Night, Daddy."

The tiny voice, thick with sleep, tugged at Riley's heart-strings, and he wanted to just sit and watch his boy sleep, but Blake was on his way to interview Leah again, and Riley needed to be present for that.

After one last look at Owen from the door, Riley softly closed it and stepped into the living room. He expected to see Leah, but she wasn't in view. Tentacles of fear squeezed him until he spotted her standing on the back patio looking up at the moon. A shaft of light caressed the side of her face, and her blond hair shimmered in the beam. Her breath came out as white puffs of smoke in the cold air.

Her beauty astounded him. Just standing there, doing nothing, she was gorgeous. Up on stage performing, she was gorgeous *and* captivating. Holding their son, her eyes alight with motherly love, she was gorgeous. Everything about her was amazing to him. Even her power to hurt him, which she held in great measure.

He slid open the patio door, the cold hitting him in the face and chilling his shirt still wet from bathing Owen. She turned to look at him. Their gazes locked in a trance. He was helpless to look away.

It was time he faced facts. He'd never fallen out of love with her. She was *the* one.

Always was, always would be.

Father, what am I going to do about her? Just what?

Leah finally succumbed to Riley's pressure to come in out of the cold. She didn't want to but agreed when she saw his wet shirt. Still, thoughts of the sheriff's upcoming questions wouldn't let her sit still. She paced Riley's living room, her mind still filled with the day's horrible turn of events. The medical examiner had arrived at Carolyn's house and said that Carolyn had been shot in the back, two bullets—just like Jill, and had been dead for some time. He would know how long after the autopsy, which he promised to perform immediately. According to Riley, that didn't happen very often. But the ME agreed to speed things up because the detective believed there was a connection to Jill's death, and they feared they were looking at a serial killer who needed to be stopped.

A serial killer. One who had a connection to her. How crazy, bizarre, and gruesome was that?

She shuddered, drawing Riley's attention. He got up from his sleek leather sofa and crossed the room. "You're thinking about Carolyn."

She nodded. "How can I not be? Especially when I don't know if the police think I'm a suspect or not."

Riley glanced at his watch. "It's been twenty minutes since Blake called. He should be here any minute to give us an update."

"Not just an update." She rubbed her forehead where tight knots were turning into a headache. "He's coming to question me, which means they likely have an estimated time of death, and because of the bad blood between me and Carolyn, Blake will want to know where I was. What if I can't account for my time? What then? What do I do? How do I handle that?" She hated that her voice was rising with each question but she was terrified of what might happen.

"Hey, hey." Riley took her hand. "It's routine questioning. Nothing to worry about."

"Easy for you to say." She huffed out a breath, but his touch did help calm her nerves a bit. "What if I don't have an alibi for the time?"

"Then you'll be a suspect."

"You make it sound so simple. Like it's no big deal." She pulled her hand free and started pacing again.

He intercepted her and stood in front of her to rest his hands on her shoulders, his gaze locking on hers. "It's a big deal to me because you're worried about it, and I don't like to see you suffer."

"I hear a *but* coming."

"No buts. I know you didn't kill anyone, and my team will find the real killer and prove your innocence."

"How can you be so sure?"

"Because my team is more than capable, and as you get to know us, you'll realize there's really nothing we can't do."

"That's mighty confident, don't you think?"

"Maybe, but we're experts in many areas. If we discover there's something we need to know but don't, we have contacts in many fields of military and law enforcement to call on." He smiled at her—a sincere, sweet smile.

It worked on her worry, lessening it, and she honestly felt hopeful again. And more. She was thankful. Grateful. And mixed with all of that, her emotions were blossoming under his gaze, and she wanted to step closer and ask him to hold her.

"There's something else," he said, looking like he hated to bring it up.

"What?"

"We need to look at Carolyn's murder another way. If she and Jill were both killed by your stalker, you could be in even more danger, and we need to up our security measures."

She gasped, and her pulse kicked up.

"Hey. It's okay." He gently stroked the side of her face. "I promise I'll take care of this for you and keep you safe. I'm yours for as long as you need me."

That was it—the end of her rope, and she all but flung herself at him. He circled his arms around her and held on like he feared she might push away. She rested her head on his chest and listened to his heartbeat. It was solid, just like he was. Solid and steady. Dependable. Loyal, no matter what she'd done to hurt him.

She looked up at him. "Thank you for being here for me. I don't deserve it, but thank you for being you and being able to look beyond our breakup to help me."

"Hey." His smile widened. "You're the mother of my child. I can do no less."

His statement sent a ripple of shock through her body. She loved hearing him say that, and she was suddenly very glad that she'd told him about Owen. Her son now had two parents to raise him, and he had this very strong and capable man as a role model.

She couldn't contain her gratitude and raised up to kiss his cheek. He startled, but quickly recovered, his gaze intense and dreamy at the same time. He gently cupped the side of her face, emotions warring in his eyes.

"Leah, I...I..." He lowered his head as if planning to kiss her then paused, maybe waiting for her to tell him to stop.

She didn't but slid her fingers into his hair and drew him closer. His lips settled on hers, the warmth of his touch nearly making her melt. His kiss was tentative like it was their first time, and his gentleness and consideration touched her.

She wanted more. So much more. She deepened the kiss. Explored it.

A loud knock sounded on the door.

He jerked back. His eyes flew open, and he blinked hard then stepped back. "Sorry...I shouldn't have...we shouldn't... that'll be Blake."

He rushed away from her. He may have regretted the kiss, but she didn't. It helped clarify her feelings. Not that she would act on them, but it was now obvious that she still had very strong feelings for him. Had never stopped caring about him. It explained why she never connected with another man since their breakup. Keeping the tattoo. Her continued trips to the firing range.

"Blake," Riley said. "Come in."

As Riley moved to let Blake enter, she took a long breath and blew out her emotions—the caring and love, and the fear of talking to Blake. Riley was on her side. She didn't need to worry about anything.

She went to meet Blake and offered her hand. He held a leather briefcase in one hand, reached out with the other. His gaze was polite but patronizing. A notch of her calm slipped.

He released her hand and looked at Riley who was closing the door. "Mind if we sit at your table?"

"Sounds good."

Riley directed them to the dining area, and Leah took a seat at the round walnut table with modern fabric chairs. Blake sat across from her, and Riley pulled out a chair next to her, straddled it, and rested his arms on the back.

Blake removed a stack of papers out of his folder and locked a penetrating gaze on Leah. "Threatening letters were found at Ms. Eubanks' residence. They were written on your letterhead and criminalists were able to lift two sets of prints. Ms. Eubanks' and yours. They were also signed by you."

Leah blinked at him, her brain unable to comprehend what he'd said.

"What's in the letters?" Riley asked calmly as he took the pages in hand while she still tried to figure out how letters she didn't write could be found in Carolyn's house.

"In the first one, Leah warns Ms. Eubanks if she doesn't sell her possessions and return the money she's stolen that Leah will make her pay. The subsequent letters explicitly threaten Ms. Eubanks' life."

"I didn't write them," Leah finally got out.

"The signature looks like yours," Riley said. "And not your autograph signature but your official one."

"Autograph? Official?" Blake asked.

"I don't use my legal signature for autographs so fans can't copy it and put it on a document like this." She snatched the pages from Riley's hands, and rapidly flipped through them, each page taking a chunk out of her confidence. "They look like my signature, but I didn't sign them."

"We can call in a handwriting specialist," Riley said.

Blake frowned. "My department doesn't have the budget for that, and I doubt PPB does either, but if Blackwell is willing to pick up the tab, go for it."

"We will," Riley said, surprising Leah since she thought he'd need to get Gage's permission first. "I don't have a source, but Eryn's friend Piper might. She's staying with Eryn this week. I'll give her a call."

"Keep me updated." Blake turned his attention to Leah. "I need to take your gun for testing."

"Was Jill or Carolyn killed with a 9mm?" Leah asked.

Blake took a slow, even breath, his expression deadpan. "I can't confirm or deny that."

Riley planted his hands on the table. "But you wouldn't ask for Leah's gun if the ME didn't retrieve a 9mm slug from one or both of them."

Blake's expression shifted for the briefest of seconds, but he didn't have to say the words.

Leah was a suspect now for sure. Panic crawled up her spine and choked the breath out of her.

Blake got out his phone and swiped his fingers across the screen then held it out to display a photo. She took one look and gasped.

"Carolyn's wrist," Blake said.

The purple-colored skin revealed a tattoo matching Jill's.

Blake leaned forward. "With the body discoloration, it's hard to see that the tat was recently inked, but the ME confirmed it was."

Riley jumped up. "Why'd you make Leah look at that, man? You could've just told her about it."

Blake sat calmly in his chair and peered up at Riley. "You're right. I could have. But I think it's important for Leah to see what leaving a dead body for days can do."

"Why? Because you think she did this?" Riley shoved a hand into his hair. "You're way off base here."

"Maybe. Maybe not. The evidence is all pointing to her." Blake drew out an evidence bag from his briefcase and laid it in in front of Leah. She took a long look at a pair of teardrop earrings she'd bought at a bazaar that sold handmade items in New Orleans. The earrings were one of a kind and there was no question that they belonged to her.

"Are these your earrings?" Blake asked.

"Yes," Leah said her stomach now swimming with acid. "Where did you get them?"

"Carolyn was wearing them."

"I didn't give them to her."

"So let me get this straight. Two women who have been murdered also stole your jewelry?"

She wrapped her arms around her body, cradling herself from additional hurt. "I don't know. I don't get any of this. If I could explain it, I would."

"Like you explained Ms. Stevenson's blood on your clothing."

"That's nothing new." Riley took a wide stance. "Leah found the body. Tried to help her, then wiped her hands on her clothes. She already told you that."

"But what she didn't tell me is that her clothes also contained gunshot residue."

"What?" Leah could hardly believe that.

"That doesn't tell you anything either," Riley said. "GSR can linger in the air for up to eight minutes. If Leah arrived right after Jill was killed, she could have gotten it on her clothes. Shoot, you could test my clothes and probably find it, too, and these results aren't worth discussing."

Leah was so thankful to have Riley standing up for her because her brain was muddled, and she could hardly think, much less defend herself.

Blake ground his teeth together for a moment then took a deep breath. "Then let's talk about Ms. Eubanks' death. The ME estimates her time of death to be three days ago. I'll need you to account for your whereabouts that day."

"An entire day? Who can do that?"

"I know it will be hard, and that's why I'll give you some time to think about it before providing your alibi."

"Thank you," she said and hoped this meant he was leaving.

"Before I go." Blake took out another set of papers. "There's one more thing I need you to explain. We've processed Jill Stevenson's house. This is a copy of a concert ticket that you mailed to her along with an invitation to attend last night's concert."

All blood drained from Leah's head, and the room spun. "No. No. I didn't mail that to her. I don't even handle those things. I don't have them available to me."

Blake arched an eyebrow. "Not available, but you could get them?"

"Yes, but not here. Not on the road."

"Who takes care of this for you?" Riley asked, his tone much gentler.

Leah didn't want to answer because she didn't want to think that Kraig sent the invitation, as he could easily get to the stationery and tickets. His assistant—who was in charge of Leah's fan mail and giving tickets to people—could be a suspect, too, but she didn't travel with Leah like Kraig did, putting her jewelry in his reach.

"Leah," Riley said. "I know you don't want to get anyone in trouble, but Blake is all but accusing you of two murders. You have to tell him who manages the tickets and stationery."

"My manager's assistant handles this from their office in California where Kraig keeps the materials. He also has access to my jewelry when he comes on the road with us."

Blake took out the notebook that Leah was coming to hate seeing. "And this manager is Kraig Moon who I interviewed the other night?"

She nodded.

Blake frowned. "Is it common for him to travel with you?"

"He doesn't tour with us on a regular basis, if that's what you mean, but he does come to concerts to meet face-to-face with other people on my team like agents, promoters, etc. Especially if there's a problem with the tour."

Blake took a moment as if processing her comment. "And is he in town because of a problem on this tour?"

She shook her head. "He's just here to schmooze."

Blake locked gazes again. "Or kill people."

Leah felt so weak that she might slide out of her chair. "I need to talk to him."

Blake snapped his notebook closed. "Not before I do, which will be first thing in the morning."

His lack of understanding made her mad, and she crossed her arms. "He's my manager. I can't sleep tonight wondering if he's a killer."

"I'm sorry," Blake said. "But I can't have you alerting him to my questions and give him time to create an alibi."

"Can Leah be at the interview?" Riley asked.

Blake shook his head. "You know protocol forbids that."

Riley furrowed his forehead. "Can she observe?"

"No." Blake held up a hand. "And before you ask, I can't share what he has to say, either."

Riley huffed out a breath. "I have the utmost respect for you, Blake, but you're not your usual self here."

Blake tilted his head. "In what way?"

"You're tougher. Less flexible."

"I have to be." He stood and shoved his notebook into his pocket. "There's no room for niceties when you're investigating one murder, much less two of them." He shifted his focus to Leah. "I'll take that gun now."

$\sim$

Riley stepped outside with Blake, the night cold, his breath creating puffy clouds in the air. Riley wanted Blake gone for Leah's sake, but he wouldn't let the sheriff leave without picking his brain first. "Sounds like you're not thinking the stalker has anything to do with these murders."

Blake dug his car keys from his pocket. "I haven't ruled him out, but so far we haven't made any progress in locating him."

"Then fingerprints from the amphitheater were a bust for you?"

Blake nodded, likely because he didn't want to verbally answer a question he shouldn't be answering. "But in light of what Leah just shared, we'll need to give Kraig's prints another look."

Riley was thinking Sam needed to do the same thing. "Can you confirm the caliber of the gun used in the murders?"

"I gotta go." Blake met his gaze. "Make sure Leah doesn't leave town."

"What?" Riley gaped at Blake. "You like her for these murders enough to keep her here?"

"Forensics point to her, and I can't ignore that." Blake opened his car door. "If anyone else was in my shoes, they'd be putting my case before the DA and seeking an arrest warrant. That's between you and me, and you aren't to let Leah know. Got it?"

Riley stood staring at Blake for the longest time before he composed himself and didn't respond in anger. "Don't worry, I won't tell her. She'd freak out. So thanks for not saying it to her."

"As much as I'd like to tell you that I held back to spare her feelings, I did it for my investigation. I didn't want to spook her and have her take off." Blake met his gaze and held on. "I'm counting on you to make sure she doesn't bolt."

"Don't worry about that either. I'll be with her twenty-four seven. You can count on that. Because I, for one, am worried that Carolyn's death means Leah is in more danger, where you seem bent on railroading her as a suspect."

Blake let out a long breath. "I'm not railroading her. Simply following the leads like you'd be doing. But you can't see clearly because you've got a thing for her, and a man in love doesn't always make the best choices."

"I don't have a—"

Blake flashed up a hand. "Save your breath. It's so obvious even a child could pick up on it."

Riley didn't think that was true, but he wasn't going to stand there and argue.

"Just make sure Leah is available when I need to talk to her, or I *will* have to bring her in."

Riley gritted his teeth. "I promise she won't be going anywhere without me."

Blake eyed him for a long time then climbed in his SUV and drove off.

Riley took a few minutes to absorb the cool air and calm his emotions. With Blake's announcement, Riley had to meet with the team tonight to update them and get them moving double time before Blake arrested Leah.

Riley stepped inside and closed the door. He turned to find Leah pacing again. He went to the sofa and patted the cushion next to him. "C'mon. Let's sit and talk about this."

"What's to talk about?" She sighed. "I didn't do this. Means we could be looking at another person on my team that I trusted betraying me. Maybe Kraig. But that's not the worst of it. He could be a killer."

Riley held out his hand and gave her a pointed look until

she sat next to him. "Do you really think Kraig killed these women?"

She shook her head. "But then I didn't think Carolyn would embezzle or Jill cheat with my boyfriend. But they did, so honestly, I don't know what to think."

"I need to get the team together for an update and to set priorities."

She glanced at the mantle clock. "Tonight."

Riley nodded. "I know you're tired, but I need you to come with me."

"Why? I'm safe here, right?" She clutched her hands together.

"The compound is extremely secure, but even a fortress can be breached, so I'd rather you be where I can see you."

She stared over his shoulder and bit her lower lip. "What about Mom and Owen? I hate to leave them alone."

"I'll call Piper. I'm sure she'll agree to stay with them while we meet."

"I hate to impose on her vacation."

"Trust me. Piper won't mind."

"But what about Bekah? Who'll stay with her while we're gone?"

"Eryn's mom usually does that, but if not, Eryn can bring Bekah over here. She can sleep in my bed as easily as her own." At least he thought that was true. When Leah didn't argue, he figured it was possible, and he dug out his phone. "Let me get things arranged."

She grabbed his arm. "Are you sure this is okay? I hate to interfere with your team's home lives."

He looked her in the eye to convey their commitment. "I promised to keep you safe. If that means no one on the team sleeps to make that happen, then we don't sleep. You're our top priority."

13

Leah used the time while waiting for Eryn and Piper to arrive to check her calendar to determine where she was the day Carolyn died. She opened the calendar program on her phone.

"Anything?" Riley asked from where he stood behind her.

She tapped the blank square on the screen. "I was in Portland that day. A break in the tour bookings."

"But you don't have a thing scheduled," he stated the obvious.

"It was only a few days ago, but honestly I don't know what I did with every minute of the day. I can talk to Mom in the morning. She'll help me piece it together."

A knock sounded on the door.

"I'll get it." Riley went to let the women in.

Eryn, carrying a sleeping Bekah, introduced Piper who wasn't at all what Leah expected. Piper's name had evoked a carefree woman with wispy blond hair in Leah's mind, but she had short, almost black hair and creamy skin plus big brown eyes. She also had an intensity about her that matched the Blackwell team members' intimidating power.

She walked with crutches, and her right foot was bandaged. Leah wanted to ask what happened, but since she'd just met the woman, that would be rude.

She looked Piper in the eye, which was easy to do since they were about the same height. "I'm sorry to ask you to do this when you're taking some time off."

She waved one of her crutches. "Are you kidding? I'm only off work because of this lame foot, and I'm not a sit-around kind of girl. I'm glad to be useful."

"Well then, thank you." Leah smiled.

"And in case you're worried that I'm not up to the job with my lame foot." She rested on one crutch and patted her gun holstered at her trim waist and grinned. "I don't shoot with my foot."

Leah laughed and took an instant liking to Piper. "Then you concentrate on that, and my mom will handle Owen's more mundane needs like water and any trips to the bathroom."

Piper nodded, and her serious expression returned.

"One thing before we go," Riley said. "I also don't want to impose on your time off, but if you don't mind, I wanted to ask if you had a source for handwriting analysis."

"No problem." She waved a hand while balancing on the crutches. "I can introduce you to someone."

"The sooner the better." Riley explained the situation.

Eryn shot him a curious look.

"Blake was just here," Riley said. "I'll fill you in on the details at the meeting."

"I'll make a few calls for you and have a name when you get back from the meeting," Piper said. "And I'm glad to facilitate getting the letters to them if you want me to take that off your plate, too."

"Thanks, Piper," Leah said. "I'll owe you big time."

"Nothing a pair of front row concert seats wouldn't fix.

Of course, I'll be bringing your biggest fan." Piper tipped her head at Eryn and laughed.

Leah smiled. "You got it."

"Any word on enhancing that dark video?" Riley asked.

Piper frowned. "I got a guy working on it. Says he can make improvements, but he's not sure how much. He thinks he'll be finished tomorrow sometime."

Leah was so thankful for all of Piper's help. "I'll owe you even more."

"A backstage pass, too?" She winked.

"Glad to. You can even come on stage if you want."

"Hey, now," Eryn said. "I'm working hard, too."

"Of course you are." Leah patted Eryn's arm. "When this is all over the three of us will get together and figure out something special."

"Oh, you know it." Eryn pumped her fist.

Leah grabbed her jacket and started to put it on.

Riley took it from her and helped her into it. She heard Piper sigh, and Leah had to agree. Nothing more attractive than a man with good manners. Except maybe seeing Riley holding their son in his arms as he carried Owen to bed. That got Leah's pulse pounding in a way she never expected.

"You two go ahead while I settle Bekah in your room, Riley," Eryn said. "And then I'll join you all in the conference room."

He opened the door for her, and they stepped into the crisp night.

"Want to walk?" Riley asked.

She nodded. She was glad for the time to clear her muddled brain of everything. She wanted to be clearheaded when she met with the Blackwell defenders who meant well but were daunting. Especially when so much was at stake, and she didn't know what conclusion they would come to. At least Riley was solidly on her side.

They walked in silence...easy, comfortable silence as if they'd turned a corner and were on more solid footing with each other. But had they? Not as far as she could tell.

She hadn't really allowed herself the luxury of looking at him for the joy of it, and she kept sneaking glances at him. It was a luxury, as he was like a fine sculpture in the bright moonlight. His profile was chiseled, his jaw like granite. But his hair reminded her of Owen's, and she knew it was soft to the touch.

The same warm emotions washed over her as when she used to watch him on a stage, singing to a small crowd, addressing each person like they were a personal friend.

Oh, man. She really was in over her head here with him. Way over her head. And the worst part was not knowing the motives behind her attraction.

Was it remembering the past when they'd been blissfully happy? Was it because she didn't want to share Owen with Riley and was fooling herself to keep him around? Or was she really and truly in love with him?

Confused, she ran a hand through her hair, getting stuck on tangles.

He looked at her and caught her gaze on him. "Do I have food on my face or something?"

She shook her head but didn't speak. What could she say? *Two women have been murdered, I might be a suspect or my manager might be a murderer, and I'm shallow enough to be noticing how handsome you are.*

Not hardly.

"What about you?" She turned it back on him. "You seemed lost in thought, too."

"I was thinking how comfortable this walk was. I'd forgotten how well we know each other."

"Yeah. We were close."

163

He quit walking and glanced at her. "Do you ever wonder what might have been if we hadn't broken up?"

All the time.

"I try not to dwell on the past." Okay, the truth, but not a real answer to his question, so she started forward again.

He took her arm and stopped her. "There's something I need to say. I've been waiting for the right time, but there hasn't been one."

He was scaring her. Was he going to share something else that would rock her already shaken world? "What's that?"

"I want you to know that I forgive you for not telling me about Owen. I get that you were thinking of what was best for him. Now that I know about him, I totally understand. If I'd been in your shoes, I would've done the same thing."

Tears sprang to her eyes, and she couldn't stop them.

"Thank you," she managed to get out as her love for this man increased. "That means so much to me."

He squeezed her arm and let go. "I'm glad. I wanted you to know so when we sit down to talk about Owen's future, that you don't think I'm holding a grudge."

Right. Give her good news then douse it with a bucket of ice water. Still, he'd forgiven her. She didn't deserve it, and she was so grateful. But he sounded like he planned on trying to take custody of Owen.

She had to face that head on. "You're not going to fight me for custody, are you?"

He shook his head. "At least not unless we can't work out some agreement between us and stick to it."

She nodded and resumed walking. He had a right to spend time with Owen, and she would have to come to grips with that. She just couldn't do it right now.

The ease between them had evaporated, and her mind traveled to the upcoming meeting.

Could she withstand additional stress, or would she fall apart in a room filled with people she'd come to respect?

Please, God, help me stay strong. This is all so over my head —please give me wisdom to know what to say.

He opened the door for her, and she was surprised to see that no one else had arrived. She sat in the same chair as their earlier meeting, and the others filtered in, taking the same seats at the table, too. So much had happened since the update meeting that Leah couldn't believe such little time had passed.

Riley stood at the head of the table, and when Gage closed the door and took a seat, Riley brought them up to speed on the latest developments. He turned to the whiteboard. "Let's first review our action items then move forward."

"Blake has the sketch," Gage said. "And he's distributed it nationally, but he hasn't gotten any hits."

"Let me know if that changes." Riley put a checkmark by the item. Then he tapped the picture where she was running, her tattoo exposed. "I showed the picture Eryn made without a tattoo to Leah's people last night and none of them recognized the area."

"I'm still trying to gather more information on the person who uploaded the image," Eryn said. "Don't hold your breath on that though. And also, I can update the stalker video from the concert venues, too, since that's next on the list. The Minneapolis video was the only one that caught the stalker and it's too dark to do much good. Piper has passed it on to experts, and if we're lucky, we'll get a clear enough shot for facial recognition."

"FYI," Riley said. "I also asked Piper to find a handwriting expert to evaluate the letters found at Carolyn's house."

"I thought she was here to rest up and recuperate from the shoot-out," Gage said.

"Shoot-out?" Leah asked.

Eryn nodded. "She was involved in an altercation with a hacker that turned ugly. She was pinned down with another agent for hours while a negotiator worked with the suspect. Piper took a bullet to the foot when she was diving for cover."

"She seems like such a nice person," Leah said sincerely. "That's horrible."

Gage nodded. "Bad things happen to good people. Which is why we have this team, and I'd like to think we're making more of a difference here than we would've in our past jobs." He looked at Eryn. "How's Piper doing?"

Eryn's eyes narrowed. "She's pretending everything will be okay, but it looks like her foot isn't going to return to normal."

"Too bad there's not a position for Piper here," Alex said.

Eryn frowned. "There would be if I gave up my job."

"Or with all you do, I could see Gage needing another person." Trey gave Gage a pointed look. "Or at least half a person. Also if Eryn decided to work part-time once our first bambino is on the way, you might need someone."

"Right, the million kids you want to have." Alex laughed.

Trey mocked offence. "I only want six, and with Bekah, that would only be five more."

Leah snorted. "Seriously. Six?"

"Yep." He slid an arm around Eryn's shoulders. "Want a huge family with the little woman."

Eryn shrugged his arm off and socked him. "Just for that comment you can sleep on the couch."

"Um, honey we aren't married yet. I live at my own place, remember?"

"You're here so much, how can she?" Alex asked.

Eryn ignored him and gave Trey an angry look that was obviously fake. "Then I'm saving this for after we're married. When you least expect it, you'll get the couch."

"Yup, this is the woman I want to marry. I wouldn't have it any other way." Trey sat back with a contented smile.

Gage cleared his throat, drawing attention his way. "What's happening with the stalker's letters you picked up today?"

"I'm processing them for prints and DNA," Sam said. "So far I've lifted several good prints that aren't Leah's." She faced Leah. "Did anyone else touch them besides you after they arrived?"

"Kraig and his assistant because they were sent to my public address which is a P.O. Box they monitor. And my mom because I was so freaked out."

"Okay, I'll need your mom's prints, too. I can get those in the morning. Where can I find the assistant?"

"She lives in L.A."

"Give me her contact information, and I'll figure out how to get them."

Leah gave her the details from her phone and made a mental note to tell Kraig about this. She planned to talk to him the moment Blake finished interviewing him in the morning.

Riley jotted the information on the board. "What about the prints from the crime scene?"

"None have returned a match in the system."

Riley made a note of that. "I'm assuming you eliminated Kraig's from the mix, but with the new developments, I need you to go back and reevaluate any place where you lifted them."

"Will do, and I can have that done by morning."

"Perfect," Riley said. "Blake will be interviewing Kraig

first thing in the morning, and I'll talk to him immediately afterward."

Riley turned back to the board. "Anything else come up in your algorithm search, Eryn?"

"Nothing of substance, but I've left it running in case anything new is posted online." She shifted in her chair. "Since Piper was acting so antsy, I had her do the measurements on Leah's tattoo in the jogging picture and compare to actual measurements."

"And?"

"And the tat in the picture is a fake."

Coop narrowed his gaze, looking so intimidating Leah almost moved back. "What do you mean a fake?"

"It's Photoshopped onto the picture."

"Wow," Alex said. "Someone went to a lot of trouble to create this photo."

"Then why put it in a comment section?" Leah asked. "I don't get it."

"Honestly, neither do Piper and I," Eryn said. "We discussed it at length, and it makes no sense. I've asked Blake to get a warrant for the commenter's user information. He's trying for it, but he's not sure if I've given him enough probable cause to get one."

"What about fan videos on YouTube?" Jackson asked. "I'm assuming fans will have posted videos of the recent concerts, and we should be looking at those for leads."

"Oh, you know I'm all over that," Eryn grinned. "I'll start the minute I get home."

"Just remember what time Bekah will wake you up in the morning," Trey said.

As a mother, Leah knew he made a valid point, but she could tell that there was nothing that would stop Eryn from watching the videos tonight.

"What have you found at tattoo shops, Alex?" Riley asked.

"You mean besides every kind of tat you could want?" He chuckled. "Nothing. Not a single person I talked to will take credit for this particular tattoo."

"You cover the whole area?"

He nodded. "I visited local places and called every place in the near vicinity. Nada."

"So we have two murdered women both with recent tats and no one in the area claiming they did the tattoo," Riley summarized.

"Maybe the killer did them," Jackson offered as he looked at Leah. "Know anyone with those skills?"

She shook her head. "I mean, not other than the person who did our tats, and I don't remember a thing about him. Not even what he looked like...other than maybe he had facial hair. And he had tattoos, but I couldn't tell you what they looked like."

Jackson leaned forward. "What about his name or the shop name?"

She shook her head. "We did this on the spur of the moment and got whoever was taking walk-ins."

"I remember the general location of the shop," Riley said. "But that's it."

Leah didn't know if this information was even important. "We weren't regular clients, and it was seven years ago. Surely he's forgotten all about us and wouldn't be stalking me."

"I agree," Riley said. "Plus tattoo artists are independent contractors who move around a lot. Even if we could remember his or the shop's name, he might not be at the same place." Riley turned to the board. "But I'll jot it down, and we can come back to it if the other leads don't pan out or if our research points his way."

"I'm in agreement." Jackson looked around the table where the others nodded. "But I think we should still consider that the stalker could be a tattoo artist and should proceed in that direction."

"How?" Eryn asked. "Check every tattoo place in the country? Even if we think he might live in the Midwest because he showed up at concerts in that part of the country, that doesn't narrow things down enough, and we can't handle visiting or even calling that many places."

"Then let's backburner this," Gage said. "And hope Piper's contact is able to give us a clear picture of the stalker because we really don't have much else to go on in finding him."

He shifted his focus to Leah. "Since the killer is targeting people you've had a falling out with, now would be the time to tell us if there are others on that list so we can make sure they're safe."

Leah didn't like his comment. "You make it sound like that's a long list."

"Is it?" Gage's eyebrow rose.

"I can't imagine you can get to where you are without making a few people mad," Coop added.

"But I did nothing to make Jill or Carolyn mad. They were the ones who wronged me." Leah crossed her arms and tried not to look upset.

"Sorry, if I offended you." Coop raised his hands. "I didn't mean anything by it, just that there has to be people who could want you to suffer or the other way around."

"Sure, but who?" She looked down at the table to avoid all the gazes locked on her and think. "One other person comes to mind. A promoter who totally screwed up my last tour. We had to cancel several concerts, and I sued him for breach of contract and won. He paid back the costs, so I have nothing against him. His name is Bruce French. He lives in L.A. I can give you his contact information."

"Sounds like he might have a grudge against you," Coop said. "What better way to pay it back than to kill people and make it look like you did it?"

"Seriously?" Leah asked. "You think he's behind the killings? That's a stretch."

"Or he could be the next victim," Riley said. "Either way, we need to let Blake know so he can take appropriate actions and another person doesn't lose their life."

14

The next morning, Riley rested his shoulder on the wall while Leah sat across a small table from Kraig in his hotel room. Riley wanted to give Kraig a fair shake, but as he sat there wringing his hands, Riley had to wonder if the guy was upset due to killing two women or because he was a suspect and Blake had questioned him.

"I don't have an alibi for either murder." He paused and swallowed, like he could swallow away his part in these murders, if indeed he had a role. "I mean I was backstage and plenty of people saw me, but can any of them vouch for me the entire time? I don't know, and I was close enough to kill Jill and get back to my spot before you found her. The sheriff must think I did it, right? I'll be accused of murder."

"Did you do it, Kraig?" Leah asked, the pain of betrayal in her voice. "Did you send those letters to Carolyn and the ticket to Jill?"

He flinched. "Are you kidding me? Of course I didn't. I can't believe you would even ask me that."

Leah crossed her arms. "Then how did the letters and ticket get to them?"

"I should have told you." Kraig ran a hand over his hair

—today he gathered a portion in a top ponytail and the back hung down to his shoulders.

"Told me what?" The suspicion in Leah's voice was cutting.

"About the break-in. Someone broke into the office. We didn't think anything was missing, but now...now I gotta figure someone took your stationery and some tickets."

Leah uncrossed her arms and leaned closer. "You're telling me your office was broken into, and you didn't mention it to me?"

"You were already freaking out on the sales numbers and the upcoming tour. I couldn't add to your stress. Besides, we didn't notice anything missing. How could we know it had anything to do with you?"

"You mean, other than the fact that you have a ton of my personal information in your office? I needed a heads up in case any of that ended up in the news."

"I'm sorry, okay?" Kraig twisted his hands so tight that they turned white. "I screwed up."

"Pretty convenient, isn't it?" Riley asked. "This break-in is suddenly a way to explain away the stationery and ticket."

"You have to believe me." He shoved up his glasses and peered at Riley. "We filed a police report. It happened about four weeks ago. I'm getting a copy for the sheriff." He shifted to look at Leah. "I'll give a copy to you, too."

"Yeah, I want to see it." Hurt strangled her voice, and she rubbed her forehead.

Riley wished he could fix it. People kept disappointing her, and she had a lifetime of disappointment before she was eighteen. She didn't need more.

"You really don't believe me." Kraig cringed. "Man, why didn't I tell you? If you want to end our professional relationship, I totally understand."

Riley didn't want to believe her manager. Riley would rather have a solid suspect, but he *did* believe the guy.

He got out his phone and opened the picture of Leah jogging and held it out to Kraig. "Do you know anything about this picture?"

He studied it. "I mean it's obviously Leah and Neil jogging, but I don't know anything else." He looked up. "Should I recognize it?"

Riley shrugged and brought up the tattoo found on Jill's arm to display it. "What about this?"

Kraig stared at the screen then looked up at Leah. "You got a tat?"

She shook her head.

"But this…"

"Is something else," Riley answered before Leah mentioned the tattoo appearing on Jill's arm. "What do you know about Bruce French?"

He frowned. "He was one of our concert promoters who royally screwed up Leah's last tour. She sued him and won."

"Do you think he's holding a grudge?"

"Yeah, sure. The guy won't arrange a tour for her again. Which is a real pain. With some promoters being regional, it makes things hard for us to schedule concerts in the northeast, but we're working around it."

"Other than making things hard for her, do you think French would try to get payback?" Riley asked.

"You mean like breaking into the office?" Kraig frowned. "No, wait. You mean like committing murder, don't you?" Kraig shook his head. "No. That's crazy. Just as crazy as thinking I did it."

Riley didn't believe either thought was crazy. Far-fetched maybe, but then, he'd seen more ridiculous reasons for murder. As far as he was concerned, neither Kraig or Bruce

French were off the hook. Not unless Blake called to say French was dead. Then that was a whole other story.

~

Not more than an hour later, Riley held Owen closer and paused at the training facility door. Riley appreciated Hannah's kindness in preparing breakfast and gathering everyone together so Riley could introduce Owen, but Riley was sweating over the announcement.

Would they respond with outrage? Disappointment? Until two days ago, Riley didn't know about Owen and hadn't kept him a secret from them, so they shouldn't react that way. Technically, that was incorrect. He did tell Hannah, Gage, and Eryn, so he *had* kept the others in the dark.

"Something wrong?" Leah asked.

"Just nervous."

She took his hand and smiled at him. "They'll be okay with this. You didn't hide it from them."

He appreciated her support, squeezed her hand, then let it go. He wanted to keep holding it, but that would draw too many questions and give his teammates the wrong idea.

"Go." Owen wiggled. "Hungry."

Riley opened the door, heard the team laughing in the conference room, and caught the smell of bacon. Usually bacon fixed almost everything, but today was an exception. He walked toward the room. He knew once he stepped in, everyone would recognize that Owen was his son. What they wouldn't know was that Leah was his mother.

He entered the room. Half of the team were at a buffet table right inside the door, the rest were seated at the conference table. Coop, sitting closest to the door, was the first to notice them. He dropped his fork on a plate piled high with scrambled eggs, hash brown casserole, and bacon. "Oh, man. Just man. Like wow."

Sitting next to him Alex looked up, and his mouth fell open. "You have a son."

Riley nodded, and one by one, the team fell silent and stared.

"You all know Leah and I were once engaged," Riley said. "I'd like you all to meet our son, Owen, who I just met this week myself."

The team openly gaped as the room got pin-drop quiet. A few of his teammates cast angry looks at Leah.

Riley didn't want to provide details with Owen in his arms so he simply said, "Leah had a good reason. I'll share it with you later."

The hostility lessened and questioning looks slipped into place.

Owen scooted closer, clinging to Riley. He hadn't thought about how coming into this group of big men would intimidate a small child. This father thing was going to take some time.

He smiled at Owen. "Hey, bud. It's okay. There are a lot of people here that you don't know, and some of them are kinda big and scary looking. But I work with them, and they're my friends. So you'll get to know them when you visit."

Owen planted his hands on Riley's face and looked into his eyes. "I want to live here with you, Daddy. I like the cabin. And Mia and David. And Barkley, too."

Riley felt Leah clench up beside him. "We can talk about that later. But now we need to eat before the food gets cold. What do you want for breakfast?"

Riley moved to the buffet table as if nothing had happened and waited for someone to start talking again.

"Did anyone catch the Timbers' game last night?" Hannah asked.

Riley could hug her for bringing up Portland's professional soccer team that was sure to get the others embroiled in a heated discussion, and the focus would be off Owen. At least for the moment.

"Riley turned to Leah. "Go ahead and get your food. I'll get mine and Owen's."

Leah looked uncertain.

Eryn approached and smiled at Leah. "Hey, take the help while you can."

Leah's face relaxed, and she headed for the buffet table.

Eryn joined Riley and gave him a big hug. "Owen is adorable. Congratulations again. You're going to be the most amazing dad ever."

"Hey, now," Trey said from behind her, a big smile on his face. "That's what you tell me."

She released Riley and turned to snake her arms around her soon-to-be husband's neck. "I meant the most amazing dad to Owen. You've already earned Dad of The Year in my book."

"Nice save, Calloway," Jackson said as he stepped into line and looked at Trey. "You're gonna have your hands full with this one."

"I know, and I'm up for the challenge." Trey planted a kiss on Eryn's head. "Are you planning to stand here all day, Glen, or get this line moving?"

Riley appreciated the good-natured jab as it meant things would be okay with the team. At the buffet table, he set Owen down next to him, grabbed two plates, and soon discovered the challenge of getting his food and filling a plate for his child.

"It gets easier," Eryn said. "Or at least the challenges change."

Riley looked at his hands. At the plates, utensils, napkins, cups, food, drinks. At Owen who reached up to stick his hand in the fruit bowl.

"Wait—" He grabbed for Owen's hand which was already fisted around something. "Hey, bud, tell me what you want and I'll get it for you."

Riley would have to take Eryn's word. Right now, being a dad seemed daunting.

Owen popped a strawberry into his mouth and smiled up at Riley. Daunting or not, Riley knew he was up for the job. He couldn't wait to really delve into the whole dad thing and become, as Eryn said, the most amazing dad ever.

Shortly after breakfast, Leah looked at the happy picture in front of her. Owen and Riley sitting on the sofa together, a book in Riley's hand. She could stand all day and watch them with their blond heads nestled together, but she had a job to do. One she couldn't ignore no matter how much she wanted to. Even if her bank account hadn't been nearly drained, she had fans counting on her. She couldn't let them down after all the support they'd given her over the years. And staff counting on their job's, too.

She joined Riley and Owen. "I need to get packed and on the road with my team."

"Wait a minute." Riley gawked at her. "You're not planning to go through with the next concert."

"I have to. My future depends on it. And so does my mom's and Owen's."

Owen looked up at her. "Can I stay with Daddy?"

Her heart creased yet one more time with her son's recent newfound preference for his father, but she knew that would abate when he realized his dad was here to stay. And after Riley took on a disciplinarian role, too.

Riley looked at Owen. "I have to go with Mommy."

"I can go, too."

"Sorry, bud. I think it's best for you to stay here with Grandma. We'll be back tomorrow."

Owen's lower lip came out. "Don't wanna stay here."

"Why don't you have Grandma help you make a list of toys you want at my cabin, and I'll get them?"

"Yippee." Owen shot off Riley's lap.

Leah cast him an admonishing look. "You need to figure out how to say no without resorting to bribery, or we'll have one spoiled child."

Riley nodded. "I was thinking..." His face turned serious. "Now that I know about Owen, I'm glad to pay child support and maybe you can work less."

She put up a hand. "I don't expect that of you when we're doing fine."

"But you just said your future was hanging in the balance."

"Only if my career tanks, and I won't let that happen."

Riley crossed his arms and eyed her. "When will *enough* be enough for you?"

"What's that supposed to mean?" She eyed him right back.

"You've succeeded. Made a name for yourself. Everyone who teased or belittled you now wishes they hadn't. They want to know you and be in your world. Isn't that enough?"

Did he think she was so shallow? That really hurt. "You really think that's the only thing that's motivated me all these years?"

His eyes narrowed. "I know you've always loved singing, and you were tenacious enough to make it to the top. But I also know having plenty of money is important to you—I thought it was because of the past ridicule."

She believed he'd once understood her, but now she didn't know. "Sure, money is important to me, but not because of what people thought of me. I was hungry every single day. I worried constantly as a kid—an innocent little kid like Owen—if I would have a roof over my head and food on the table. I was always scared that social workers were going to take me away." She shook her head. "I won't have that for Owen."

Riley shot to his feet and planted them firmly on the wood floor. "I would never let that happen."

"My father once said something like that to my mom. And where was he when we needed him? Where is he now? We don't have a clue. So I need the security of a large bank account. My popularity is already waning, but if I can amass enough savings and live a modest lifestyle like I'm doing now, we'll be set when my celebrity status fades. We both know it's just a matter of time before it does. It's already on a downward swing."

He rubbed his forehead as if she was giving him a headache. "Where does your faith play into this?"

"Faith? It doesn't. That's separate. After all, God wasn't there when I was hungry, why should He be here now when I'm not?"

Riley dropped his hand. "But you still believe in Him."

"Sure I believe in God. I question a lot of the things He does, but I believe. But I also know He gives people abilities and skills and expects us to use them the best way we know how. And singing is what I know, so I will do it to the best of my ability and make that nest egg for my boy until I can do it no longer."

"God doesn't tell us to lay up oodles and oodles of money just in case. Like my father, hoarding it when using the cash to help others could do much more good. Instead, God says to trust Him to provide for each day."

She crossed her arms. "And there you have it. Trust. I don't trust anyone but myself. The school of hard knocks taught me that, and it will take something major to make me change on that point."

Riley blew out a long breath. "So here we are again. Where we keep finding ourselves. Our philosophies of life are completely different and money stands between us."

"I never pretended I'd changed, Riley."

"But you hoped *I* had, right? That I could now see things your way?"

"Sure, yeah. Since we're now parenting a child together, it would be nice."

Riley frowned. "How will we ever do that and not saddle Owen with all of our baggage?"

"We have to figure it out, or I'll have to go back to parenting alone."

His mouth fell open. "You can't mean that."

"I wouldn't want to do it, but Owen comes first, and I have to do what's best for him."

"And you think keeping his dad away from him is best?"

"I don't know...I just don't know." She felt like pulling her hair out but settled for running her fingers through it. "What I do know is my team is leaving soon, and I'll be on the bus with them for the drive to Pelican Point so we can perform tonight."

Feeling sadder than she had in years, she hurried into Riley's bedroom. His minty scent lingered in the space, and that brought tears to her eyes. Huge tears rolled down her face, and she couldn't stop them. She swiped an angry fist under her eyes and started throwing items into her suitcase.

Why couldn't she just do as Riley said? Trust God. Trust anyone.

Because people kept letting her down. Not in little ways. That she could handle. But the major things of life is where she had to draw the line.

And here she thought she'd taken a big step toward God and wanted to do what He wanted for her life. Not a day had passed since her commitment, and she'd failed. Had she really drawn closer to Him? If so, she needed to trust Him, here, too.

"Leah," Riley's voice came from the doorway. "I'm sorry. We seem to always push each other's hot buttons. I want to make this work. Let's find a way to get along and care for Owen."

She turned around. "Me too. I don't want to be like this. I just can't let it go." She looked at him and his contrite expression made her tears flow faster.

"Hey, don't, honey." He rushed over to her and drew her into his arms.

She should push him away, this man who was totally wrong for her in almost every way but was totally right when it came to love. But she didn't. She rested her cheek against the softness of his cotton work shirt and traced the embroidered team name to distract herself from the overwhelming emotions crashing through her body.

His hand came up to clamp on hers, stilling her fingers. She glanced up at him, and his awareness of her as a woman burned in his eyes—the last thing she needed, but her heart betrayed her and sped up.

"I..." she said but didn't continue because she didn't know what to say.

"Yeah," he whispered against her hair. "Me, too."

He continued to hold her, and she let him, loving the feel of security and safety in his arms. But as time ticked by, she knew she needed to get going.

She pushed back. "I've gotta pack."

He released her and stepped back. "About that. You'll need Blake's permission."

"Why?"

"Because you're a suspect, and he told me you weren't allowed to leave town without telling him."

Fury flashed inside of her. "And you decided I didn't need to know this?"

"I thought it would worry you more."

"Well, you're right. It does. But it's my worry, and you have no right to make decisions like that." She put her fists on her hips. "Did you *neglect* to tell me so I would be forced to stop performing?"

"No, no! I—"

"Is there anything else you're keeping from me?"

He shook his head fervently. "I'm sorry if I made the wrong decision, but I did it with the right reasons in mind. Honestly, I wasn't trying to sabotage you."

This was getting more complicated by the minute. She blew out a breath. "Well, you need to get that permission from Blake right away—I'm keeping all of my commitments. Now I need to pack."

"Okay. And I'm coming with you. You know that, right?"

"Yes, that's fine."

"I still want Owen and your mother to stay here where they're safe."

She really wanted Owen nearby, but she had to listen to her own convictions and put Owen first. Maybe it was better that way since she'd be busy with his father...a man who she adored one minute and was furious with the next.

15

Riley couldn't think of an instance when not having a helo at his disposal was a good thing, and a few hours later when they touched down at the small airport outside of Pelican Point just up the Oregon coast a few hundred miles, it was no exception. He'd convinced Leah to let her team bus go on without her and let Coop fly them to the concert location. He'd take the helo back to the compound, but Riley wouldn't be alone in protecting Leah. He'd brought Alex along for reinforcement during the day as the others had to remain at the compound either working on this case or teaching classes. Didn't mean they wouldn't be on protective detail at the concert that night. Coop would ferry them all to the venue in plenty of time to secure the place and stand watch.

Leah pointed out the window at Felicity who leaned against the hood of her electric blue Ford Focus. "There's Felicity waiting for us."

Riley nodded, and was fine riding in Felicity's little Focus to the hotel where the SUV Riley rented should be waiting for them. An inch taller than Riley, Alex might grumble about Felicity's car, but Riley would let him ride shotgun where his knees might not be in his nose like Riley would experience in the back seat with Leah.

Coop left the rotors spinning, and Alex got out first to circle the area, looking for any issues.

"You'll be back here by five," Riley confirmed with Coop before taking off his headset.

"Roger that," Coop replied.

That was all Riley needed to hear to reassure him that Coop knew his mission. Riley could count on his teammates in every situation. Every single one. They had his back on the job and in life. He'd never really had that before except with Leah, and that had ended so badly it had taken some time for Riley to trust anyone. But the men and women of Blackwell Tactical made it easy to trust them, and he did. Now Leah was back, bringing up all that old anxiety again.

Alex gave a thumbs-up, and Riley hung up his headset and hopped out. He helped Leah down and stayed close to her, his head on a swivel as they crossed to Felicity. She wasn't paying any attention to Leah, which was odd, but her gaze was locked on Alex who was so focused on their surroundings that he wasn't even looking at Felicity. She pushed off the car and slowly ran her gaze up and down Alex's body.

Riley had seen this look many times before. Not only for Alex, but for men Riley had worked with in law enforcement and on the team. They carried themselves with such a presence and confidence that women took notice. Of course, Alex was also very good-looking. Put those qualities together and it made perfect sense that Felicity was captivated. And Alex was a consummate professional, so it made sense that he wouldn't react when he was part of Leah's protection detail.

"Felicity, this is Alex." Riley didn't linger on introductions but walked to the car. "We should get going. Leah you're in back with me. Alex in front."

Riley opened the door and ushered Leah inside. He took one last look over the tarmac, and satisfied she wasn't in danger, he wedged himself in beside her, his knees pressed against the passenger seat.

Alex looked inside. "Mind if I move this seat back?"

"Go ahead." Riley eyed him. "If you have a death wish."

Alex laughed and managed to get himself inside. "Remind me to make travel arrangements next time."

"I should have thought about the car size," Leah said. "Sorry."

"I'm not." Felicity winked in the rearview mirror then cast a flirty smile at Alex who was looking out the window and not paying any attention to her.

If she kept flirting with Alex, Riley suspected it was going to be a long ride for all of them.

Riley's phone rang, and seeing Sam's name on the screen, he eagerly answered. "Tell me you have good news."

"Sorry. I reviewed Kraig's fingerprints from the crime scene, but they don't reveal anything of value."

Riley had to admit he was disappointed. Even if Kraig *was* innocent, he would be a perfect suspect to take the focus off Leah. "Thanks for reviewing them so fast."

He disconnected and called Piper. "Just checking in. Any word on the video yet?"

"Sorry, not yet."

"You'll call me the minute you know anything?"

"Absolutely."

As Riley hung up, frustration over every dead end had him slamming a fist into the back of the seat.

Alex jerked forward. "Whoa, buddy, easy back there."

Leah watched him, but he didn't care. He was reaching

the end of his rope. He had to think about something positive. The video could still pan out. He sat back and tried to think of anything they might have missed. But he came up empty, and soon Felicity was pulling under the hotel's portico.

The car had barely stopped moving, and Felicity hopped out before Alex could even unfold his legs. Riley took equally as long to get out. If there had been a threat to Leah, neither of them would be much good. Riley wouldn't let Felicity drive them back to the helo. He would take the rental vehicle and arrange to have it picked up there.

"I'll get the room keys," Felicity called over her shoulder.

Riley glanced at Leah. "Stay in the car until I tell you."

"Sure."

He appreciated her compliance, but honestly, her determination was part of her personality that had drawn him to her. This attitude felt almost as if she was giving up.

He signaled Alex to scout out the south side of the building and parking lot, and Riley surveyed the north side, all the while keeping Leah in view. When he was satisfied that it was safe, he sent Alex inside to clear the lobby.

Riley remained by Leah's door until Alex stepped outside, nodded, and positioned himself between the car and entrance.

Riley opened Leah's door. "Stay by my side and head straight inside."

She nodded and complied, which he was grateful for. Standing by the desk, Felicity turned to them, room keys in her hand. She gave one to Leah and one to Riley.

"Are the rooms adjoining?" he asked.

Felicity snickered and nodded.

Riley didn't like the implication of Felicity's response, and Leah seemed to like it less, but she didn't say anything.

Felicity turned her attention to Alex who'd hung his

sunglasses in the V of his shirt. "Since I didn't know you were accompanying Riley, I didn't book a room for you. But I'm assuming you need to be near Leah, too. They'll have to clean a room for you. Should be ready in an hour or so. You're welcome to hang out in my room if you want."

Alex's mouth opened like he planned to say something, then he snapped it closed. With his dry humor, Riley could only imagine what he'd almost said, but Riley was thankful Alex thought twice before speaking. No need to make things even more uncomfortable.

"He can hang with me, and you can deliver Alex's key there." Riley faced Leah. "Let's get you upstairs."

"I'll arrange to have the luggage delivered to the rooms," Felicity said. "And Leah, we have some details to iron out. Do you want me to come up to your room once I take care of Alex's room and the luggage?"

Leah smiled at her assistant. "Sounds perfect."

Alex and Riley walked on either side of Leah to the elevator and escorted her safely to her room on the third floor.

Riley handed his room key to Alex. "Let's get the connecting door open and then you can head back to the lobby to finalize our rental car."

Alex frowned, a rare thing for him. "You better hope Felicity isn't still down there or you'll owe me big time."

"So you noticed the flirting." Riley grinned.

"Could anyone have missed it?" Alex shook his head, a bemused look on his face.

"I'll have a talk with her," Leah offered.

"Nah, don't bother. I'm used to it and can handle it just fine." He spun and exited the room.

Leah's gaze tracked him as he walked away. "I can see Felicity's fascination. He's real pretty."

"Pretty? Don't let Alex hear you say that." Riley chuckled.

She laughed with him, and for a moment, things were easy between them. A reminder of the past. One he shouldn't dwell on.

She suddenly sobered. Maybe the same thoughts darted through her brain.

"I hate to ask this, but would you mind if I took a nap? Concerts take a lot out of me, and I need to rest up."

He blinked. "Why would you hate to ask that?"

"Because you and your whole team are working so hard on finding my stalker and the killer. I feel guilty napping."

He waved off her concern. "We don't have to perform tonight. You do."

"Not perform, no, but you'll be working. Keeping me safe."

"Hey, don't worry about it. Take your nap, and I'll be right next door if you need me."

She nodded, but still didn't look convinced. He crossed the room and on his way to the door, stopped to look her in the eyes. "I honestly want what's best for you, honey. The very best. Don't ever doubt that, okay?"

She nodded and took his hand to lift it to her mouth and plant a kiss. Her tenderness caught him unaware, and he tugged her into his arms, a place she was ending up far too much for either of their good. He wanted to linger, but it felt wrong with everything unsettled between them.

He set her away and left the room, his heart staying with her, and he wished things could work out between them. But it was just a wish, and life experience taught him that wishes rarely came true. Especially ones related to Leah.

Leah tried to sleep, but she couldn't quiet her mind. Sure, the murders weighed heavy on her, but it was the tender hug and the lingering look that Riley gave her that she couldn't forget.

She groaned over her traitorous mind, pushed out of bed, and wandered the room, pausing by the connecting door, her hand raised, ready to knock.

But why? What would she say to him?

"I know we have the same old struggle, but I still love you and want you in my life" was what she wanted to say. But what would be the point of it? They still couldn't be together.

She groaned again and walked to the window to look out. The beach lay silent and deserted in the bright sunshine, sparkling waves rolling in. She needed to think, and what better place to do it but there? She couldn't take Riley. Couldn't take Alex or even Felicity.

She needed to be alone. She went to her suitcase. Grabbed her baseball cap and large sunglasses and slipped into bulky sweats. Her disguise. She'd used it hundreds of time to avoid the press and fans. Surely, it would work for her stalker.

She pocketed her key and slowly turned the doorknob. A quick glance down the hallway told her it was empty, and she softly closed the door behind her, making sure it latched. She raced for the stairwell and jogged down. Outside, she looked around. Sure she was alone and not watched, she bolted for the beach.

Heading to the shoreline, she took off her shoes and let her feet sink into the cooling sand. As the granules oozed between her toes, she let her mind have its way and filled it with the first song she would sing that night. Humming, she found a secluded spot among the tall beach grasses and dropped down. She lifted her knees and hugged them, softly singing her songs and watching the calming roll of the waves.

Music had always been a balm for what ailed her. Music and solitude. She got a lot of the first in her life, but very little of the second. She was always on display. Always performing, even when she wasn't on stage. An interview. A PR gig. An award show. Even a walk to her car. The public wanted to see her. Wanted to know her. And social media brought them closer. They thought they were part of her life, but it was carefully staged by her publicist to make it seem real. So her fans believed they knew her, when it was all a lie.

And she was tired of living a lie. So tired.

She laid back, her arms behind her head, feeling the remaining warmth of the sand, gazing up at the bright blue sky with slowly moving puffy clouds. She sighed out her stress. Repeated it and inhaled the salty ocean air.

A day at the beach had always reminded her of God and His amazing creation of the earth. The magnitude of it always made her problems seem so small, but not today. Her life was crumbling around her. She didn't think it could get much worse, and if it did, she wasn't sure she could survive. At least not alone. With Riley at her side, she could survive anything. She knew that as much as she knew how to breathe.

But he isn't at your side, is he? Not permanently. You put him aside long ago.

She couldn't think about that. Wouldn't think about that now. She closed her eyes and concentrated on breathing. That sleep she'd needed beckoned, and she soon fell into it.

"Are you okay, miss?" A male voice came from above.

She woke to a dark shadow lingering over her. He stared

down at her. Dark glasses. A baseball cap. He was as hidden from her as she was from him. Was he her stalker?

She scrambled back.

"Hey." He held up a fishing pole. "It's okay. I'm not some creep trying to come on to you. I've been fishing for the last hour or so, and you didn't move, so I just wanted to make sure you were okay."

An hour? She'd been sleeping for an hour? "I fell asleep, but thanks for asking."

He nodded and turned back to the water. She jumped up and ran for the hotel. She had no idea how long she'd been gone, but she had to hope that Riley didn't discover that she was missing or she'd have to deal with that, too.

She slipped into the building unnoticed and climbed the stairs. The hallway was empty and quiet.

Perfect.

Her shoes dangling from her fingers, she ran silently over the floral carpet and slid the key into the lock. The door snapped open, and she quickly entered.

She'd made it. She was safe, and her mind was clear. No one except the fisherman would know she'd gone for a walk alone, and even then, he had no idea of her identity. She almost laughed. She'd successfully pulled off her version of *Ferris Bueller's Day Off*.

Sitting at the desk in his room, Riley heard the lock on Leah's door click and the door open.

He charged for his door and looked in the hallway in time to see her step into her room, the door closing behind her.

Had she gone somewhere alone? But where and why when he'd warned her not to leave without him? Maybe she'd heard a noise and was simply looking into the hallway.

Right. Like he believed that.

He stepped back into his room and went to the adjoining door. He started to knock but heard her shower running. Wherever she'd gone, she felt a need to shower afterward. Or maybe this was just her routine before a concert, he didn't know. But the moment she was dressed, he would ask her.

He went back to his computer where he'd been reviewing several YouTube videos of her last concert, looking for anyone in the crowd who stood out. He'd viewed countless files while she'd napped, or had maybe gone somewhere, but none of them provided anything to go on.

His phone rang, and seeing Eryn's name, he answered. "Whatcha got?"

"A couple of things. First, the handwriting analysis is in. The expert claims Leah signed those letters."

Riley's heart dropped. "They're one hundred percent sure."

"Handwriting analysis is never a hundred percent. But it's the expert's opinion that Leah signed the letters. Still, you should know that handwriting analysis has come under scrutiny lately, and she could be wrong."

Riley liked hearing that last bit. "And the second thing?"

"This is odd, so I wanted to run it past you. One of the first things I look at when reviewing a computer hard drive is recently deleted files. I figure if someone is guilty of something they might try to cover it up by deleting files and think they can't be recovered."

"When they typically can, right?"

"Right, and in this case, I restored the recently deleted files on Leah's laptop. I was shocked to find GPS tracking software. Before it was removed, it was logging data from a specific tracker. Not a cell phone, but an actual GPS device."

"That's odd."

"Yeah, and even odder and most suspicious is that the last address for the tracker is Carolyn Eubanks' house."

Riley jumped to his feet. "Leah was tracking Carolyn's movements?"

"Yes. For almost two months."

His gut cramped hard. "And yet, she failed to mention that."

"Exactly." Eryn sighed. "I thought I'd gotten to know her a bit and never expected her to do something like this, but the evidence is there in black and white."

Riley didn't want to comment. Couldn't comment because he was stunned.

He started pacing. Had he been all wrong about Leah? Did he let his past connection and his current feelings blind him to the present-day woman?

No. She wasn't a killer. But she still could've tracked Carolyn. Maybe she had a good reason for it.

"I'll ask her about it." His phone beeped, signaling an incoming call. He glanced at the screen to see Blake's name. "I gotta go. Blake's calling. If you have anything else, call me back, okay?"

"That was it."

He disconnected and clicked over to Blake's call.

"Where are you?" Blake asked.

"The hotel, why?"

"Leah with you?"

"Yes," he said and asked why again.

"Because I just got a call from dispatch. Leah's makeup artist, a Helen Carpenter, was murdered sometime in the last hour at the concert venue. She was shot in the back and has a Leah tattoo on her wrist. I wanted to make sure Leah was with you and had an alibi before I started investigating."

Riley dropped to the chair, his legs weak. He should be her alibi, but he'd seen her sneak into the room and immediately take a shower, which was suspicious. So if she hadn't met up with someone, she had no alibi, and a warrant for her arrest was imminent.

16

The nap and shower were invigorating, and Leah felt rejuvenated and ready to face anything. She could handle this stress now. Handle being with Riley. Handle just about anything.

She grabbed her purse and knocked on the adjoining door. Riley quickly opened it as if he'd been waiting for her knock. His forehead was knotted, his expression thunderous.

"Where did you go?" he demanded.

"Excuse me?" Surely, he couldn't be talking about her stealth trip to the beach.

"Before your shower. I saw the door to your room close and you disappear behind it."

He'd seen her. Of course he had. He was good at his job.

Why did she think she could have pulled this off? "I went to the beach to clear my head."

"Alone?"

"Yes," she said and waited for him to explode.

But he didn't. He went quiet and contemplative instead.

"Look, I know I shouldn't have gone out alone. But I

wore a disguise I often wear in public and no one recognized me, so it's fine."

"Fine, it's hardly fine." He fisted his hands.

"I got back safe and sound, so let it go. Please. I won't do it again." She felt like a wayward teenager pleading not to be grounded.

He looked shocked. "Then you haven't heard."

"Heard what?" she asked, knowing by his expression that she didn't really want him to answer.

He closed his eyes for a moment. Opened them and locked gazes with her. "While you were on your little jaunt to the beach, Helen Carpenter was murdered at the concert venue."

"Helen? Oh, no. No." Leah dropped her purse and clutched Riley's arm. "Tell me you're kidding."

"She was shot in the back," he said bluntly. "A tattoo was branded on her wrist like the others."

Leah's ears started ringing, and her vision faded. Her legs wouldn't hold her, and she slid to the floor. Helen was the sweetest young girl. In her early twenties, she'd barely finished cosmetology school, much less experienced life. And now...oh, now, the sweet girl was dead. *Murdered.* Unbelievable.

She looked up at Riley. "Please tell me they caught the killer."

He shook his head.

"Then at least someone saw him?"

He shook his head again and didn't speak.

Tears pricked her eyes, and she swallowed hard to stop them. "How is this person getting away with so many murders? Right there in public like that?"

"Perhaps it's someone these people recognize and it doesn't raise a question."

"You mean someone on my staff?"

He shook his head. "No, I mean you."

"Me?" She gaped at him. "You think *I* did this?"

"Do you have an alibi?"

"I was at the beach. I fell asleep." Her brain searched for something that might help. "Wait. There was a fisherman. He saw me. Talked to me. He could still be there."

She jumped to her feet, ran to the window, and jerked open the heavy drapes. She scanned the sand and water, looking for him. She saw no one.

"He was there." She pointed at the ocean. "Fishing. He came over to me. Said I hadn't moved for an hour and asked if I was okay. Please believe me. He was there. We have to find him."

"We can try, but honestly, if your disguise is as good as you claim, all this man can say is that he talked to a woman on the beach. Not that he talked to you."

He was right. She had no way to prove her whereabouts, and the only thing that she could prove was that Riley saw her creeping back into her room. That would make her look completely guilty, and she expected Blake to barge through the door any second to arrest her.

That should be what she worried about most. But what was tearing her apart right now was that Riley seemed to believe she was capable of murder.

An hour later, Leah hung up from calling her mother to arrange for Owen's care in case Blake arrested her after the interview. She gathered her things together and gazed longingly at the bed. She wanted to crawl under the covers instead of going to the venue. To cocoon in a ball, hoping all of this would pass, but she couldn't. She had to face it head on like she'd faced most everything else in her life. Find the strength she had before Riley delivered that blow.

Riley and Alex would escort her to the venue where she would sit down and be questioned by the intimidating sheriff again. But this time, she knew in advance that he might slap cuffs on her and haul her to jail.

She wished she was back on the beach. Back when she'd thought things couldn't get worse. But now she knew they could—and had.

"Ready?" Riley's steel eyes and cold attitude made her feel like a felon.

She wanted to cross over to him. Caress the side of his face to loosen the rigid muscles and look into his eyes and force him to see she was telling the truth. But there was no point. He'd made up his mind, and she was on her own now.

He opened the door, and she stepped out to where Alex stood waiting. He didn't give even a hint of what he thought about her, but his usual joking demeanor was gone, a locked-down expression in its place.

"Follow me," he said and headed inside.

Riley came up beside her but didn't say a word. As the elevator whooshed down, both men put on aviator sunglasses to prepare for the bright lobby with large windows that would be lit with the fiery ball of sun making its way toward the horizon.

Belief in her innocence or not, they would guard her from any foe that might still be out there. For that she was grateful.

Thank you, Father for bringing this amazing team into my life. Please help me clear my name because they don't know the truth. You do, and I desperately need You to fight for me. And help them catch this killer right away.

The door split wide, and Alex stepped out. Leah exited

next with Riley by her side. The front doors swished open and paparazzi rushed her.

"Is it, true, Leah?" A gangly man shouted as he shoved a microphone at her. "Did you kill your makeup artist because she knew about your secret child, and she revealed your secret this morning?"

Leah gasped, and her feet stilled. She couldn't move. Not a muscle. The news of Owen was out. Given to the press by another person she trusted. How had Helen even found out? And why tell the reporters?

Money. It was always about money in this business. And now an innocent little boy was going to suffer because someone wanted to make a buck off her life.

Oh, Owen, sweetheart. How can I protect you from this?

Her heart shredded, the pain nearly taking her down to her knees again. Riley must have sensed her distress, as he cupped her elbow and held her firm. She looked up at him. His jaw was clenched, his eyes angry, and he fended off the reporter with a raised arm. "Ms. Kent needs to get through. Please stand back."

He kept hold of her elbow and muscled his way through the crowd that Alex was parting in front of them.

"Did you murder the other women, too?" A woman yelled. "Are you that self-absorbed that you can't handle it when someone wrongs you?"

Leah wanted to answer, but even if she could, she knew better than to feed them by any response, even a "no comment."

They got to the car, and Leah hurled her body into the back seat. Riley climbed in beside her, and Alex quickly got them on the road.

Riley faced her. "Did you know Helen knew about Owen?"

She shook her head.

"Why don't I believe you?"

"Because you want to think the worst of me. If you believe I can commit murder, why not believe I'm lying to you?" She grabbed his hand and held on even when he tried to pull back. "I'm not lying to you. I have no idea how she knew. And I didn't know she'd gone to the press."

He pulled his hand free and ran it over his face. "I really don't believe you're a killer. It was a knee-jerk reaction. I was mad because you went out on your own. That you don't trust or respect me enough to do what I ask."

"I do," she said, but then considered it. "Maybe you're right. The music business is terribly cutthroat, you can't even trust the people you believed were on your side."

"I'm not in the music business. I'm not just anyone." He glanced at Alex then looked back at Leah and lowered his voice. "I'm me. The man you once loved. Why can't you remember that man?"

She could. Easier than he might think. But with the remembering came pain—gut-wrenching pain that she didn't want to go through again. So maybe she didn't want to remember. Didn't want to trust him, because if she did, she would have to admit she'd never loved anyone the way she loved him. That she was still wildly in love with him, wanted a future with him, and couldn't have one.

That, more than anything she was facing, would destroy her.

∿

"More press," Alex announced bringing Riley out of his thoughts to look around.

He had to get a grip. He was on Leah's protection detail, no matter what had transpired between them. No matter what he was feeling. Thinking. Stewing over. Her safety had to come first.

"When I looked at the building plans, I saw a second side entrance," he told Alex. "Head to that side, and Leah can call Felicity to let us in."

"Roger that," Alex said.

Riley turned to Leah, but she was already arranging their arrival with Felicity. Riley should have been prepared for the press to swarm her after word had gotten out about Jill's death. In fact, he should have expected them even sooner. Maybe not at the hotel, as they'd booked her team in a different hotel and had chosen one for her in a nearby city to keep her location under wraps.

Helen probably spilled that, too.

He wanted to be mad at her, but she'd lost her life because of her actions. A huge price to pay for betraying Leah. Betrayal. Another one. Riley should've cut Leah some slack. Maybe tried to comfort her, but what did he do? Treat her like a killer.

Nice one, Glen. Way to be supportive.

Leah lowered her phone. "Felicity will meet us at the door."

His forehead furrowed. "I need to ask you something first. Do you have the knowledge...or, well, have you ever tattooed anyone?"

She jolted back. "No! And I certainly wouldn't duplicate our tattoo. That was...special, significant." She looked him in the eyes. "You have to believe me. I've never once thought of shooting a person, and I've never thought of tattooing anyone. This is all just crazy."

"I'm sorry." He grabbed her hand and squeezed it. "I really am. Like I said, I never really believed you could kill Helen or anyone. I was just mad that you'd taken off."

"I'm the one who's sorry. I really botched things, didn't I?"

"You certainly didn't help, but I'll go to bat for you with Blake and try to keep you out of jail."

Her eyes suddenly glistened with tears. Maybe because he'd said aloud what she'd been thinking, and that made it more real to her. But he didn't regret saying it as there was a very good possibility that Blake would arrest her for this murder, and Riley could do nothing to stop it.

"You should know," he said, hating that he had to give her additional bad news. "Eryn called me. She's reviewing your computer files."

"And?" Leah asked, sounding innocent enough.

"And she found GPS tracking software that had been deleted. It was used to track Carolyn for the last two months."

"On my computer? No. No one has access to that but me, and I leave it at home. Not even my mom has the password."

"You know how that sounds, don't you?"

"Like you're guilty as can be," Alex said.

Riley glared at Alex in the rearview mirror. "Thanks for that."

"What? It's the truth."

"Someone must have gotten into my house and installed it to make me look guilty."

"Do you realize how contrived that sounds?" Alex asked.

"Yes, but it's the only option because I sure didn't track Carolyn. Even if I knew how to do it, which I don't, why would I want to do that?"

"To know where she was so you could kill her," Alex said. "Not that I think you did it, but the sheriff will."

Riley shook his head. "No. He doesn't know about this yet, and we won't tell him. He has a copy of your hard drive, and his team can find it on their own."

"What if it's the lead that blows this case wide open?" Alex challenged. "You can't withhold that."

"He's right." Leah met Riley's gaze. "I don't want another nail in my coffin, but you need to tell him."

Riley didn't want to be the one to pound in that last nail. "I'll see how the interview goes and play it by ear." He grabbed the door handle and waited for the vehicle to stop.

"You're making a good case for your innocence right now by urging him to hand this over." Alex pulled up to the side entrance, thankfully press free.

Felicity opened the amphitheater door.

"Ready?" Riley asked Leah.

She looked like she wanted to say no, but she nodded, and he whisked her inside.

"It's true, isn't it?" Leah stopped right inside the door and looked at Felicity. "Helen was murdered."

Riley didn't know why Leah needed to confirm it after he'd already done so, but she did.

"It's horrible." Felicity grabbed Leah in a hug. "Just horrible."

Riley saw Leah's shoulders shaking and sobs followed. He could barely stand by and watch her in distress without pulling her from Felicity's arms and into his, but with their emotional turmoil, Felicity was likely a better person to do the comforting. He hated to admit that to himself, but it was the truth. Especially after he all but called her a murderer.

Blake stepped into the hallway from one of the dressing rooms. "Good. Glad you're here. You see the press outside?"

Riley nodded. "They mobbed us at the hotel, too. Someone leaked that Leah has a son."

"It's not true, right?" Felicity jerked back. "I mean if you had a son you would've told me."

"I'm sorry," Leah said the color draining from her face. "He's four."

Riley might not be the right person to hold her right now, but he could support her. "He's our son."

Blake's mouth dropped open, but he quickly recovered and closed it.

Leah smiled her thanks at Riley. *Good.* She apparently appreciated his admission.

"I think we should keep that between us for now," he added. "Until Leah can decide how or if she wants to announce it."

"Why didn't you tell me?" Felicity asked, the hurt obvious in her eyes.

Before Leah could speak, Blake guided her toward another dressing room door. "Let's step in here to talk."

Leah went first, and as Felicity started to follow, Blake gave a quick shake of his head. "Sorry, this is official business."

She crossed her arms and glared at him.

He ignored her and motioned for Riley to go in.

"Why does Riley get to be included? He's not even a friend. Just a guy who dumped Leah when she needed him." Felicity shot him a resentful look.

"We can talk later," Riley said.

She glared at him.

He felt bad for her, but he couldn't do anything for her when Leah needed him more. He entered the room and went to the love seat where Leah sat, hands clasped.

He took a seat next to her. "I hope it was okay to tell them I'm Owen's dad."

"Yes, and I'll have to make a statement soon, so you need to decide if you want that to be public knowledge."

"It's going to come out eventually, right?"

She nodded.

"Then better it comes from you."

"But your father..."

"We'll figure that out when the time comes," he said, hoping to sound confident when he was anything but. His father would hate being embroiled in a public scandal, and Riley couldn't predict what his father might do.

Blake stepped into the small room and closed the door. Riley felt like the air had been sucked out of the space. By the way Leah's face paled, he could tell she was having similar feelings. He took her hand and cast a defiant look at Blake.

He wanted the killer found. Wanted him brought to justice. Wanted to help Blake, but Leah came first, and Riley made a promise right there—with God as his witness—that right along with Owen, she would come first in his life, no matter what he had to do.

17

Blake perched on the edge of the makeup table as he had yesterday, and Leah held her breath in wait for his questions. Just one day had passed. A mere twenty-four hours and another woman was murdered. This time it wasn't someone Leah had a falling out with, but it was a young woman she cared about.

Sweet Helen. Such a sweet girl. Sure, it looked like she told the press about Owen, but Leah really didn't believe it. Helen wasn't that kind of a person. At least Leah didn't think so. Maybe the killer had something to do with releasing that information. It sure looked like he wanted to destroy her life by hurting her, and letting the world know about Owen was a great way of doing so. But it didn't appear that he knew about Owen at first. So what was the point of killing all these women? Jealousy? Retaliation for something? Destroying her career and her personal life forever? Who would go through such drastic measures—even inking a tattoo on the victims—to implicate Leah? She couldn't figure it out.

Blake took out his notebook and pen. "Tell me about your relationship with Helen."

Leah's emotions were so raw she couldn't imagine telling him about the special one-on-one times she shared with her makeup artist. "I'm not sure what you want to know."

He looked like he wanted to sigh, but he calmly asked, "Were you friends?"

"Friendly as in an employer with her employee, but not personal friends. I did care about her, though. Does that make sense?"

Blake nodded and softened his tone. "Tell me about that."

"She'd worked for me for only a year. It's funny how we met." The memory made Leah smile. "My regular makeup artist left to have a baby and wasn't coming back. I had some artists referred to me, and Helen was the assistant to one of those candidates. But as I talked with her boss after she'd done my makeup, Helen kept giving me odd looks. She didn't even realize she was doing it. But I had to know what was fueling it. So I finally asked her. She told me my makeup was all wrong, and she gave me reasons and a plan to fix it."

That part of the memory wasn't pleasant and Leah paused for a moment. "Helen's boss fired her on the spot. I felt bad for her and gave her a chance to prove her theory. She redid my makeup, and she was absolutely right. From that day on, she worked for me. She was dependable and always a true supporter." And sweet. And kind. Simply a delightful young lady.

"Any idea why she outed you to the press, then?" Blake asked.

Leah shook her head. "No idea at all, and no idea how she found out about Owen. I bet the killer is the one who actually did it."

Blake looked up from his notepad. "I've contacted the reporter who broke the story. According to him, Helen had written an email to him saying she overheard a conversation you had with your mother."

Leah shook her head. "I tried to be so careful. It's like the picture of my tattoo when I was out running. I knew I didn't make a mistake, and Piper proved that image was fake. Maybe the email came from someone else, too."

"Or maybe not, and you didn't want Helen to go to the press."

"Of course I didn't. If I wanted them to know, I would have told them."

"So you killed her to stop her, but what you didn't know is the damage had already been done. Is that what happened?"

Leah shook her head but didn't speak. What did one say to such a ridiculous accusation?

Blake took a long breath, and she knew she wouldn't like the next question any more than the last one. "Why did you want to keep your son a secret?"

She didn't want to speak badly of Riley's father. She looked at him for guidance. His eyes were narrowed, his face ashen, but he nodded.

She explained, being as kind as she could about her telling of Philip Glen's actions. She finished and watched Blake, trying to decipher his thoughts.

His face was stony and unreadable as he came to his feet towering over her. "Then you had high stakes—the risk of losing your son—riding on keeping his existence undiscovered."

She nodded. "But I wouldn't kill anyone over it."

Blake took out his phone and showed her a picture.

She took a quick look. *No. Oh no.* Someone snapped a photo of her creeping back into the hotel from her beach visit. Her stomach twisted.

His gaze intensified. "Looks like you didn't want anyone to know you were out of your room."

She didn't think anyone saw her. She should have known better. There was always someone there. Looking. Prying. Always. "This doesn't prove anything. I often wear this disguise to hide from the paparazzi. Even to go get a bucket of ice down the hall."

"Thank you for confirming it's you."

She'd played right into his hand.

"But it's not the disguise that's the key here." He wiggled the phone. "Look at the timestamp on the photo. It proves you weren't in your room at the time Ms. Carpenter was murdered. You had motive and means to kill each victim. Opportunity is another thing. Can you account for your time the day Ms. Eubanks died?"

Leah and her mother had figured it all out except a few hours and that would be enough of a gap for him to believe in her guilt. "Not the entire day, no. I was home all day, but there was a few hours in the afternoon that I took a nap while Mom and Owen ran errands, and I was alone."

"Plenty of time to drive to Ms. Eubanks' house and fire off two shots. And you have no alibi for Ms. Carpenter's time of death either."

"Enough!" Riley stepped forward and matched Blake's combative stance. "I've stood by without saying anything, but I can't anymore. Leah couldn't have shot Helen. You have her gun. And she doesn't know how to create tattoos."

"I'll deal with the tattoos in a minute." Blake shifted his focus back to Leah. "Do you own another gun?"

She wanted to lie, but he would find out. "I still have the one Riley gave me."

"A Sig Sauer P250." Riley looked at her. "You kept it?"

She nodded but didn't comment. Now wasn't the time to

go into the fact that she'd kept the gun because it was from him.

"The Sig is a 9mm," Blake said. "Your Luger didn't match the bullets retrieved from the bodies. Means your Sig could be our murder weapon, and I need you to turn it over."

She almost sighed in relief over the Luger not matching, but she had to go through the same process with the Sig and wasn't out of the woods yet. For all she knew, the killer could've stolen it and used it to frame her. "I'm glad to give it to you, but it's at my house in Portland."

Blake cocked an eyebrow and stared at her. He obviously thought she had the gun here and had just used it. "Then I guess we'll pick it up when we do our search of your hotel room and your house."

All the privacy she'd worked so hard to build was now being violated.

Why, Lord?

Riley shook his head. "You're searching her house?"

Blake nodded.

"How can you seriously believe Leah killed these women?" Riley took a step toward Blake, looking like he might deck him.

She held out a hand to Riley. "It's fine. I have nothing to hide."

Riley met her gaze, and his anger dissipated a fraction.

"Where's the gun located?" Blake asked.

"In a gun safe in my bedroom closet. The combination is 0721." She glanced at Riley.

He was watching her carefully. Of course, he was. The safe combination was his birthday. She'd had the safe since he bought the gun, and she never changed the combination. Another thing that probably meant something, and she had to think everything she'd kept in her life regarding him. But not now. Not with Blake still staring at her.

"Despite Riley's defense, you know how this looks, right?" Blake asked. "Add to it the fact you had Ms. Stevenson's blood on your clothing along with GSR. That all victims are tattooed with your name. And—"

"Unbelievable," Riley snapped. "You think Leah could've left the hotel, gotten the tattoo done, killed Helen, and still made it back to the hotel without me noticing she was gone?"

Blake lifted his shoulders. "I do, if she did the tattoo herself."

Leah rolled her eyes. "As Riley said, I don't know how to do tattoos."

"Hmm," Blake said. "Seems odd when we found this in your dressing room."

He held out his phone and displayed a photo of a basket of tattoo equipment sitting next to her jewelry box.

She shot to her feet, nearly toppling Riley. "That's not mine. Someone planted it."

"She's being framed." Riley's deadly intense tone raised Leah's apprehensions.

"Forensics say otherwise."

"But it's all circumstantial," Riley declared. "You don't have anything to put Leah at the crime scenes."

"I don't have anything that doesn't put her there either. And I have a list of evidence that I can recite. Ms. Stevenson's blood on your clothing along with GSR. The letters to Ms. Eubanks have been verified as being signed with your signature. The victims wore your jewelry. All victims are tattooed with your name. Can you refute any one of these points?"

Breathing hard, Blake stared down on her. He seemed like a giant, and someone she had to battle. She felt like David looking up at Goliath. David wasn't a match for Goliath, and she wasn't a match for Blake. She'd come to the end of what she could do for herself. Totally the end. Caput. She finally had to put her trust in God. She was ashamed it had taken her this long to get here, but she was there now and raised her face in prayer.

"Leah?" Blake asked.

She finished her plea, and with her carefully controlled life disintegrating in front of her eyes, the first real comfort she'd ever experienced in her life spread through her. No knot in her stomach. No lingering worry. The nagging ache that warned of imminent disaster that she wasn't even fully aware of carrying every day until now. She could do nothing, and with that came the knowledge that she didn't have to try harder. Something she'd been doing every minute of every day. God didn't want her to try harder. He wanted her to do her best with the gifts He'd given her, put her trust in Him, and let go. Start trusting and watch Him work.

"Leah," Blake said. "Please answer my question."

"No," she said. "I can't refute them, but why would I implicate myself by putting my own jewelry and tattoo on the victims if I was trying to get away with murder? That doesn't make any sense. But if you need to arrest me, I understand and won't make a scene."

"What?" An incredulous expression claimed Riley's face. "You can't give in like that. You didn't do anything wrong except trust people who betrayed you, and now someone is singling them out and killing them."

Blake shifted his gaze to Riley. "Is that your head or some other part of you talking?"

"Everything in me believes in Leah. She's not a killer. She's a strong, amazing woman and the mother of my child. I'll put all the resources of Blackwell Tactical behind keeping her out of jail."

"Is that so?" Blake challenged.

Riley planted his feet, Leah's defender in action, warming her heart. "If you want to test me just go ahead."

Blake shoved his notebook into his pocket and took his time clipping the pen on the fabric before looking up and meeting Riley's gaze. "I have to take this to the DA. I have no choice. It's my job. But if you promise to keep an eye on Leah, I can cut her some slack and not detain her until the DA issues the warrant. If you come up with something to clear her before the warrant is issued, then I'm glad to reconsider."

Yes, Leah was most certainly at the end of her abilities. Only God could keep her out of jail now.

Riley couldn't believe what was happening. He had an hour —maybe less—to prove Leah's innocence, and he had nothing to go on. He'd even had to tell Blake about the tracking software. He didn't want to, but Leah insisted they be aboveboard and trust God no matter the consequences.

"It's okay, you know," Leah said to him from where she sat calmly on the love seat. "I'm trusting God to clear my name."

She'd obviously turned a corner in her faith, and he was so proud of her. If only he could round the same corner, but trust didn't come easily for him. Not after years of living with a father who had ulterior motives.

"You could do the same thing," she said softly.

"Could I?"

"I get it. I really do. My life had to fall apart for me to place my complete trust in Him. I hope you can figure it out before you have to reach the same spot."

He hoped so, too. "Still, trusting God doesn't mean you give up and don't fight with everything you have."

"But see, that's the problem," she said, her voice even quieter. "I don't have anything left. Nothing at all, but I can rest and leave it all in His hands."

"Well, I can't." Riley jerked his phone from his pocket and dialed Sam. "Where are you?"

"At the heliport, why?"

He told her about Helen. "I think Leah is being set up, and it has to be someone who consistently has backstage access."

"I can evaluate Helen's murder scene if you want me to. Maybe something will jump out at me as being staged."

"Yes. But hurry. We're on a deadline." He hated hearing how panicked he sounded, and he took a cleansing breath before he explained about the imminent arrest.

"I'm on my way," Sam said quickly. "Tell Leah I'm on her side."

"Is Eryn with you?" he asked before she could hang up.

"Yes."

"Have her call me once you're on the road."

"Understood," she said and the call went dead.

Riley faced Leah. "Sam's on her way. She wants you to know she's supporting you. When she gets here, she'll evaluate the scene to see if it's been staged."

"You mean like someone putting the tattoo equipment in my dressing room? We both know I didn't put it there."

"Exactly."

His phone rang, and it was Eryn. That meant that the team had really hustled to get on the road this quickly, and he owed them big time. Maybe when they arrived, they could brainstorm and come up with a way to keep Leah out of jail.

He answered the call. "I'm sure Sam told you about Helen as well as Leah's pending arrest. So please tell me you've found something that might help."

"Maybe. At least I've got something interesting. My algorithm found a post and picture in a fan forum where a guy uploaded a photo of his arm and hand. He's holding a gun, and he's got the infinity tattoo on his wrist with Leah's name."

"That's great! Which wrist had the tattoo?"

"His left wrist. I'm searching for other posts he might have made to see if we can get a look at his face."

"You've got to work faster," Riley snapped.

"I'm doing all I can, and Piper is helping, too."

Eryn didn't deserve for him to lose it on her. "I'm sorry for getting mad. It's just...we have a limited time."

"If you let me go, I can work on enhancing the image on our way there and maybe find an actionable lead."

"Okay. Thanks." He disconnected and relayed the information to Leah.

She narrowed her gaze. "This is so odd. I'm certain *two* people couldn't know about my personal tattoo. I think this is all being done by my stalker."

"Then maybe it's time we consider the guy who did our tats, as he's the *only* other person who could know about the tattoo."

"Honestly, that's the only thing that makes sense. Could we be lucky enough that he works at the same place? If we can figure out the shop where he worked, that is."

"Odds aren't good, but maybe we can come up with the name of the tattoo shop and then contact the owner. If this guy has moved on, maybe the owner will know where he is now."

The door flew open, and Blake stormed into the room. He eyed Leah. "Well, you got a reprieve."

"I did?" Leah stared up at him.

"Thanks to your celebrity status, the DA won't act until I have more evidence. It's an election year, and he doesn't want to risk the bad publicity for falsely arresting a superstar."

Riley's mood soared with the news.

"I'm not that big of a star," Leah said. "But I'm glad for the reprieve."

"Forget I said that about the DA." Blake looked between them. "Both of you. I should've taken the time to cool off before coming in here."

"I won't say a word," Leah said, sounding relieved.

"I can't promise not to share with the team, but you know they'll keep it to themselves."

Blake nodded and stepped closer to Riley. "I'm taking off my sheriff's hat and talking to you as a friend. I need you to keep an eye on Leah. For her sake, not mine."

"You don't think she's guilty."

"I didn't say that."

"You didn't have to." A weight lifted off Riley's back.

"Just know that no matter what or who this investigation reveals, I will do my sworn job. Friend or no friend."

"I know you will, but I also know you'll be fair about it." A hint of optimism found its way into Riley's heart. "This is probably pushing things with you, but if we can figure out the tattoo shop where we got inked, I'd like to take a quick trip to Portland and take Leah with me."

Riley held his breath in wait for the answer. Sure, he could send another team member to Portland, but he felt compelled to do this.

"Okay." Blake turned to Leah. "You're not to go into your house for any reason. Got it?"

"Yes. I don't need to go there."

Blake faced Riley, his gaze narrowed. "Whatever you do, don't make a fool of me here for trusting you, Glen."

"I won't." *I hope.*

18

Not even ten minutes later, Leah had to put aside Helen's murder. Put aside Blake and his warnings. She had to deal with her performance tonight. The show must go on. So Kraig gathered her along with Riley, Felicity, and Gabby on the stage. She expected the band would be there waiting for her, but the stage was empty save a few stools.

Gabby was perched on one, Felicity on another. Felicity glared at her, obviously still upset, and she had every right to be. Leah would have to work hard to repair that relationship, but the good news was she could be totally honest with Felicity now and they could become real friends.

Leah sat on the open stool next to Gabby. "We need to make this meeting quick and get the band warming up."

Gabby frowned. "I'm sorry, Leah, but we can't hold the concert tonight."

Leah didn't like Gabby's dire tone of voice. "What do you mean we can't hold the concert? I understand not doing it out of respect for Helen, and I'm glad to cancel for that, but it sounds like you're saying it's cancelled for another reason."

"Your promoter is threatening to drop you and wants to

reevaluate," Kraig said, not pulling any punches. "And even if he didn't, after today's publicity about Helen's murder, you can't possibly perform tonight."

She swallowed down her mounting worry. "I understand about tonight. It's probably not a good idea to go on, but surely we can find someone else to replace this promoter if he bails."

Kraig shook his head hard, his long hair swishing back and forth. "Not in the middle of a tour, no."

She slouched on the stool, feeling as if the weight of the announcement was pushing her down. "So he's like everyone else then. He thinks I'm a murderer."

Gabby sat forward and met Leah's gaze. "Actually, that's not it at all."

"Then what?"

"The fact that you hid your son is blowing up all over social media. He's seeing people threatening to boycott your concert, and he doesn't want to be associated with the bad publicity."

"Seriously?" Outrage had her shooting up on her stool.

"Seriously." The word whispered out of Gabby's mouth.

"In this day and age, I can't imagine they're upset about me having a child when I wasn't married," she said, though honestly, she was mortified by it and had always been so.

"That's not it either," Gabby said. "Your fans feel betrayed."

"Betrayed, but how?"

"I can answer that one because I feel the same way," Felicity chimed in. "I thought I knew you. That you were open and honest about your life. But here's this big, I mean really big—huge—thing you didn't tell us about. We believed you were genuine. The real deal. We can't trust you to be genuine anymore."

"And the thing today's generation hates more than

anything is lack of authenticity," Gabby added. "They thought they knew you, and you betrayed their trust."

"But I had good reason. Ril—" She started to mention Riley's father, but she wouldn't do that to Riley. Even if she lost her career, she wouldn't throw his father under the bus. Not because she was worried about going against his father, but because she cared about Riley and didn't want him to have to go through more hounding of the press than he would likely already experience.

"This will be hard to come back from." Gabby squeezed Leah's knee. "But I'll work with my team to come up with something to save your career."

"You're kidding, right?" Leah gaped at Gabby while she tried to wrap her head around this mess. "My whole career is in danger because I didn't share about my son?"

"Yes," Kraig said. "You're like social media kryptonite now, and no promoter will touch you until this blows over. If it ever does. I'm sorry, but that's today's world of social media where fans think they're part of your life."

Leah didn't know what to say. What to feel. She'd just gotten over the stress of not being arrested, and now this? And she thought she'd come to the end of herself. *Hah!* God had even more of a work to do in her life. She'd been so cocky, having mastered peace for only a second before telling Riley that he should embrace it. And now, here she was. Her peace gone.

She obviously feared losing her career more than going to jail. How could that even be?

"We'll get to work now and try to repair this as best as possible." Gabby stood and patted Leah's shoulder. "Hang in there, okay?"

Leah nodded, but honestly, she didn't know how to hang in there when her life had totally exploded.

"Ditto what she said." Kraig squeezed her shoulder and left the room with Gabby.

"I'll go, too, but not to help them," Felicity said, her expression tight. "I'm done with you, and I'm going back home to Portland. I wish things were different, and I could support you, but right now I have to put some distance between us."

"I understand," Leah said. "And I'm sorry I hurt you. I didn't mean to do that. I was protecting my son. When you have children, you'll understand."

"Maybe," Felicity replied, and shaking her head, she exited the stage.

"Thank you," Riley said the moment she was out of earshot. "For not mentioning my dad. He deserves to be outed in public, but I appreciate that you didn't do it."

Leah turned her focus to Riley. "I couldn't hurt you that way."

He came over to her. "It could cost you everything."

"Then it will."

He tipped his head, smiling. "Your newfound trust in God in action again?"

She shook her head. "I'm not feeling that peace anymore. More like resignation. But if I'm going down, I don't have to take you with me."

"I can't believe God wouldn't honor your integrity and work this out."

"Seems I can trust Him with clearing my name, but when it comes to my career and money, I don't know. It's got me by the throat. I need to figure out a way to lay it down. Who knows? Maybe that's what this is all about."

"Maybe." Riley took her hand. "Just know I will always be thankful for your consideration here. When I tell my parents about this, they'll be thankful, too, and Dad won't take any action."

"Actually, I fully expect him to say I'm lying about having come to see him back then. After all, I don't have any proof, and if there's anything I've learned this week, it's that you need proof when someone calls your actions into question." She thought back to that day. "I suppose I could describe his office, and I'd never been there before."

He squeezed her hand and let go. "Your word is all I need."

She dredged up a smile for him and moved on to more pressing things. "Do you think since I have fallen out of the public's favor that the DA will be more apt to file charges against me?"

"Yeah, I think it's possible."

"So, can we get out of here before the sheriff comes looking for me?"

Riley nodded. "If we figure out the tattoo shop, I'll arrange for us to go to Portland tomorrow, and with the hotel being closer, we might as well stay here tonight."

"Sounds good," she said, but nothing sounded good right now. Nothing at all.

Riley bent closer and looked her in the eye. "I know it feels like your life is out of control, but you need to have faith that God will work all of this out."

"Sounds like you're suddenly the one trusting Him."

He shrugged. "Maybe I am. But here's the thing. It's easier to trust God with someone else's life than your own."

"I get that." She sighed. "I just wish I knew how this will be resolved."

"That would be nice, wouldn't it?" He gave a wry smile. "But if we knew the future, then we wouldn't need faith, now would we?"

~

Riley couldn't sleep. He kept waiting for his phone to ring or a knock on his door, or hearing Blake at Leah's door, arresting her. Leah was probably going through the same thing. Maybe pacing the room as she typically did when stressed.

He tossed off his covers and glanced at his phone to make sure he didn't miss a call or text, but the screen was blank. He went to his computer to check his email. Seeing Eryn's name and an attachment, he hoped the image of the tattooed man had been improved enough to give them something to go on.

He clicked on the message and quickly scanned it to discover she had indeed lightened it. The name of a bar where he was sitting when the picture was taken was displayed behind him. Excitement building, Riley entered the bar's name in Google Maps and sat back stunned.

The bar was next door to Everlasting Tattoos. The name sounded familiar, but Riley wanted it to be, so maybe he was letting the power of suggestion get to him. He looked at the man's picture again. The guy could very well be Leah's stalker. Well, at least his arm, and he was holding a Walther PPS. A 9mm. Could be their murder weapon.

Riley searched for Everlasting's website and opened the main page. He clicked on the link for tattoo artists and the page opened with the names and profiles of the artists, but no photos of them.

One guy's name—Milo Belcher—stood out. That could just be because it was an unusual name. Which made Riley think he was wrong, too, because odds were better that an unusual name like that would stick in their memory, but he didn't know if the guy had even mentioned his name.

They would just have to hope that tomorrow when they walked into the shop, he was there. They might not remember his face, but they would surely recognize the Leah tattoo on his arm.

19

Riley approached the tattoo shop on foot. He'd flown Alex and Leah to Portland in the helo, touched down on Lee's property, and used the ratty old truck to get to a car rental place for a more reliable vehicle. He didn't want their would-be stalker to bolt when he saw Leah, so Riley left the others in the SUV in the parking structure.

The minute he stepped into the tattoo shop, he knew it was the right place. The scent of strong incense still clung to the air, and the interior hadn't change much in the last seven years. A curved reception desk sat in the front with a Kelly green countertop. The walls were filled with tattoo designs. Behind the reception area were small half-wall booths with paisley privacy curtains on top.

Three artists were in their booths, one woman and two men, one man bent over, the other two looking up when Riley walked in. The guy—who was bald—instantly frowned. As a former police officer, Riley still carried himself with the same presence an officer held, and the guy likely recognized that.

He got up and moved slowly toward Riley. He stroked his left hand over a long beard in a muddy brown color then ran the back of his hand over his mouth. Riley fixed his gaze on his arm, noting it was clear of any Leah tats, and he wasn't their suspect.

He stepped behind the counter and pointed at Riley's shirt. "What's Blackwell Tactical?"

Riley considered making something up, but he figured this guy would see through it. "We're a group of former members of the military and law enforcement officers who help out people in trouble."

"Figured you for a cop."

"Good eye. I was a PPB officer for a lot of years."

"What can I do for you?" He was outwardly wary now.

"I need to speak to the shop owner."

He jabbed a thumb at his chest. "That's me. Jared Bones."

Riley took out his phone and opened the picture Eryn had located. "I'm hoping you recognize this guy's arm."

Jared stared at the picture and didn't respond verbally but curled his fingers tightly on the Formica countertop. "What's he done now?"

"You know him, then?"

He nodded and frowned. "Was an artist here until about six months ago. But he had some mental health issues, and I had to ask him to find another place to work."

"What kind of issues?"

He narrowed his eyes. "Exactly why do you want to know?"

"I think he's stalking my client and may have murdered three women."

"Man, seriously? He's a manic depressive who didn't like to take his meds. I mean when the mania took control he was a different person...but a killer? Nah, I just don't see it."

"Then maybe you can help me clear his name," Riley

said trying to make this guy's sharing of information a positive thing. "Like starting with his name?"

"Milo Belcher."

So Riley was right last night. Interesting. "Do you have a picture of him?"

"Might have."

Riley tapped his phone to bring up Leah's sketch of her stalker. "Does he look like this?"

"Man. Yeah. That's him."

"Would you be willing to look for an actual photo?"

Jared stroked his beard again. "This won't be a problem for the shop, will it? I'm barely making it as is and couldn't handle bad publicity."

"If Milo is the person we're looking for and it makes the news, I'll make sure that everyone knows about your cooperation and people will know you did the right thing."

"Thanks, man." He offered his hand for a fist bump.

Riley obliged him. "About that picture."

"I'll get it now." He hurried toward the back of his shop and soon disappeared behind heavy green curtains.

Riley took the time to look at the tattoo drawings on the wall, trying to see if the infinity design was still there. He'd like to claim that it was a unique design he and Leah thought of, but they found it here. He kept looking and finally spotted it on the top row. Number eighty-seven.

Jared returned with several pictures. Riley flipped through them and anger flared in his gut. He should be happy because they now had a name and could hopefully find this guy. But the guy looked even more threatening than the sketch portrayed, and Riley could easily imagine the man stalking Leah and killing the women.

Riley's stomach twisted in a knot. "These are perfect."

"We used to have pictures on our website, but we took them down. These are from the photo shoot."

"Can I take them?"

Jared nodded.

"Do you have an address for Milo?" Riley asked.

Jared opened a drawer below the cash register and lifted out an old tattered address book. "I'm old school. Don't like Big Brother having access to all my records."

He swiveled the book to display the address.

Riley entered it into his phone. "Any idea if Belcher still lives there?"

Jared shook his head. "He used to hang out at the bar next door, but I haven't seen him in months. Still, you could check with the owner. Her name's Windy Washington. Tell her I sent you. We're kind of a thing, and she'll help you out."

Riley offered his hand for a shake, and then headed for the door but turned back. "Just curious. If Milo doesn't work here anymore, why's his name still on your website?"

"Oh that. Costs too much money to have our web designer change things so I left it. But if what you're telling me is true, I'll pay anything to have him removed."

Leah stared at the photos, fear taking hold, and her stomach churning. The dark parking garage didn't help. Could Belcher be following them? Lingering in the dark? The bar owner had told Riley that Belcher still lived in the same place and stopped by the bar regularly, but that Riley would likely find him this morning in his apartment sleeping off a night of binge drinking.

She searched into the shadowy spaces. The murky corners. Between cars. Looking for him. For this man who might be a killer and might want her dead.

"Leah, is it him?" Riley asked from behind the wheel. "Your stalker?"

"Yes." She jerked her focus away from the garage.

"You're sure?" Riley asked.

"Yes. It's really him. You found him, Riley. Thank you." She grabbed his hand and held it tight. If Alex wasn't climbing back into the car from making a phone call she would kiss Riley's hand. Maybe kiss him, because with finding the stalker's information this could all be over soon, and she could go back to her regular life.

Hah! Like that was an option. Her regular life could very well be gone. Her hope for providing for her son gone. What would she do if the promoter dropped her? She'd never held another job except waitressing and working at the college cafeteria. Not that there was anything wrong with doing either of those jobs. They just didn't pay the kind of salary a single mother needed to be able to send her child off to college someday. And she didn't have any skills that could gain her a better paying job.

Is this it, God? You wanted me to come to the complete and total end of myself? Well, I have. Now what?

Riley's earlier conversation came to mind. God wouldn't show her what was going to happen. She had to woman up and have faith that He would work things out. Trust Him. Totally trust Him.

Problem was, her old insecurities were buzzing around her brain like angry wasps, and she didn't want to get stung again.

"Leah," Riley said. "Did you hear me?"

"Sorry, no. What did you say?"

"Alex and I need to head to Milo's apartment. I don't like leaving you in the car alone. Alex has a buddy who's a DEA agent. That's who he was calling. His buddy's on vacation this week. He's home and has agreed to let you hang with him."

"Okay," she said, but the last thing she wanted to do right now was go to some stranger's place and make small talk.

"Don't worry," Alex said. "You won't likely even know Devon's there. He's not big on talking. You won't have to worry about entertaining him or answering a bunch of questions."

"Let me just get Eryn started running a background check on Belcher." Riley took out his phone and tapped the screen. "Eryn, good. I'm glad I got you. We have the stalker's ID. A Milo Belcher."

He took a breath and gave her Belcher's address. "Alex and I'll pay him a visit after dropping Leah off at Devon's house for safety. I need you to gather as much information as you can on Belcher in that time, and I'll call back once we're at Devon's place."

Riley said goodbye and stowed his phone. "Okay, let's do this. Can you put Devon's address in your phone's GPS to give us directions?"

Leah nodded and couldn't miss the excitement in his eyes, likely fueled with adrenaline. She was excited that her stalker, maybe the killer, could be in custody in a few hours, but she had so much else going on in her life and brain that she couldn't really embrace the excitement.

On the drive, Leah listened with interest as Alex and Riley discussed their plans to handle Belcher and how they would protect the scene if they located evidence of his stalking.

"We can't do anything that will jeopardize a successful prosecution," Riley said. "No way I'll let this creep walk. That means hands off everything and wearing gloves and booties."

"That's what's in the tote bag you brought along?" she asked.

"Among other things."

"Sam's really drilled into our heads the importance of preserving crime scenes," Alex added. "Riley here already knew what to do, but those of us with military backgrounds weren't as cognizant of the procedures. Now we are."

"Cognizant?" Riley looked in the rearview mirror. "If you mean not rolling onto a scene like an armored tank as you did in the past, then yeah, you've been more *cognizant.*"

Leah glanced at Alex who rolled his eyes good-naturedly but didn't say anything.

Leah loved the team comradery and witty sparring. She didn't have that with her team. Probably because she was always on guard to keep from revealing anything about Owen. That was one good point about the public knowing about Owen. She could let that guard down with her team now. *If* she had a team to go back to. That was a big if.

And if she lost the promoter, a group of wonderful and dedicated people would be out of a job. Her bus drivers, equipment truck drivers, stage crew, even her band and backup singers.

Father, please, for them. Please let me at least finish this tour. Their families are counting on the income as much as I am.

At a stoplight Riley looked over his shoulder at Alex. "We'll call in PPB the minute we have any concrete evidence that Belcher's our stalker. And when I want to beat the crud out of Belcher, I need you to be the voice of reason and stop me. You hear?"

"Got it."

"I mean it, Alex. He's stalked someone I care about very much, and I'm sure you can't even begin to understand how I feel about the guy."

Alex leaned forward. "You want me to go as far as to physically restrain you?"

"Do it if you have to, but don't let me hurt this guy."

"Hey, man, trust me. I'll be glad to put you in a hammerlock." Alex grinned, revealing a mischievously handsome smile.

Riley shook his head and when the light turned green, he got them moving again. His comments had given Leah a lot to think about. He said he cared about her. Very much. Cared as in present tense. Not *once* cared about. Not cared about in the past. But cared about. And then the rage burning in him over the stalking was a shock, too. He'd hidden it well. Staying calm most of this time when it had likely been simmering in his gut.

She didn't like that he was this upset, but she did love that his anger on her behalf was because he cared for her.

She glanced at him. He looked at her and smiled. A sweet, *I'm glad to be with you* smile that he'd always greeted her with in the good old days. She didn't think beyond the fact that she liked it and reached out to take his hand.

Surprise flashed in his eyes, but he didn't withdraw his hand until he pulled up in front of a small white bungalow in an established city neighborhood. He gave her fingers a squeeze, that sweet smile materializing again, and then all that tenderness vanished into a hard expression as he assessed the area through the windows.

"Let me check things out, and I'll come open your door." Hand on his holster, he walked with Alex, and they surveyed the area.

A moment ago he was her supporter. Now he was her defender. In both cases, he was fierce and just plain amazing.

Thank you for bringing him back into my life. I couldn't have survived this alone, and he's the only man I trust to protect me.

He opened her car door, stood back, and then walked her up to the tidy and manicured yard. The house was well-maintained, too. Leah trailed Alex up the steps to the small front porch.

He pounded on the door. "Open up, Dunbar, or I'll break it down."

Leah thought Alex was being overly dramatic, but it was likely some private joke between them.

The door cracked open, and icy blue eyes stared at them from the face of a darkly dangerous man. He cocked an eyebrow and stared at Alex. "Oh, it's you."

He started to close the door, and Alex pushed inside. "Seriously, this is getting old."

"Not for me." Devon smiled.

Leah stood for a moment under the power of his captivating smile. He was a handsome man with blackish-brown hair and a scruffy beard. She could see where the ladies would like him, but he wasn't her type. She'd always fallen for blonds, but she noted he didn't wear a wedding ring, and she suspected he'd broken a bunch of hearts over the years.

He held out his hand to her. "Devon Dunbar. Friend of Alex, sometimes, and DEA agent when I'm not forced to use my vacation time."

"Leah Kent. New friend of Alex's and singer, songwriter."

He released her hand and tapped his chin with his index finger. "Hmm, I think I might have heard your name somewhere."

He laughed and stood back giving her access to small living room filled with contemporary furniture, a wall with built-in shelves filled with records, and an expensive turntable nearby. She went straight to his records and perused the titles.

She turned to look at him. "A jazz man I see."

"Totally."

She faced Riley. "Okay, this will work. We can talk music, so you can go now. Just make sure you apprehend my stalker."

"You can count on us."

Alex nodded. "Yeah, what he said."

"Man." Devon grinned at Riley and Alex. "I envy the lack of red tape you guys can avoid in making a bust."

"It's great, as I always tell you. Go and get yourself shot up and you can join the team, too." Alex chuckled.

"Yeah, sure, I'll get right on that."

"Okay." Riley squeezed her hand. "We're out of here. Call me if you need anything, and I mean *anything*. If we're apprehending Belcher, I'll have my phone on silent and won't answer right away, but I *will* call you back a soon as I can. You can count on that."

Riley was headed into potential danger, and she didn't care if there were others in the room. She slid her arms around his waist and drew him close. He held her tightly.

"Be careful, okay?" she whispered. "I can't lose you."

"I promise we'll be fine."

Yeah, fine like when he took a bullet and lost one of his kidneys. She couldn't say that to him, so she gave him one last hug and stepped back. "You be careful, too, Alex."

"What's the fun in that?" He grinned and stepped outside.

Maybe that was a glimpse of why he was single. He was a daredevil, and it would be hard to be with someone like that unless you had an equally fearless personality. That wasn't her. It hit her then. She was the exact opposite. She'd been living with fear and anxiety since she met with Riley's father. Was on her own with a child to support. She'd lost every bit of her fun side. How she missed that. Could she get it back?

"Wow, something's got a hold of your mind," Devon said.

She'd forgotten he was in the room with her. "Yeah, I'm working through some things."

"When Alex asked if you could spend a few hours with me, I looked for you online. You know, to get an idea of who I was protecting."

"And?"

"And you've got some real haters out there right now. Gotta be hard to handle."

"You have no idea," she said, tears nearly breaking free, but she willed them away and vowed to use this time to find a way to save her career and figure out the rest of the life she'd once had all mapped out.

Belcher's apartment was within walking distance from Everlasting Tattoos. It was a second-story walk-up over a vintage clothing store. Access was up worn wooden stairs in a grungy alley, and he and Alex cringed with each creak of the wood. But if Belcher truly was sleeping one off, surprising him would likely be successful.

They reached the bright blue door with peeling paint, and Riley pounded on it, using the side of his fist to make a noise loud enough to wake the hungover guy. Riley didn't want Belcher not to answer, so Riley didn't announce himself. He stood to the side of the door and waited, tapping his foot with each second that passed. At the count of fifty, he pounded again and didn't stop.

Belcher didn't answer.

"You think he's passed out?" Alex asked.

"Could be."

"Or he might not be here."

"If he is, I'm not leaving without talking to him." Riley grabbed the doorknob and gave it a twist. It turned in the palm of his hand. "It's unlocked. I'm going in. Make sure you have my back."

He drew his weapon, his years of training as a police officer taking over. He kicked the door open, gun raised, and ran his gaze over the small kitchen with old metal cabinets and faded linoleum floor. A small green table and one chair sat near the wall. Dirty dishes and takeout containers covered every surface, and the smell of rotting food was enough to make Riley gag.

He entered and quickly moved to the inner doorway that led to a short hallway with two doors before opening into a living area. Riley flung open the door on his right side and found a small bathroom with a clawfoot tub and old porcelain sink on rusty metal legs. It was empty. Figuring the other door was the bedroom and they'd find Belcher in there, Riley gave Alex a questioning look, asking if he was ready for this.

Riley received a swift nod in response and couldn't miss the excitement burning in Alex's eyes. Riley figured if he wasn't here, Alex would've already burst into the room. His swashbuckler personality didn't fit his former job as a recon Marine where he had to be slow and meticulous. Riley never understood that contradiction.

Riley kicked the door open. Belcher lay facedown on a bare mattress, his eyes closed and his mouth hanging open, but Riley couldn't take his focus off Leah's tattoo on his arm. Here he was. The living breathing creep who'd made Leah suffer. Given her sleepless nights and intense emotional pain.

Riley could easily grab Belcher by his stained T-shirt and pummel him senseless. It would feel great to release all of his pent-up rage...but then what? He'd be in major trouble as well as have beaten a defenseless man. What long-term satisfaction would that bring? None, and it would have all kinds of negative consequences.

He grit his teeth, indecision still clouding his judgment.

Alex nudged Riley and pointed at the wall behind the door. Thankfully, Riley managed to shift his attention before he exploded and went for the guy's neck.

The wall was covered with pictures of Leah. At concerts. At the park with Owen. Shots through the front window of her house where she was playing with Owen. Personal photos. Her tattoo exposed. And emails and forum posts were tacked around the pictures. This was the proof they needed of his stalking, and Riley should back out of the room. Call PPB.

But he spun. Saw Belcher. Saw red. He started for him.

Alex rested his hand on Riley's shoulder and whispered, "Don't do it, man."

Riley shrugged Alex's hand off and moved forward.

"One more step, and I use the hammerlock," Alex said, louder now, but Belcher didn't stir.

The urge to move ahead nearly blinded Riley. He had to defend Leah's honor. Let this jerk know what he did wasn't acceptable. He'd hurt the woman Riley loved, and he couldn't stand that.

Wait. Loved? He loved her? Not as in *once* loved her. He really did love her. It wasn't in question at all.

His anger vanished as swift as an ocean wave crashing into a dune. He loved her. He did, and it felt good to admit it. At least to himself. But what about telling her? How did she feel?

Belcher stirred, and Riley dragged his attention back to the man as he rolled and belched then settled on his back.

"Watch him," Riley said. "While I call in a detective buddy of mine. This jerk is going down and not by my hands, but by the law."

20

___

On the other side of his living room, Devon put a new record on the turntable and looked up. Leah had expected him to leave her, but he didn't seem ready to do that.

"You look like you want to be alone," he said.

"Sorry, I don't mean to be rude." Leah smiled, but she had to admit it was forced. "I've got a lot on my mind. The stalker. The murders. Losing my career."

He leaned against the wall, his ankles crossed, acting like he might stay and talk when Alex said just the opposite. She didn't know how she felt about that.

"Sounds like maybe the first two issues will be solved in the next little while," he said.

"Yes, thanks to the Blackwell Tactical team. But there's nothing they can do to counterbalance the social media outrage. I think time is the only thing that can fix that. And even then, I'll be a has-been playing small venues for a pittance."

"Maybe you need to reinvent yourself."

"If only it was that easy."

"I didn't say it was easy. But I've been where you are. In a big mess, thinking my career was over. And it was. But I made the hard decision to leave the SEALs and became a DEA agent. It's not as exciting, but it's rewarding."

"Why'd you leave the SEALs?" she asked, as she knew nothing about the military. "If you don't mind me asking."

"Actually, I do mind, but I'll tell you anyway," he said, surprising her even more. "I left for a woman. She couldn't handle a relationship with me being deployed, and I chose her over the team."

She looked at his hand. "But you're not wearing a ring, so I assume you didn't marry this woman."

He pushed off the wall, looking uneasy. Had she pried too much?

"Turns out she couldn't handle a relationship with me even when I wasn't deployed." He snorted. "In hindsight it was good to learn before the *I do's*. But, man, at the time it was awful." He shook his head. "Don't know how you got me started. I don't ever talk about this."

"I appreciate you sharing. I wish I had another career I could do. I mean moving into law enforcement is sort of natural for former military, right?"

He nodded.

"But for me, there's no real career path."

"What about changing genres?"

"Like suddenly do jazz or something, you mean?"

"I don't know anything about the music business, but it's just a thought."

"Thanks," she said, but couldn't imagine what genre she could move to.

"I'm gonna give you some time to think about this. You want me to leave the music on?"

She nodded.

"Let me know if you need anything." He left the room.

She leaned her head back on the sofa. Tried to remain

still and absorb the music's sultry undertones, but she couldn't. Not when Riley could be in danger.

She got up and paced the living room. She watched her feet travel over the lacquered wood floor, each step of worry clarifying her feelings for him. She loved him, and it was time to admit it. But what she did with that knowledge, she didn't know.

Her phone chimed a text. She quickly dug it out. The message was from him.

Belcher arrested. Evidence in apartment proves he's your stalker. Searching now for proof of his involvement in murders. Hang tight. It might take some time.

Success! Her mood soared to beyond joyous. She typed her response.

Celebrating his arrest! I'm fine here. Take your time.

She exhaled the final remnants of her fear and stowed her phone. Riley was okay. Not hurt. And Belcher had been arrested. The stalking was over. Hopefully the killing, too.

Thank you. Thank you. Thank you.

A rush of adrenaline left her body, and her legs wobbled. She dropped onto the sofa and closed her eyes to listen to the music.

The notes smoothly rose and fell, like a ballet dancer whisking and leaping across the stage. Her heart swelled with the crescendo. Could she do what Devon suggested? Find another genre that might be more accepting? Maybe she could start anew. Her only other musical experience was at church where she and Riley used to play in the worship band. Her pastor had once suggested she pursue a Christian recording career.

Could she do that? Did she want to do that, or had the whole career been simply to prove her worth, like Riley kept telling her? She certainly had proved it, but it was all super-ficial and then people turned on her. It really meant nothing. Like the harsh treatment of her peers growing up. What did any of it mean in light of eternity?

If she ever considered Christian recording, then she would do it for the right reason. To proclaim God's Word, not to make herself popular. Could she even do this and still share custody of Owen with Riley? Or might she and Riley possibly get back together?

She sighed. She really had a lot to think about.

A loud knock sounded on the front door, scaring her upright. Devon charged into the room, his hand on his sidearm as he approached the door and looked out the peephole then came back to Leah. "It's a woman. I don't know her. Blond. Pretty and dressed very fashionably. Not carrying anything like she's trying to sell something or take a survey."

"Can I look to see if I know her?" Leah asked.

Devon nodded.

Leah went to the door, and when she saw Felicity standing there, she could only stare for a moment. "It's my assistant."

"Did you call her?"

Leah shook her head.

Devon frowned. "Guess you should let her in, and we can see what she wants."

Leah opened the door.

"Sorry to show up unannounced." Felicity smiled, easing Leah's worry that she'd lost her friend. "I'm sorry for bailing on you when you needed me and want to make it up to you."

Leah returned the smile, and she was once again thankful for her assistant's support. "How did you find me?"

"Riley. I called him and told him I wanted to surprise you. To make up with you. He said Belcher was arrested for stalking you, and they found the murder weapon, too. They have the killer in custody, and Riley wants to get back to Owen as soon as possible. So he asked if I would drive you to the helicopter. I thought we could talk on the way. I honestly think that was his whole point in asking me. He really cares about you and wants you to be happy."

Leah should be touched by Riley's consideration but she couldn't think about that quite yet. "Belcher's the killer?"

"Oh, right." Felicity absently scratched her cheek. "I guess Riley didn't have time to tell you yet. He said the place was chaos, and I could tell he was in a hurry to get off the phone. I guess he planned to tell you when he saw you. To celebrate it with you. Don't tell him I said anything. I don't want to ruin it."

"Belcher is the killer. It's all over. Resolved." Leah felt like she could float away, and she reached out to hug Felicity. She stiffened. Right. They had some work to do to repair their friendship. Leah really wanted that. Especially now that she didn't have a secret to hide. She could include Felicity in her private life, too. The drive would be good for them.

"Let me grab my purse." Leah turned to find Devon watching them carefully.

"Maybe you should call or text Riley to confirm this is what he wants," Devon suggested.

"You think I'm lying?" Felicity's lips pressed into a white slash. "Why would I do that?"

"Exactly," Leah said. "Felicity is my friend. She would never lie about something like this. And besides, he's busy, I don't want to bother him and delay his departure." She grabbed her purse but saw Devon take out his phone and start tapping the buttons.

"You're texting Riley?" she asked, a bit irritated that he thought he had to do so.

He nodded. "Something seems off here."

Leah appreciated his considerate care, but she had nothing to fear with Felicity. Still Leah gave Riley a few minutes to respond. When he didn't, she headed for the door.

"Leah, wait," Devon called after her. "Give Riley a chance to get back to me."

"What's the point? Felicity is a friend doing him a favor. And as a bonus we can reconnect. It's all good."

"No, it's not. I—"

"Let me know if you hear from him," she said over her shoulder. "But until then, I'm headed for the heliport to go back home to my son, and no one is going to get in my way."

Outside Belcher's apartment, Riley climbed behind the wheel of his rental vehicle, and Alex took the passenger seat. Riley had heard his phone chime several times while he was in the middle of interviewing Belcher, but he'd ignored it to concentrate on Belcher's statements. Riley grabbed his phone to check his texts, but it rang with a call from Eryn before he could.

"What's up?" He answered quickly on speaker, hoping Eryn might have a lead on the murders. They'd found nothing to show Belcher had any part in them, and he claimed he was innocent.

"I just finished reviewing the files on Leah's phone." She took a sharp breath as if she was about to announce bad news. "Someone installed a spyware app. It tracked her location, along with recording all calls, texts, and Internet use."

Riley had been upset before, but this was an extreme invasion of privacy. "Who installed it?"

"I don't know yet, but it had to be someone with access to her phone."

"Is the app still tracking her location?"

"I'm sure it is, unless she found it and uninstalled it."

Riley didn't like the sound of this. Not one bit. "Belcher didn't have access to her phone, so who could have done this?"

"Anyone who's close enough to Leah to get to her phone. And know her password."

"Like maybe the killer who had backstage access and no one seemed to notice them," Alex said, tossing Riley a pointed look that sent Riley's gut cramping.

"Exactly," Eryn replied with force. "I'll keep after it and should have additional information soon."

"Call me the minute you know something." Riley disconnected and looked at Alex.

"I'm seriously thinking Belcher isn't our killer," Alex said. "With the way he didn't care about hiding the fact that he was stalking Leah, seems like he wouldn't have worried about concealing murder either."

"Could be." Riley checked his phone to see who texted him. "Devon texted me twice. Said Felicity showed up at his place claiming I told her to pick Leah up."

"Odd," Alex said. "Maybe Devon got it wrong."

"Maybe." Riley dialed Devon and put him on speaker so Alex could listen in. "I didn't talk to Felicity."

"It seemed odd to me, and that's why I texted you." Devon sounded concerned.

"Tell her not to go anywhere. I'm on my way."

"I can't. When you didn't reply, she left."

"She what? No. No." Riley gripped the steering wheel tightly with his free hand. "You thought something was off. Why didn't you try to stop her?"

There was a long pause. "You mean like forcibly restrain her? You might do that with a woman you've just met, but I won't."

Riley's chest tightened with frustration. "I didn't mean that."

"Then what?"

"Try to talk her out of leaving until she heard from me."

Devon snorted. "Have you tried to convince Leah of something? Because if you have, you know she has a mind of her own."

Devon had a point, but still Riley wanted to rail at him for failing to keep her there.

"Leah seems to think Felicity is a friend, so why is it so bad that Leah is with her?" Devon asked.

"Because I didn't tell her where Leah was. You, Alex, and I are the only people who knew that."

"Maybe Leah called Felicity," Alex said.

"No," Devon replied. "I asked, and she said she didn't. So how did Felicity find Leah? And how did she know about Belcher?"

A sick feeling spread through Riley's body. "Eryn just told me that someone installed spyware on Leah's phone. It had to be Felicity and she would've seen my texts to Leah."

"But my address?" Devon asked. "How did she get that?"

"GPS," Alex said. "Felicity could track her using the spyware, and if not that way, she could also see that Leah plugged your address into her phone to get directions."

"Why would Felicity even take Leah?" Devon asked.

"Because maybe..." Riley had to swallow hard to get the next words out before his throat closed. "Just maybe she isn't the friend she claimed to be, and she's the killer we've been looking for."

Leah sighed in relief, thankful the killer and her stalker had been caught. Her ordeal was over. She was finally safe. And

245

she wouldn't be arrested. A massive weight had been lifted from her shoulders. And now she was headed to the heliport to meet Riley and fly home to her son. *Their* son.

After Owen was in bed, she and Riley would work out arrangements for Owen's care and hopefully her career would resume and life would go back to the way it was before the stalker and the murders. But did she want the way it was? Or did she want Riley in her life again?

The sight of Riley carrying Owen to bed popped into her mind. Seeing them together was just plain bliss and she would love to see more of that.

"What are you smiling about?" Felicity asked.

"Just that the killer and stalker has been caught, and I can go back to my life." Leah picked up the mocha that Felicity had bought and took a long sip. Leah considered the gift of her favorite drink as a peace offering from Felicity and hoped they could make up and move on. "Thank you for getting this for me, and for giving me a chance to explain."

Felicity glanced at Leah, and for a moment she was taken aback by the anguish in Felicity's eyes.

Leah felt so bad. Keeping her secret had come at a high price. "I really hurt you, didn't I?"

"You have no idea."

Nervous that she might not be able to fix things with Felicity, Leah sipped on the drink to moisten her mouth. "Now that the truth about Owen is out, we can be true friends outside of work, too. Don't you know how many times I wanted to tell you?"

Her eyes narrowed. "And yet, you didn't."

"I couldn't, but I can't tell you why."

"More secrets." Felicity's face darkened with deep red blotches.

She was mad. So mad.

Leah took another long sip of the coffee, and then a second one for good measure, enjoying the warm chocolate sliding down her throat. "I guess so. But it really has nothing to do with us."

Felicity cast Leah a wary glance. "Other than I don't know when you'll keep things from me in the future. Things I should know. That a true friend would know."

"Hey," Leah said, a sudden wave of sleepiness washing over her. "Friends don't tell each other everything. I'm sure there are things you haven't told me over the years."

"Like what?"

Leah tried to shake her head, but dizziness spun her world. "Something's wrong. I'm feeling really weird."

"Weird how?"

"Sleepy. Dizzy. My eyes are so heavy. The world is spinning."

"Probably the adrenaline wearing off."

"No, no. Thissh, ish..." At the bizarre sound of her slurring words, she stopped talking, and the world turned faster. She rested her head back and noticed she was still holding the coffee cup. She tried to put it back in the holder but it fell from her hand.

What was happening?

She turned her head to look at Felicity.

"Help," she got out before paralysis took over her mouth.

Felicity slowed at the stop light and smiled, but it was a sickly-sweet smile that scared Leah. "Just relax, sweetie. Let the drug take hold. When you wake up, I'll explain everything."

Drug? The coffee. She'd spiked the coffee. She knew Leah would never refuse a mocha.

"I..." She tried to argue, to beg, but she couldn't keep her eyes open and slipped into the black void.

21

Still sitting in the car, Riley tapped Leah's phone number, his hand shaking. The call went straight to voicemail. He tried again. And again. Then he dialed Felicity. No answer.

Was Felicity really the killer, and had she abducted Leah, or were they sitting somewhere hashing out their differences?

The first. His gut said it was the first.

He looked at Alex whose worried expression told him he wasn't overreacting.

Riley struggled for breath, fearing he would hyperventilate, but he slowed his breathing and tried to hold it together as crazy thoughts pinged through his brain. "You're thinking Felicity is our killer."

Alex nodded. "We have nothing on Belcher, plus he would've stood out backstage. But Felicity had access to Leah's jewelry and knew Leah's every movement. She also knew Leah had argued with Carolyn and Jill, and Felicity could've even pretended to be Helen and leaked news of Owen to the press."

Riley didn't want to agree, but he had to. "But how would she have found out about Owen?"

"You can't keep a secret like that forever. Especially from people you work with every day. It was bound to come out."

"Maybe, but with as careful as Leah was, I can't imagine she slipped up."

"You could be right, but Belcher knew about Owen."

Riley grimaced. He thought about the leads they'd uncovered. "Yeah, and she probably wrote the letters. She could have figured out how to forge Leah's signature well enough to fool a handwriting expert."

Alex nodded. "What about the tattoos? Could she do that? And even if she did, why put the tattoo on the girls?"

"No point in speculating on that. Felicity is looking good to me for the murders." Riley shoved a hand into his hair. "Why didn't I see it before?"

"Because Felicity appeared to be a good friend, and there was nothing that pointed to her as a possible suspect."

"Still, I should've seen it."

Alex frowned. "Why? No one else did. And I still can't come up with a motive, can you?"

Riley shook his head. "As far as I know, they've always been good friends until Felicity found out about Owen. Maybe she discovered it a while ago, and she's been planning this for some time."

"We can speculate all we want, but the fact is, we need to figure out where Felicity would've taken Leah. Maybe Eryn can track her phone."

Riley called Eryn, and when she answered he didn't waste time saying hello. "We think Felicity's the killer, and she's taken Leah. Can you track her phone?"

Eryn gasped, but didn't speak.

"Well?" he demanded.

"No."

"What about using the spyware app?"

"I'd need to have Leah's actual phone, not just an

image." She paused for a moment. "Sorry, Riley. The only way it can be done is to have someone in law enforcement ping cell towers."

Right. Something that would take a warrant and time—time they didn't have. "Could Piper help us get that done quickly?"

"I'll ask her and get back to you."

He hung up, his heart heavy, his brain mush. Where could Leah be? "I doubt Felicity took Leah to her apartment or even to Leah's house, but we should check them both out first."

"Also someone should interview Leah's manager."

"We need help. You get the team on a video call while I head to Leah's house." Riley grabbed his iPad from his tote bag and handed it to Alex then got the car on the road.

He wished for the first time in a long time that he was still a PPB officer and could run with lights and sirens. But there was no point in wishing. He had to face facts.

He'd failed Leah. She was missing. Depending on him. And he had to find her.

He heard Alex getting the team members to log into their secure video conferencing program as Riley wove in and out of busy Portland traffic. He tried to keep his full focus on the road, but his mind kept wandering to Leah and the danger she was in. It was hard for him to imagine Felicity as a killer. He just didn't see it.

"Maybe we're wrong," he said to Alex. "Maybe they really are just driving to the heliport."

Alex didn't answer right away.

Riley glanced at him.

His brow was furrowed. "What?

"If Felicity hadn't abducted Leah, why are neither of them answering their phones?"

"Because they're talking things out. Making up and they don't want to be disturbed. Or they're out of cell range."

"Could be."

"But you doubt it."

"Yeah," Alex answered. "You can't discount the fact that Felicity knew where Leah was when no one else could know."

"Okay, but I still think we should check the heliport. Can you call Lee and have him look for them?"

"Sure." He changed his focus to the iPad. "Hang on guys, I need to make a quick call."

Riley made a mental note to thank Alex for his help after they found Leah safe and sound.

What if you don't?

No. He couldn't think that way. Just couldn't. If he lost her—if Owen lost his mother—it would be too painful to bear.

Leah faded in and out of consciousness, her brain churning, grasping, trying to figure out where she was. What was happening. She heard music playing. It was "Never Let You Go," Riley singing the chorus bold and strong.

Loving you. Holding you.

Never let it end.

Never let you go.

You and me, it will always be.

Riley? Was he here? Singing? She loved the timbre of his voice. Loved him.

A female voice broke into the song, taking Leah's part. She knew that voice but couldn't place it. She worked harder to wend her way out of the murky darkness and up to the surface. She blinked her eyelashes. Blinked again. She was in a chair on a stage. But where?

She turned her head to look. Dizziness bombarded her. She closed her eyes and waited. Opened them again and moved her head slower. A fraction of an inch at a time until she could see her surroundings better.

The floor was worn wood, the front of the stage round. Balconies on both sides were held up with white pillars, the paint peeling. She knew this place. Loved it. It was an old movie theater remodeled to be a concert hall, now closed and in disrepair. The place where she and Riley played their first real concert. The place where their manager discovered them. Where their future could have blossomed.

The song continued. Riley only. Comforting her.

A smile came as memories washed over her. Memories of the joy of harmonizing with him. Of putting herself into the lyrics. Open and vulnerable. Something she hadn't done since they'd broken up. Sure, she put emotions into her songs, but they were never *those* emotions. Those were reserved for Riley.

The female voice came closer, the strum of a live guitar mixing with the recording behind her as the crescendo heightened the mood and the song raced toward the end.

No. Leah should be the one singing. Playing. She tried to turn her body, but she couldn't. She was tied to the chair with thick ropes.

What in the world? Was she dreaming?

"So you're awake." The woman's tone was ethereal and odd. She started singing again.

That was the voice Leah knew. It was Felicity. She was singing. Leah hadn't heard her sing in many years.

Why now? Why here, and what was up with the ropes?

"What's going on? Why am I tied up?" Leah asked when the song ended.

Felicity moved around front. She was holding Leah's favorite guitar. A Martin that Riley had given to her when they'd first met. He'd bought the same model for himself, but his was black and hers was mahogany and Brazilian rosewood. She hadn't used hers since they'd broken up and had stored it in her recording room at her house. She often wondered if Riley had kept his.

"How did you get my guitar?" she asked, still trying to clear the fog from her brain.

"It wasn't hard to lift your key and have a copy made while you were rehearsing." Felicity held her head high in a haughty pose.

"And Owen? How did you find out about him?"

"For someone with such a big secret to keep, you're very careless with your phone."

Her phone? What did that have to do with anything? "That's not true. I guard it carefully and have a strong password."

"Really?" She scoffed. "Do you hide your fingers when you enter the password? Do you take your phone onstage with you?"

"No, but it's in my locked dressing room."

"And who usually holds that key while you sing?"

"You, but I trusted you."

"And I looked out for myself."

Leah was so confused. "Why are you doing this?"

"The very fact that you have to ask should tell you everything."

Leah couldn't comprehend this. It was unfathomable. "I don't understand. We're friends. Sure, I didn't tell you about Owen, but otherwise our relationship was perfect."

Her eyes hardened into shards of granite. "Hah! Perfect for you maybe. Not for me. Never for me."

"You're unhappy?" Leah shook her head as she tried to understand. "But you never said anything."

"Because what would have happened if I did? You'd move me to another job. Or let me go."

"No. No, that wouldn't have happened. I would have fixed things. You're the very best assistant, and I know I told you that all the time."

She got in Leah's face, her sour coffee breath nauseating. "I. Don't. Want. To. Be. Your. Assistant. *I* am the star. Not you. *You* are mediocre at best. I would shine. But you killed my chance to shine, didn't you?"

This accusation was even more ridiculous. "What? When?"

"Wray Tipton heard me warming up the band for you earlier this month. He asked if I ever thought about performing. And what did you tell him?"

Leah had no idea what the record exec had to do with this, but she would play along to get the answer. "I told him exactly what you told me. That you quit performing years ago because you didn't want to do it. That you still liked the music business, and that's why you became my assistant."

She jerked her head up and strummed an angry, harsh chord on the guitar. "I didn't want to be a backup singer, hidden in your shadow. I was *so* over that. But a chance at being a headliner? I would've jumped at that, and you ruined it. You should have come to me and asked."

"I'm sorry I messed up, but if you'd told me, I could have fixed it. I might still—"

"No!" she shouted with another strum of the strings. "I already tried. Called Wray. Told him I was interested. He said he'd already signed someone new and wanted to focus on them." She got in Leah's face again, an ugly sneer taking away her beauty. "You ruined my life. Now I'm ruining yours and you're going to go to prison."

"Prison?" Leah gaped at her for a moment as the implication registered. "Did you...please say you didn't kill Jill and the others."

She grinned, evil and sick.

Everything suddenly became clear to Leah and blood pounded in her ears. "You stole my jewelry. Wrote the letters. Sent the ticket. But the tattoos?"

"Did those, too. Wasn't hard to learn to do such a simple design."

"But why do them?"

"I wanted to make it clear that the murders were connected to you. And it pointed the police away from me. Because I mean, why would I do a romantic tattoo?"

Leah's throat went dry. "So you abducted them all. Made them sit while you tattooed them. Then shot them in the back."

"Jill was the best. I told her you made me do the tattoo, and you demanded she attend your concert afterwards. She stormed backstage and was all set to let you have it. Instead..." She shrugged. "Carolyn was easier because it was at her house. I didn't have to come up with a story. Just let her think she was getting away and pumped two bullets in her back."

Leah didn't know what to say so she just stared. She recognized this woman standing before, her longtime friend, but the words coming from her mouth were unbelievable.

Felicity shook her head. "Don't look so shocked. They both deserved it. You know they did."

No one deserved that. Not even a cheater and a thief. "What about Helen? How could you hurt such an innocent woman?"

"Because. I had to make you pay." Felicity stabbed Leah in the chest.

"By killing people in my life." Leah glared at her. "That makes no sense."

"It would have if Riley hadn't butted in. The sheriff would already have you in jail, railroading you to a conviction."

"This is unbelievable. They died because you want me to go to prison for murder."

"My life working with you has been a prison for years. You deserved to know what that was like."

"If you were so unhappy, why didn't you leave?"

"And go where? Do what? I want to be a superstar, and I thought my best chance of making that happen was with you. I may not have known your exact secret back then, but I did know you were hiding something. I knew it would be exposed, and once it was, I'd be there to go on stage for you. It was only natural with the band knowing me from when I sang during warm-up because you wanted to baby your precious little voice. Doing your songs better than you did. Not your backup singer. Not your assistant with a passable voice. But *me*. Felicity Ivan. The next star who would take over when you failed."

Leah could barely believe all of this and had no idea what Felicity had planned now. "But you made a mistake, right? You took it too far by telling the press about Owen. It all backfired on you, didn't it? And Riley will fight to the death to clear my name, so your plan won't work. Not at all."

She huffed out a long breath. "And that's why we're here. I've had to go to Plan B. You've written a lovely suicide note, and you will end it all here. Where it all began. You will take your own life using the gun that killed the others."

"But you'll be blamed. Devon told Riley you were picking me up. They'll all know you lied."

Felicity glared at her. "Don't you know by now that I'm smarter than you? While you snoozed, I used my GPS to enter your home address and made a quick trip there to pretend to drop you off. Then you sent me a farewell email thanking me for picking you up from Devon's place and taking you home. For being so wonderful to you all these years, and suggesting I be considered by the label for a record deal."

She stopped to laugh in delight. "Then I told the GPS to go home and drove there as well just to be sure I covered my tracks. Once there, I opened your email, and since you told me you planned to end things here, I put this address in my GPS and hurried over here where I found you."

Leah was shocked. Beyond shocked. Felicity had gone to unbelievable lengths to achieve her goal and if Leah didn't come up with something, she would succeed.

She stood staring at Leah, her eyes a mixture of pride and elation, looking like she was mentally patting herself on the back. "I thought of everything. When the police arrive, I'll be so distraught. Give the performance of my life. Tell them that, yes, I lied about Riley wanting me to pick you up because I knew you wouldn't come with me otherwise, and I was desperate to make up with you. Then I'll show anyone and everyone who matters in this business your recommendation and give them my demo. I will easily step into your shoes, and my career will begin at last."

"That's not how a star is born, Felicity. You know that. The record execs will think you're tainted by your association with me. They won't want to have anything to do with you."

She strummed madly on the guitar and then looked up, her eyes wild, a bead of sweat slithering down her hairline. "It will work. I decree it." Her smile was as cold as death.

Leah couldn't believe what she was seeing. This woman wasn't her assistant. She was a crazed psychopath, and she really would end Leah's life. Just like she described.

22

Riley raced through Leah's house. "Leah, are you here? Leah?"

He couldn't control the desperation in his words, and he didn't care if Alex knew the level of despair he'd sunk to. He could hardly think. It was sheer adrenaline that had him going right now.

"She's not here," Alex stated the obvious.

"Then let's get out of here." Riley shoved his gun in his holster, bolted for the car, and pointed the vehicle toward Felicity's house. No need to go to the helipad as Lee had called to say they weren't there. And Gage interrogated Kraig, but he didn't have a clue about where Felicity might have taken Leah.

Riley tried desperately for about the thousandth time to figure out where she was. He caught a flash of metal ahead. Blinked hard. He was coming up too quickly on another car. He slammed on the brakes.

Alex pitched forward and planted a hand on the dash. "Hey, man. We can't help Leah if you kill us on the road."

"Sorry." Riley swerved around the car and floored it again but kept his speed within reason for the traffic.

Alex sat back. "So you're still in love with her then."

Riley glanced at Alex, who for once wasn't joking. If Riley admitted it, he wouldn't be deemed objective, and Alex would insist on taking charge. Something Riley wouldn't allow no matter what. But for some unfathomable reason, he felt like answering.

"Guess I am." He took a quick look at Alex to gauge his reaction.

His expression didn't change, but he shifted to face Riley. "What do you plan to do about it? Long-term, I mean."

That was the question of the hour. Week. Maybe year. And Riley felt lightheaded over the implications it held. "Not much I can do."

"Why not?"

"I'm not leaving Blackwell, and she doesn't stay in one place for long."

Alex watched him for a long time, his gaze as penetrating as a laser. "Ever think she might if you asked her?"

"No."

"Maybe her being on the road isn't as much about being a big star as it's running from whatever happened between the two of you back in the day."

"Nah," Riley answered quickly, as he didn't even need to think about that one. "You got that wrong. She never really cared about stardom, other than to show those who dissed her in her past that she'd amounted to something. She grew up dirt poor and craved the security that money provided. I would never make the kind of salary she needed, so she used her talent to find that security. With Carolyn's embezzlement, Leah lost most of her money, and she'll work hard to get it back."

Alex frowned. "I don't know, man. Sounds to me like the perfect time for you to step in and offer that security."

"Right." Riley rolled his eyes. "Like we're getting rich on

our salaries. I'm not complaining. Gage pays us very well, but it's not superstar kind of money."

"Not talking about money. I'm talking about security. You're like the rock of the team. Solid and steady. That's what she needs."

Riley glanced at Alex again. "When did you get to be Dr. Phil?"

"Been around Hannah too much I guess." He chuckled.

"I should probably be asking myself what Hannah would tell me to do."

"Hey, man, I thought I was channeling her just fine." Alex grinned.

Riley frowned. He felt like they were betraying Leah with this lighthearted banter when Felicity might be planning to harm her. Might have already hurt her. "You could be right. Could very well be right, but instead of thinking about this, I need to find Leah before something bad happens to her."

Riley pressed the gas pedal and nearly sang out for joy when they reached Felicity's house. Within seconds, he was out of the car and up the walkway. He wanted to kick in the door, but he had to determine if Leah was in danger first. He looked in the garage window. No car, but it was filled with stacks of bags, boxes, furniture, all piled high with narrow walkways between.

"Looks like she's a hoarder," Alex said from behind.

"I would never have expected this from Felicity. She seemed organized. Like a real neat freak."

"Nothing neat about this space." Alex moved back from the garage window. "No car. I doubt they're here."

Riley moved to the side window looking into the family room. More piles of stuff. "Seriously, she has a problem, but no sign of them. I say we go in and scout the place out."

"Agreed."

Riley went to the front door, kicked it in, and entered. The house smelled of rotting food, and there was only a narrow hallway between boxes, baskets, and furniture piled ceiling high in the rooms on both sides. He listened for a moment. Heard nothing. He crept down the narrow aisle, careful not to bump anything. If he disturbed one item, it could start an avalanche and bury them in a mound of trash.

He reached the kitchen area, which was actually pretty clear of debris except for dirty dishes filling the sink and a meat wrapper laying on the countertop, the source of the bad smell he supposed. The kitchen was open to the family room where one chair, an end table, and a television sat among tall piles of trash.

He found his way to another hallway, and Alex followed. They passed two bedrooms he couldn't even step foot inside and one bathroom. He opened the last door. The master bedroom. The space was clear of all debris and a neatly made queen-sized bed sat in the middle of the room. Three guitar cases were neatly lined up in one corner.

Riley glanced into the adjoining bathroom. "Clear."

Alex went to the closet door and jerked it open. "Whoa. Look at this."

Riley joined him. His mouth fell open, and he froze on the spot. The back wall was plastered with pictures of Leah, her face gouged out with a sharp object. Felicity also posted concert clippings and press releases where she crossed out Leah's name and inserted her own.

"Man, this is freaky to look at," Alex said. "Felicity wants to be Leah. Looks like we found her motive."

Riley didn't care about that right now. "Knowing her motive would be good, but knowing their location is what I need."

"We should look for a computer."

Riley spun and saw a laptop sitting on the nightstand. He ran across the room, passed the guitars, and sat on the bed to open the computer.

"Felicity's a musician?" Alex asked.

"She was once one of Leah's backup singers."

"Why'd she quit?"

"She and Leah didn't really say why."

"Well, she must still value music. Otherwise these guitars would be buried in her junk."

"Yeah, and if she wanted to become Leah, Felicity was likely keeping up on her skills in the event that a chance presented itself."

"Or she made a chance present itself."

Riley glanced up. "You mean like framing Leah for the murders or even leaking about Owen? Abducting her now?"

"All of the above."

Riley turned his attention back to the computer and looked in Felicity's email but found nothing of interest. He opened her Internet history. He pointed at Felicity's search for information on Rose City Theater. "Look at this. It's an old movie theater that was remodeled to be a concert hall. It closed years ago."

"And it's significant, why?

"Not sure, other than it's where Leah and I played our first real concert and our manager discovered us there."

"Why would Felicity be searching for it?"

Riley scrubbed a hand over his face. "I just don't know."

"If she's wanting to be Leah, it might make sense that Felicity would go back to where Leah's career began."

"It's a stretch but if we don't find any other lead, I say we go there."

"We have to look for something more promising. Something actionable." A lump grew in Riley's throat as he got to his feet. "I have a feeling we don't have much time to find her before Felicity does something terrible."

$$\sim$$

Felicity stepped to center stage and adjusted the microphone. She glanced back at Leah. "I've listened to you like how many times? A zillion and one. So now you're going to listen to me."

"For how long?" Leah asked hoping to figure out how much time she had to find a way out of this or for Riley to discover her location.

Felicity sneered. "Until I get tired of performing. With all your hits, it'll be several hours at least."

Perfect.

Felicity began singing "Never Let You Go" again, and Leah looked down at the rope holding her snuggly to the chair. She tried wiggling, but Felicity had done her job. She'd secured the rope tighter than Leah thought possible.

Felicity had placed Leah's arms by her side, her hands resting on her lap, making them nearly useless. She looked down to search for the knot, hoping it was in reach. It was dead center of her body but higher than Leah would've liked. Still, she shifted until she could touch the knot with the tips of her fingers.

The haunting melody of the song was reaching the finale, and Leah dropped her hands back to her lap. She didn't want Felicity to catch her trying to escape. With Felicity's fragile hold on reality, Leah didn't need added incentive for her to kill her.

Felicity glanced back at Leah. "That was so much better than your rendition, don't you agree? You've become lax. Stale and uninteresting. That's why your career tanked. Okay, maybe it also had to do with the fact that I didn't follow up on so many promotional things that Gabby assigned to me." A snide grin snaked across her mouth. "Now. The next song. My favorite."

She launched into Leah's second hit song, and Leah didn't bother to listen but put her full attention on the ropes. She shifted, and hunched down, moving the knot lower. She strained against the ropes. They cut into her arms, but she pushed harder.

Yes! She got hold of the knot and dug her fingers into it. No movement. She tried again. Digging harder, the scratchy rope ripped into her tender flesh, but she didn't care. She dug deep. Got it moving. A fraction of an inch, but at least it released some. She kept going.

Yes! Yes! She was doing it.

She pushed harder and opened the knot enough to slide her finger in then tug. The loop loosened. Leah almost cried out with joy but bit her lip to stop. She shimmied her shoulders to release the rope. It started slipping, but she had to catch the ends with her hand and flip the cord around to keep it going.

The end of the song was coming.

She was nearly there. She had to work. Harder. Faster.

Hurry! Hurry!

Frantic now, she got it moving at a good clip.

Grab. Flip. Wait for the rope to come around. Grab. Flip again.

Only a few circles remaining, she hefted her arms high, pushing the rope up and around her neck. She jerked it over her head and got to her feet.

Only a few more lines of the song remained. She turned and crept as quietly as she could across the floor. Each creak, each click of a heel made her stomach churn with acid. She reached the backstage area and ran for the door. The sight brought her up short.

No. Please, no. Not chains.

"That was foolish, Leah," Felicity's voice came from the stage.

Oddly calm, it scared Leah even more. She shot a look around. Searching. Looking. Where to go?

The catwalk. She remembered it led to another exit on the other side of the stage. She ran for the steps. Climbed up the rickety metal stringers. The structure trembled under her weight.

Please let them hold. Please!

She reached the top. Stepped out on the catwalk, an even more unstable venture. She thought to turn back. Saw and heard Felicity on the steps. Leah had no choice. She had to go forward. She slid her foot ahead, gripping the handrail tightly. Inch by inch she moved.

"Where do you think you're going?" Felicity asked, her voice coming from the bridge. "I have a gun and won't hesitate to use it."

She'd shot three women in the back already, so Leah knew it was the truth. She came to a stop and turned around. Felicity stood, gun raised, that glare of hatred in her eyes.

"But you have to let me go," Leah said, feeling confident. "If you shoot me at a distance it won't look like a suicide, and your plans will all fail."

Felicity tilted her head in thought, then a revolting smile slid across her lips. "There's more than one way to end your life."

She tucked her gun in her waistband and hung onto the railing then started stomping on the catwalk, shaking Leah. The metal groaned and started swinging.

Leah held tightly to the railing.

Felicity stomped harder. Harder. And harder, putting her whole weight into it.

Leah heard a rending of metal, and the structure beneath her suddenly let go. She clung to the railing but it went too, plummeting her toward the stage floor.

She screamed, her lungs aching with the force, but what good did it do? Even if she survived the fall, no one was there to hear her.

23

The scream was high-pitched and terrified, and it tore at Riley's heart.

Leah. She was in trouble. Was he too late?

Please don't let her be hurt.

Riley slipped through the concert hall door, and quietly entered, Alex hot on his heels.

He heard Felicity hysterically laughing from above. "That'll teach you to cross me. You're already losing strength. Won't be long now, and it'll be over."

Footsteps sounded on the metal stairs ahead. Descending. Coming closer.

Riley took cover on one side of the hallway behind a metal pillar, Alex the other side. Footsteps tapped on the wood floor heading their direction. He soon heard Felicity humming, her tone joyful.

That meant only one thing in Riley's book. Felicity had killed Leah. He felt sick to his stomach and wanted to hurl on the spot.

No. Don't think that way. Trust God. For once in your life, trust Him.

Riley took a long breath, held it, and directed Alex to

take Felicity down. Alex nodded. Riley held his breath. Waited. Her footsteps tapped closer. Came even with Riley. Passed. Alex pounced and took her down.

"Leah. Where's Leah?" Riley demanded.

Felicity laughed, her tone hysterical again. "Wouldn't you like to know?"

"Leah!" Riley yelled at the top of his lungs. "Leah, where are you?"

"Here. Help. Take the catwalk steps."

She was alive. Alive! He nearly dropped to the floor with relief. But she wasn't safe yet. She needed him.

He ran in the direction of her voice. He found the stairs. Saw the twisted metal structure dangling above the stage floor.

"Leah?"

"Climb the steps. I'm holding on. Barely."

"Hold on, honey, I'm coming." Riley wanted to pound up the stairs, but they were shaking, and he didn't want to risk hurting Leah.

"Hurry." She pleaded, creasing his entire body with anguish. "I'm slipping."

He reached the top. Found her hands gripped on a barely intact railing, the end pulling from the brick wall as shards rained down on her.

He quickly assessed the situation. He couldn't remain standing and reach her. He got on his belly. Hooked his feet into the side rails. Lowered his upper body over the edge. Stretched out. Reached for her hand and came up short.

He shifted, easing his feet forward another few inches, still too short, but if he moved ahead even another inch or two he'd be at the wrong angle and couldn't pull her up.

"You have to let go with your upper hand and reach up to me," he said making eye contact.

"Let go? No. I can't."

"You have to, honey. I can't lower myself any further."

"But I'll fall."

"I won't let that happen."

"I don't..."

He met her gaze and held it, conveying confidence. "Trust me, honey. Trust me. Trust God. You can do this. On three. Reach up and I've got you. I've always got you."

She bit her lip for a moment, tears mixing with terror in her eyes. "Okay. I'll try."

"Here we go," he said infusing his tone with confidence for her benefit. Maybe his, too. "One. Two. Three."

She jerked her arm free and raised it high. He grabbed her wrist. Her other hand slipped. She swung like a clock pendulum. His arm felt like it was ripping from the socket, but he held.

Her life was literally in his hand. And it started sweating.

She was slipping. Falling.

No. *God, help me hold on.*

"Lift your other arm," he shouted.

She raised it.

He strained harder. Touched it but couldn't hold on.

He stretched out more, his muscles aching with the exertion. He caught hold of her other hand. Held. Her swaying stopped.

"Now what?" she cried out.

"I'll pull you up until you can touch the platform and crawl over me."

She looked uncertain, but he couldn't let that impact him. He would not fail her. Never again. "Ready?"

"Yes."

"Okay, here we go." He lifted her, the muscles in his forearms burning and his back screaming. He kept lifting. She let go and grabbed onto the platform.

"Okay, I can do this." She got a foothold on the dangling railing and climbed up, landing on top of him.

He let out a long sigh and offered a prayer of thanks.

When she scrambled over him, he pulled himself up and turned. Every muscle in his body shook from the exertion and he gulped in long breaths to calm his racing pulse. She was *alive*. She sat trembling at the top of the steps, her back to him. He scooted forward and slid his legs around her to draw her back against his chest, wrapping his arms tightly around her. He pressed his forehead against her soft hair, and if he could find a way to hold her closer he would.

He'd almost lost her.

Thank you, God. Thank you.

Emotions whirred in his body. He couldn't pinpoint what a single one of them meant—except guilt. "I'm so sorry I let you down. I will never let anyone hurt you again. I promise."

His words came out more forcefully than he intended, and she startled for a moment before looking over her shoulder at him.

She met his gaze. Held it. She didn't say a word. She didn't have to. Her expression said it all. She didn't plan to be around long enough for him to keep that promise, so it made no difference.

Three hours after Felicity was hauled off to jail and the police had interviewed Leah until she was about ready to scream, she stood toe-to-toe with Riley in his living room. One would think that after the near-death experience they could work things out, but no. They'd reached the same impasse again. She needed to go back to work, which meant traveling. He wouldn't go with her. Old news. Old problem.

But now they had another one. A big one. She didn't want to have this conversation, but it was a must.

"We need to work things out for Owen's sake," Riley said, his face stony and unreadable.

"I…" Leah couldn't get any more words out, so she touched his cheek.

He pulled in a sharp breath, and his gaze locked on hers. Gone was the animosity, and love lit his eyes, making her bold.

"I love you, Riley," she said with every ounce of conviction she could muster. "I'm sure I always will."

He drew her into his arms, holding her like he might never let her go, and she reveled in the feeling. Reveled in it too much.

"I love you, too," he whispered against her hair and drew back to cup the side of her face.

His head lowered. He was going to kiss her.

She wanted him to. How she wanted him to, but she couldn't allow it. No matter her love for him. They couldn't get over their differences.

She pushed free of his arms and stepped back. "I'm sorry. I can't. I wish things were different, but I guess it's not meant to be."

His expression hardened to solid granite. "I'd hoped for Owen's sake that you might consider staying here. You wouldn't have to live with me, but if we were in the same town it would be easier to share custody."

Shared custody. The thought still turned her insides into tight knots. "It would be extremely hard for me to travel from here. I need to be near an airport."

"I could fly you to Portland in the helo."

"I'm sure Gage won't want his helicopter used for our personal business."

"Then once you get back on solid ground you can buy a small helicopter." He was starting to sound desperate.

She hated that she'd put him in this position and wished it could be different. "You'll get tired of having to shuttle me to Portland."

"Fine." He fisted his hands, lifted one, and looked like he planned to punch the wall, then let if fall with a resigned sigh. "Then we'll set a custody schedule, and Owen will alternate his time between here and Portland, but once he's in school that's going to be an issue."

"We'll figure that out when we have to." Her phone rang and she was thankful for the interruption, though it wouldn't change this conversation. Nothing would.

"That's Kraig's ringtone." She dug out her phone and lifted it to her ear with shaky hands. "Tell me you have good news for me."

"I do." His voice was more animated than she'd ever heard. "Turns out when the fickle public heard about Felicity trying to kill you, they forgot all about Owen and are supporting you again. Our promoter wants to resume the tour."

"Are you kidding?" She shrieked. "When?"

"Tomorrow. The crew and staff are already on the road."

"That means I have to leave around lunchtime tomorrow."

"Gabby's got major magazines and a couple of news stations calling for live interviews with you—she's working them into your schedule. And I've already been searching for a new assistant for you. Until then, I've brought in a temp to help you out."

Leah's head spun. Her fans wanted her again. The public wanted her. She had interviews and concerts lined up for her. What wonderful, shocking news! Her career was unexpectedly taking off, and she could finally make up the money that Carolyn stole from her. "Wow. I...yes! Thank you. I'll make my travel plans and email the information to you."

She disconnected the call and found Riley staring at her.

"You're leaving?" His voice held a finality she could hardly bear.

She shoved her phone into her pocket and took a moment to find the right words, but there were none. "The fans have turned in my favor again. Seems Felicity trying to kill me brought them back to my side, and the tour is on again. Even the magazines and news want to interview me."

"When do you have to go?"

"After lunch tomorrow."

He clenched his jaw and the muscles worked hard. "And what about Owen?"

She hadn't even had a chance to think about that. "Normally, I'd take him with me, but would you like me to leave him with you? I mean, if you want me to."

His eyes darkened with emotions she couldn't read. "Of course I want."

"And you're sure you can handle that with your work schedule?"

"Hannah and Eryn will help out."

"My mom could help, too, if needed."

"Thanks."

There. Done. She was going. He was staying.

She considered reaching out to him. To touch him one last time, but if she did, she wouldn't go. "I better get going on my travel plans and spend some time with Owen before I leave."

Riley nodded, but didn't speak. She was suddenly back in his apartment years ago, walking out on him, and she could barely breathe. She hurried to the bedroom before she broke down.

You're doing the right thing for Owen and his future. And for your band members, the crew, their families. You will be helping so many people while keeping your commitments.

She had to do this.

Then why did she want to curl in a ball on the bed, pull the covers over her head, and never come out?

The next morning, Riley pulled his guitar case from under his bed. Stickers from the many places he'd played with Leah decorated the case. He ran his fingers over them. Let the memories flow until he couldn't think about the past any longer.

Did him no good. She was leaving. Walking out on him again. And leaving Owen as a consolation prize. Riley could hardly believe it. He was in love with her, and she was leaving. Going away. Tossing him aside.

How had this happened to him again? How had he let it happen?

He flipped the latches and jerked out the guitar, the black finish still glossy after little use, and concentrated on tuning it to keep his mind busy. Then he tried a few cords. His fingertips were soft, his calluses from holding chords gone long ago, but it felt good to play. Weird, because when Leah left him before, he could barely stand the sight of this guitar. Too many memories. Now he thought it might soothe him.

He launched into a favorite song. Not one of theirs. A pop song. Started singing and lost himself in the music.

There was a knock on his bedroom door.

"Come in," he called out, expecting Leah or her mother, but Hannah poked her head inside.

"Wow," she said, her eyes wide with admiration. "You're really good."

"Thanks, but I'm just a hack."

She shook her head. "No, you're not, and you know it. You should play at our cookout down at the beach today."

Their lunch cookout was only a few hours away. He couldn't just perform after all this time. "I'm so out of practice."

"Would you do it for me?" Her pleading tone was one he'd heard often enough and at times had even given into.

As he would do now, because he couldn't bear to see another woman disappointed in him. "Sure."

"Mind if we talk a minute?" she asked.

Yeah, he minded when his emotions were so raw, but she was a good friend, and he needed a good friend right now. He patted the corner of the bed. "I've been expecting you."

A delicate eyebrow went up in surprise. "You have?"

"Yeah. You butt in whenever one of us has a personal issue, so I figured you'd want me to talk about it." He grinned at her.

She rolled her eyes and sat on the corner of the bed, her slight weight barely making the mattress move. "You never said why you and Leah broke up the first time."

The familiar pain settled in his gut, and he had to take a breath before answering. "I loved music but never the way she did. I played to relax and spend time with her. But we caught the eye of a record label executive, and they offered us a recording contract."

"That's amazing."

"Yeah, it was...until it wasn't."

"What happened?"

He looked down at the guitar, the memory as real as if it had happened yesterday, and he recounted the story for

Hannah. "They wouldn't offer her a solo gig. I essentially killed her career before it started, and we broke up."

She shook her head. "You didn't kill it. Look how successful she is."

"Yes, but it took a few more years for her to get there."

"Then that was what God wanted."

"Why does what God wants have to be so hard sometimes?" He sighed. "I loved her, you know. Man, I really did and sticking to my guns, knowing she would leave?" He closed his eyes for a second, the memory painful. "Was the hardest thing I've ever had to do."

"You still do love her from what I can see," Hannah said. "So why are you letting her go?"

"She needs to leave."

"She might not if you ask her to stay," Hannah said softly.

Hannah was a wise woman, and he wanted her to be right, but that was only wishful thinking. "It's not that simple. Nothing has changed between us. Leah still needs the security of making money. Which means travel and concerts—and now she's got the public clamoring for interviews and all. I don't want to live that life."

He shrugged. "Maybe if we'd reconnected right after I'd been injured and left PPB, things would be different. But now I'm here, and I'm not leaving. We're a family, you know. And now, thanks to you and Gage—all the others, too—I can see what I'm missing in life. I want to settle down. Enjoy raising Owen. Stay here. Not take endless trips in buses and spend nights in hotels. I love her, but I can't deny who I am. And what I believe God wants for me."

"I applaud that, Riley, I really do. A man who knows his mind and is willing to follow God's will no matter the consequences is a powerful thing." She squeezed his arm. "Just know that it will work out. It always does."

"Yeah, you're right. But it could mean a world of hurt before it does."

~

Leah trudged across the sand dune toward the music floating into the salty ocean air, shocked that the morning had flown by and the whole group was gathered around a campfire. She was drawn to the music as much as she was repulsed by the sound. Riley was playing the first song they'd written together. A song of love and a future that they'd never had. The melody drew her like the Pied Piper's flute, and she wanted to forget her career. Forget her need for security. Forget the fickle public and untrustworthy people surrounding her. Throw herself into Riley's arms and stay. Broke and poor...just stay. Be loved and give love.

Oh, Riley.

The pain was almost more than she could bear, and she dropped to the sand warm from the overhead sun. It cradled her knees and reminded her of the hours of lazy summer fun with Riley. She'd splash in the ocean as he surfed, and then they'd build a fire and noodle around on their guitars, creating music that no one had ever heard. What she wouldn't give to have such blissful days again, Owen at their side.

Her alarm sounded on her phone. Abrupt and sharp it pealed into the open air, belying the quiet comfort surrounding her.

Time to go. To climb in her taxi and leave. Leave all of this behind.

She dried her tears and rose. She climbed the dune, knowing the Blackwell team members were having lunch on the beach. As she crested the top, she stopped dead in her tracks. Riley had quit playing and singing. He was holding Owen. Showing him chords on the glossy black guitar that was part of their matching pair.

Their son's pudgy face was alive with such joy, such happiness, she had to take a breath or risk hyperventilating. She took another one. And another. Owen was a happy child on the whole, but this look—the love in his face mixed with a sense of belonging—was new to him. To her. She'd never had this with her father. The man who walked out like she meant nothing.

She didn't want Owen to have to experience any pain when it came to his father. She wanted him to know joy and happiness and the love of an amazing man. And Riley was just that. An amazing wonderful, awesome, godly man who would never leave Owen. Never leave her.

Oh, man. She'd been such a fool. Thinking money would secure her son's happiness. It wouldn't. Being with his father full-time might not either, but it was a step in the right direction. And being with his mother, too? It would bring her happiness as well.

She took out her phone and dialed Kraig before she changed her mind again. "I've had a change of plans. I won't be able to make it today. We can discuss the remainder of the tour, but I've got something to do right now that can't wait. I'll call you tomorrow." She quickly hung up and silenced her phone because she knew he would call back. She shoved it into her pocket and jogged down the dune to where the group sat around a blazing fire, some roasting hotdogs others already eating theirs. Laughter and witty banter flowing through the group.

One by one, they looked up, caught sight of her and conversation stilled. Gazes narrowed. A few were angry. She got that. She'd hurt one of their own, and she was a pariah in their group now. But she couldn't let that deter her.

She headed straight for Riley and Owen.

"Mommy." Owen squirmed free to grab her legs and hug them.

Riley frowned. "Did you come to say goodbye?"

"No," she said and took his hand to tug him to his feet. "I came to say hello."

His uncertain expression sent an ache through her heart.

She smiled to ease his apprehension and took his guitar to gently lay it in the case. "We need to talk alone for a minute."

He stood staring at her. Not moving, a hard kind of certainty in his eyes. Certainty that they were over. Her fault. She'd hurt him so badly again, but had she left things too late?

And how did she proceed? She hadn't planned this out and everyone was watching them. Now uncertain herself, she glanced at the others.

Hannah met her gaze and offered an encouraging smile, bolstering Leah's confidence.

Hannah held up a bag of marshmallows. "Owen, do you want to make s'mores?"

"Yes!" Owen ran to her.

"Thank you," Leah mouthed for Hannah's support and turned back to Riley.

She took his hand. He tried to remove it, but she held tight and dragged him away from the group. She kept going until they were out of earshot. She'd rather not still be in full sight of the others, but with a flat, wide-open beach, she had no choice.

She faced Riley and drew in a breath to reinforce her determination.

He freed his hand, his expression tight. "What's going on, Leah?"

"I've come to ask you to marry me." She smiled and tried to take his hands.

His eyes narrowed, and he stepped back. "I'm not in the mood for jokes."

Not the reaction she expected at all. She stepped closer to him. "No joke. I've been so dumb. Choosing the wrong thing when the right thing was right in front of me. I want a future with you. A family with you. Owen and more children."

"And how did you reach that conclusion?" His lips pressed flat.

She didn't think this would be so difficult for him to accept, but she deserved his suspicion. "Seeing you and Owen just now. His expression. I kept telling myself that financial security would ensure his future, but a father who loves him will do far more to ensure that. I thought this was all about me making our future secure. But it's not about that."

She paused and breathed deeply to go on. "It's about my father bailing on us and me vowing to always provide for Owen, not trusting anyone else. But you aren't like my father. Nothing like him. You're trustworthy and loyal, and I know I can count on you. I don't have to do this alone." She paused, tears wetting her eyes. "If you'll have me after everything I've put you through, I would like us to make this work and be a real family."

He tilted his head and stared at her. "You really mean this? You're not going to change your mind?"

She shook her head emphatically. "No, I'm positive. You have every right to be skeptical. I would be if I was you. But I already called Kraig and told him I wasn't coming. I owe it to my fans and team to work out the rest of this tour, but maybe Gage would give you some time off and you and Owen could come with me."

"What about all the interviews and people wanting your story? You've got everyone's attention now. Your career will really take off."

She pulled her hand through her hair. "Well, I was thinking maybe I could do remote interviews...maybe from here? I don't have to do too many, and Gabby can handle the social media news. I just owe it to my fans to give them the truth of what happened—otherwise all kinds of crazy stories will come out. I don't want that to be my legacy...for Owen's sake. Then I will be done with this life and settle down. I want to be far away from that crowd and be a good mother to Owen." She paused. "You're already a wonderful father. I want us to be a family together."

He met her gaze and watched her carefully.

"I love you, Riley," she rushed on. "I've never stopped, and I promise I never will."

He started to reach for her hands, then let his arms fall to his side. "What about your music when the tour is over? You love performing, and I don't want you to resent me someday because you gave it up to be here."

"I haven't thought that far." Devon's suggestion came to mind. "Do they have churches around here?"

"Of course, why?"

"I could fill that need by playing in a worship band, if one would have me. Maybe playing with you again and writing songs. Just for fun. Or maybe we could sell the songs. I don't know, but I *do* know I'll be okay and never resent you."

His eyes were wide now and glowing. "You really mean this, don't you?"

"I do. So what do you say, Riley Allen Glen?" She looked up at him, knowing her love equaled the light burning in his eyes. "Will you marry me?"

"Yes. Yes. Yes!" He lifted her into his arms and spun

around until he dropped to the sand, cradling her against the fall. "Yes. I'll marry you. Today if you want. Or tomorrow. Or the next day. Any day." He held her snugly in his lap and kissed her with abandon, and she kissed him right back, getting lost in his love for her.

"What's the matter, Mommy?" Owen's voice came from nearby. "Did you fall down? Are you hurt? Is Daddy kissing it away?"

"Yes, Daddy has kissed all my hurt away." Leah smiled at Owen. "And if you get hurt in the future, he'll kiss your hurt away, too."

Riley tugged her to her feet, scooped Owen up into his arms, then pulled them together into a family hug. "Any hurt we face in the future, we face together. The three of us. Forever."

Waves of joy left Leah breathless. Being held in this man's arms, him by her side loving their son, and God completely in control of their lives was all the security she would ever need.

∼

Enjoy this book?

Reviews are the most powerful tool to draw attention to my books for new readers. I wish I had the budget of a New York publisher to take out ads and commercials but that's not a reality. I do have something much more powerful and effective than that.

A committed and loyal bunch of readers like you.

If you've enjoyed *Cold Fear*, I would be very grateful if you could leave an honest review on the bookseller's site. It can be as short as you like. Just a few words is all it takes. Thank you very much.

Dear Reader:

Thank you so much for reading COLD FEAR, book five in my Cold Harbor series featuring Blackwell Tactical.

Book 1 - COLD TERROR
Book 2 - COLD TRUTH
Book 3 - COLD FURY
Book 4 - COLD CASE
Book 5 - COLD FEAR
Book 6 - COLD PURSUIT
Book 7 - COLD DAWN

I'd like to invite you to learn more about the books in the series as they release and about my other books by signing up for my newsletter and connecting with me on social media or even sending me a message. I hold monthly giveaways that I'd like to share with you, and I'd love to hear from you. So stop by this page and join in!

www.susansleeman.com/sign-up/

Susan Sleeman

She's on the run...

When Whitney Rochester's brother-in-law kills her sister, Whitney fears for the life of her niece and nephew. She can't leave them in her murderous brother-in-law's care so she goes on the run with the children to be sure they're out of his reach. Or so she thinks until a killer shows up— weapon in hand—at the ski resort where she works and targets her.

But he's in pursuit.

Former Recon Marine Alex Hamilton is working an undercover investigation at the resort when a crazed man wielding a gun takes out a guy in close proximity to Whitney. Despite not having the support of the Blackwell Tactical team, other than their forensic expert, Samantha Willis, Alex isn't about to let the shooter harm Whitney or anyone else. When a blinding snowstorm triggers avalanches in the area, it's too dangerous for the police to reach the secluded resort to stop the killer. Alex and Sam must protect everyone at the resort while they feverishly work to figure out if Whitney or the victim were the intended target. As Alex and Whitney grow close and the killer strikes again, Alex has to find and take down this madman, even if it means risking his own life.

~

Chapter One

One Month Earlier

Whitney's mind spun frantically. *Take the children. Run. Now. Fast. Far.*

But how, when a monster with a gun held her captive?

Looking for an escape, she shot a look around the deserted alley. Angry clouds darkened the noon sky, and heavy rain pelted down on her, icing her to the core.

Percy backed her up against the alley wall, a gun barrel jabbed into her stomach. His mouth thinned into a hard, unforgiving line. "Where are my kids, Whitney? They're mine, not yours, and I *will* have them back."

She tried to escape, but he pumped iron on a regular basis, making him strong. Crazy strong. An indestructible wall of cruelty. He glowered at her with hard brown eyes, wet strands of coal black hair falling in his face.

Her breath stilled. She tried to take another. Gasped. Couldn't manage it. The hospital Emergency Department, her place of employment, was merely a few feet away. No one would see her die right outside of their doors.

"Please," she choked out.

He sneered at her. "Just tell me where the kids are, and I'll let you live."

He was lying. *Get a grip. Do something. Save yourself.*

He shoved a corded arm against her throat, his arm crushing her throat.

She opened her mouth. Tried for a breath. Even the tiniest sip of the chilly, wet Portland air. Nothing got through. Nothing but rasping in the back of her throat.

Panic settled in, clawing its way into her core, warning of death.

She felt her eyes bulging. Growing in their sockets.

She raised her hands in defense. Gun in her abdomen, she shouldn't try to fight him, but she had to. Her arm shot up and clawed his face—nails digging, slicing, drawing blood.

He swore, a long curse filled with venom, and back-handed her face, the strike splitting her lip. He stepped back and swiped at the blood on his hand, rain smearing it.

Her lungs unlocked, and she gulped in a sharp breath. Too much too fast, and pain sliced through her chest. Her jacket and scrubs were soaked, and she shivered, gasping for air.

A sudden glassiness in his deep eyes was even more alarming, a slick grin following. He jammed the cold barrel against her temple. "Tell me where they are. You have until the count of ten."

She would never reveal the children's location. No matter the pain he inflicted. No matter if he killed her. She was their protector now.

She didn't move except to breathe.

"Ten," he snapped, a conqueror gloating over his prey. "Nine...eight..."

She tuned him out. So much could happen in ten seconds. Like Percy—her brother-in-law—escaping from jail as he awaited trial for murdering her sister. Her sweet, loving sister, Vanessa.

Escaped. He'd really escaped.

Overpowered a deputy on the way to the courthouse. Now here he was to claim his kids.

And to kill Whitney, as she was the reason he'd been arrested.

"Seven...six...five." He shifted on his feet, drawing her attention.

I'm going to die. Right here. Here, where I can practically reach out and touch my coworkers.

"Four." His face tightened, reminding her of the night three weeks ago when she'd found him standing over her sister's broken body at the base of the stairs in their comfortable suburban home. A glare in his eyes. His chest heaving with anger. His face red, his hands fisted.

She'd run to her sister, checked her pulse, and when she found none, she called 911. He tried to calm her down and claim it was an accident, but Whitney knew differently and told the police as much. He'd been arrested, and as the police hauled him off, he threatened to make her pay.

And now he would.

"Three." He grinned. He was enjoying this. The sick, sick man. No way would she ever let him find his children. Not while she was breathing—which might be only three more seconds.

"C'mon, Whitney. There's no need for you to die." He abruptly stroked the side of her cheek.

She flinched.

"Two." Gone was the smile, a raging inferno burning in his eyes.

He really was going to kill her. Her heart slammed against the wall of her chest.

Please. Please. The kids need me. They can't handle another loss.

Panic crawled up her spine. Her chest froze. Maybe her heart stopped.

He opened his mouth. She waited for the number. For *one*. For death.

A car careened around the corner and screeched to a halt by the ED door. Percy whipped around, mouth still open, that word—*one*—never uttered.

A lumberjack of a man jumped out of the vehicle. He was huge. Could overpower Percy. Not a bullet, but...

Scream!

She screeched with all her might. "Help!"

The driver spun, his eyes catching the scene. "You there. Leave her alone."

Percy jerked back. His gaze darted around.

The monster-sized man came at them with big lumbering steps, bellowing and waving his hands. "Get away from her. Now. I mean it. Move."

Emotions waged war on Percy's face. He glanced at the gun. Lifted it.

"No!" She slammed her shoulder into him. Knocked him off kilter. He stumbled. Caught his footing.

Lumberjack man reached out to grab Percy. He slithered out from under the big beefy arms and sprinted away. Down the alley. Into the fog.

Lumberjack went after him. The sound of Percy's sharp footsteps snapped into the air. Lumberjack's solid thuds followed.

Whitney hyperventilated and fell back against the wall, rain cascading over her hair and running down her face, her mind a jumble of thoughts. She'd only known this level of terror one other time—the day she'd discovered her sister.

She wanted to drop to the rain-soaked ground, but she had to rescue the kids. She'd get to them before he could.

No. No. You can't. The kids needed her to get it together. Act. Move.

Where could she go?

288

Think, Whitney. Think.

Not home. No way. Percy would find her there. Take her niece and nephew.

He obviously didn't know which daycare she'd selected for nine-year-old Isaiah and three-year-old Zoey. She had to get to them. A plan forming in her mind, she scrambled around until she found her purse on the wet asphalt where she'd dropped it when he'd grabbed her. She snatched up the strap and ran for the parking garage. This could be the last time she ever saw this place since she started her nursing career eight years ago. She couldn't even let them know she wouldn't return.

She would have to cut all ties. Even with her parents.

She found her little Honda in the garage. Fumbled for the keys. Dropped them on the concrete. Scrambled to locate them and get the car open. Inside, she raced the engine and pointed it toward the nearest ATM. She couldn't go home for anything and would need to take out as much cash as possible to survive until she could figure out how to get more. Change her identity. The kids' identities too. And get a job. She couldn't continue to work as a nurse. It would be too easy for him to find her that way.

How in the world would she support the three of them?

A wave of hysteria bubbled up inside.

How had her life come to this? Nearly dying. Planning to assume a new identity. Running with two young kids to... where? She started hyperventilating again. She wasn't strong enough for this.

"Help me, God!" she cried out.

Calm down. Freaking out won't help anyone.

Yes, she had to stay calm. For Isaiah and Zoey.

"Call 911," she said to the car's infotainment system.

The dispatcher answered, and she quickly recounted the attack, swiping at her tears, her voice catching, stopping and swallowing hard too many times to count, but she got out her story. All of it. Every necessary word.

"I've dispatched an officer to the scene," the serene dispatcher said, her voice soothing, almost entrancing. "He'll be with you soon."

"I'm not at the hospital. I left. I have to go now. Find him. Please. Arrest him. He wants to take the kids. I can't let him." She ended the call and had the system dial her mother.

"Percy escaped from jail," she blurted out. "Tried to kill me."

A gasp filtered through the phone. "No. Oh no. It can't be true. Are you okay? Where are you?"

"It's true, and I'm fine," Whitney replied, barely able to believe it herself as she recalled the attack. "I'm on my way to the daycare to pick up the kids. Then I'm taking off. Not sure where I'll go, but I can't tell you or he might try to get it out of you."

"You think he'll come here?"

Whitney hated hearing the frantic fear in her mother's voice, but there was good reason to be afraid and hopefully it would help keep her parents safe. "Yes, and I think you and Dad should get out of town for a while, too. Try not to leave a trail that he can follow."

"Oh, dear...no...oh my."

"Go *now*, Mom. After me, you're his next target."

"Yes. We'll go. I love you, sweetie."

Tears came full force now. Whitney could barely see to drive. "I love you, too, Mom. I'll keep watching the news and call you the minute he's back in custody."

She ended the conversation on that positive note. She had to believe law enforcement would find him and arrest him again.

She instructed her car to dial the daycare center. The phone rang. Once. Twice. Three times.

"C'mon. C'mon." She slammed a fist into the wheel.

One more ring and the director's cheery greeting rang out.

"It's Whitney Rochester." She tried to sound calm, but panic edged through her tone. "Isaiah and Zoey. Are they okay?"

"Fine, why?"

"My brother-in-law has escaped from jail." When she'd registered the kids, she told them all about Percy as the staff had to understand the potential danger. "He knows nothing about your place, but I wanted to alert you and tell you I'm on my way to pick up the kids."

"We should call the police."

"My next call," she said. "I'm ten minutes out. Hide them if you have to, but make sure they're safe. Please. Please. Don't let anything happen to them."

"You know we'll do our best." Her sincerity was comforting, but what could a petite little woman of bird-sized proportions do against the anger-driven Percy should he show up?

Whitney floored the gas, the tires spinning and spitting over the rain-slicked road and prayed that their best was good enough to keep the precious children out of a rampaging killer's hands.

Available now at most online booksellers!

For More Details Visit -
www.susansleeman.com/books/cold-pursuit/

BOOKS IN THE COLD HARBOR SERIES

Blackwell Tactical – this law enforcement training facility and protection services agency is made up of former military and law enforcement heroes whose injuries keep them from the line of duty. When trouble strikes, there's no better team to have on your side, and they would give everything, even their lives, to protect innocents.

For More Details Visit -
www.susansleeman.com/books/cold-harbor/

THE TRUTH SEEKERS

People are rarely who they seem

A twin who never knew her sister existed, a mother whose child is not her own, a woman whose father is anything but her father. All searching. All seeking. All needing help and hope.

Meet the unsung heroes of the Veritas Center. The Truth Seekers – a team, that includes experts in forensic anthropology, DNA, trace evidence, ballistics, cybercrimes, and toxicology. Committed to restoring hope and families by solving one mystery at a time, none of them are prepared for when the mystery comes calling close to home and threatens to destroy the only life they've known.

For More Details Visit -
www.susansleeman.com/books/truth-seekers/

HOMELAND HEROES SERIES

When the clock is ticking on criminal activity conducted on or facilitated by the Internet there is no better team to call other than the RED team, a division of the HSI—Homeland Security's Investigation Unit. RED team includes FBI and DHS Agents, and US Marshal's Service Deputies.

For More Details Visit -

www.susansleeman.com/books/homeland-heroes/

WHITE KNIGHTS SERIES

Join the White Knights as they investigate stories plucked from today's news headlines. The FBI Critical Incident Response Team includes experts in crisis management, explosives, ballistics/weapons, negotiating/criminal profiling, cyber crimes, and forensics. All team members are former military and they stand ready to deploy within four hours, anytime and anywhere to mitigate the highest-priority threats facing our nation.

www.susansleeman.com/books/white-knights/

ABOUT SUSAN

SUSAN SLEEMAN is a bestselling and award-winning author of more than 35 inspirational/Christian and clean read romantic suspense books. In addition to writing, Susan also hosts the website, TheSuspenseZone.com.

Susan currently lives in Oregon, but has had the pleasure of living in nine states. Her husband is a retired church music director and they have two beautiful daughters, a very special son-in-law, and an adorable grandson.

For more information visit:
www.susansleeman.com

Made in the USA
Columbia, SC
21 November 2020

25152972R00181